PRAISE FOR
A WORLD WITH NO SHORE

"Luminous. A writer you feel envious of.
The beautiful prose weaves a net of wonder around you."

—NIKKI GEMMELL, author of *The Bride Stripped Bare*

"I thoroughly enjoyed this taut rumination on grief, memory
and human connection. Hélène Gaudy's exquisite prose
will hook you from the very first line, and Stephanie Smee's
thoughtful translation perfectly captures the cold beauty
of the Arctic regions. This book is a real gift."

—LAUREN CHATER, author of *Gulliver's Wife*

"Hélène Gaudy provides a profound and thought-provoking
meditation on the human need to explore and discover,
in a book that blurs the boundaries between
history, fiction and reportage."

—KATE FORSYTH, author of *Bitter Greens*

NOVELS IN FRENCH BY HÉLÈNE GAUDY

Vues sur la mer, Les Impressions nouvelles
(2006)

Si rien ne bouge
(Éditions du Rouergue, 2009)

Plein hiver
(Actes Sud, 2014)

Une île, une forteresse
(Inculte, 2016)

Un monde sans rivage
(Actes Sud, 2019)

A WORLD WITH NO SHORE

A Novel

HÉLÈNE GAUDY

Translated from the French
by Stephanie Smee

ZEROGRAM
PRESS

Los Angeles, 2022

ZEROGRAM PRESS
1147 El Medio Ave.
Pacific Palisades, CA 90272
EMAIL: info@zerogrampress.com
WEBSITE: www.zerogrampress.com

Distributed by Small Press United / Independent Publishers Group
(800) 888-4741 / www.ipgbook.com

First Zerogram Press Edition 2022
Originally published in 2019 as *Un Monde sans rivage* by Actes Sud (Arles, France)
Copyright © 2019 by Hélène Gaudy
English translation copyright © 2022 by Stephanie Smee
Text design and typesetting by Tristan Main
Cover design by Pablo Capra
Cover art: *The Explorers* by Mark Cappellano (2021),
    www.instagram.com/cappellanoarts

PUBLISHER'S CATALOGING-IN-PUBLICATION DATA

Names: Gaudy, Hélène, author. | Smee, Stephanie, translator.
Title: A world with no shore / Hélène Gaudy ; translated by Stephanie Smee.
Other Titles: Monde sans rivage. English
Description: First Zerogram Press edition. | Pacific Palisades, CA : Zerogram Press,
    2022. | Translation of: Un monde sans rivage. Arles : Actes sud, 2019.
Identifiers: ISBN 9781953409089 (paperback)
Subjects: LCSH: Arctic regions--Discovery and exploration--Swedish--Fiction.
    | Ballooning--Accidents--Arctic regions--Fiction. | Andrée, Salomon August,
    1854-1897--Fiction. | Frænkel, Knut, 1870-1897--Fiction. | Strindberg, Nils,
    1872-1897--Fiction. | LCGFT: Historical fiction.
Classification: LCC PQ2707.A94 M6613 2022 | DDC 843.92--dc23

Printed in the United States of America

CONTENTS

III
WHAT REMAINS

Everything plunges into a world with no shore,
a world that defies any definition and in the
face of which, as so many have already said,
any affirmation is a loneliness, an island.

H. G. Adler, *A Journey*

CONTACT

Copenhagen, November 2014

They are standing in front of a dark shape: an immense fallen balloon, as still as an animal washed ashore. There is, in the taut fabric, a breath of wind to be felt, as if some enormous mouth were still inflating it. One of them makes as if to move, the other is motionless, already. They were in mid-air and now here they are, contemplating the inert mass of their dream.

The image bears all the uncanniness of those early days of photography, of the first portraits of strangers and spectres. It is riddled with a multitude of insect-like dark flecks. Its surface is velvet grey, glimmering with the vague reflections left behind by the light, smooth as cloth, deep as the sea, a scattering of abstract constellations, markings, sooty crackling, edges leaking like ink, traces of too powerful a light that obliterates the landscape, or vapour that dissipates every nuance of black.

If you look past these blemishes, if you try to lift them like a veil, what remains, next to the mass of the balloon, black on white, are two silhouettes, dangling in the void as if by an invisible hand. You can only tell where the ground stops, where the sky starts, by the position of their feet. Without those figures, you might just be looking at an icy cliff or a sugar lump held between two fingers.

There is nothing to indicate their sex, their age, only what we have all understood since childhood to represent a human shape: two arms, two legs, a blockish torso, a small head. And yet quickly we sense they

1

are men – is it because of the weapons, black dashes at their belts? Or because at the turn of the twentieth century there were so few women photographed anywhere except in front of a painted backdrop or salon wall-hanging? If there are two of them in that image, there must be a third holding the camera, another man, invisible, to whom we owe the photograph.

It stands out, among others, at Copenhagen's Louisiana Museum – an elegant, white structure, colonnades and terraces reminiscent of the state of Louisiana which, you might guess, has lent this place its name when in fact it was named after the three successive wives of its founder, all called Louise, and all of whom you can easily imagine strolling one after the other across the luscious lawns that tumble down to the Baltic.

Across the water is Sweden. On a fine day, you can just make out the coastline.

Sometimes, an image breaches the unspoken agreement entered into with all the others – that we see them as surfaces, as memories, that we accept that what we are looking at only exists now behind a frame of glass or paper. Every now and then, one of them makes us pause. Our eyes are used to taking in everything without seizing on anything; this eases their task, allows them to rest. Sometimes we stop. To look.

And then the vast rooms of the museum release the space hinted at by the photograph, the growl of the sea intrudes more and more, bringing with it fragments of a northern land that is as unknown as it is familiar, of some white void that might be carried like an island within us all. There might be a lake, a glacier, fir trees and reindeer, then fewer and fewer trees, nothing but the cold and the light.

Things have changed scale; the image now takes over the room. The beginnings of a story seem to be hidden within it, something spills out from it, something unfinished, the outline of narratives to be rewritten, working backwards, since the image has just become the new point of departure.

The eye is a photographic plate which is developed in the memory. There are other images to be found, somewhere there, between lens and imprint.

I
THE DISAPPEARED

REVEALING

Royal Institute of Technology, Stockholm,
September 1930

The image is not yet complete, it is still just a fragment, caught among so many others, fragments of a film that has spent years under the snow, in one of the most remote landscapes on earth. It is so water-logged that the sensitive material adheres to the finger touching it. It has suffered significant deterioration. It is well past its expiry date. One thing is certain: there is very little hope of being able to decipher from it anything resembling a narrative.

A man is holding it in his nervous hands, his expert but nervous hands, trying to stop himself trembling. His name is John Hertzberg. He is an experienced photographer and technician. On this particular day, he is dealing with an entirely unprecedented set of circumstances: hidden within that film is a mystery that has unsettled all of Sweden for over thirty years. He has it in his hands, but the slightest careless gesture by those same hands could consign it to darkness. It is up to him, as he himself wrote, to firm up these traces, to restore life to the scenes remaining hidden within.

There is a gravity in this moment, taking place behind the thick walls of Stockholm's Royal Institute of Technology. With the greatest of care, Hertzberg unrolls the films which are all pressed together.

In addition to these blank rolls, one of which is wrapped in a scrap of the changing bag from the darkroom, soon he is looking at a roll of film taken from the body of the camera and, in copper canisters, another seven rolls, four of which have been exposed.

Each strip includes forty-eight 13 × 18 centimetre format images.

There is often little faith in the enduring nature of photography – exposed to the atmosphere, materials deteriorate and any contrasts could well vanish, be lost, leaving nothing behind. It does not share the noble and enduring reputation of painting, whose very substance reveals the stages, the regrets, the artist's signature behind the land-scape, the vestiges of preparatory drawings, layer upon layer for whomever wishes to notice them.

A photograph, you might say, generates itself, it appears fully formed, and it is only when you develop it yourself – when the paper is plunged into stop baths, when it takes on varying degrees of contrast, of intensity, when you experiment with the numerous possible ways it can be handled – that you understand the significance of the actions which have brought it to life, understand its fleeting nature, attributable to choices made, to mishaps.

Hertzberg is well aware of the power he wields over the images. He has mastered a new procedure: using autochrome plates on which, with the help of microscopic granules of potato starch, it is possible to re-create every colour under the sun. He knows how to filter the light and bring out the tints on the plate through the subtle interplay of the powders, much as the pointillist painters do. He knows how to create the most faithful print possible from what was once living, indeed even how, after the event, with some delicate handling, to give it the precision it was lacking. But he is also readying himself to discover the surprises it may be keeping in store.

Hertzberg works painstakingly, he is on edge. This message that has been sent to him through the mists of time must not be impaired. He is after a product which will reveal rather than damage, strip the superfluous without erasing the essential. He opts for pyrocatechol, to oxidise the silver bromide, absorb the blue and purple spectrum, intensify the salts.

Soon he has dozens of photographs before his eyes. He is the first custodian of these remnants, and he will remain the only person to have had contact with them when there was still something dynamic about them, when it was as likely they be ruined as be revealed – a flame that the slightest gesture might have extinguished. Later, the negatives, poorly conserved, will deteriorate, taking with them the sharpest contrasts, those areas that had remained hazy, the miniscule details that his methods, no matter how meticulous, had been unable to bring to light. All that remains of those images is what Hertzberg himself was able to detect in them. Should something have escaped his attention, that something has been irretrievably lost.

Some of them are much too pale, others overexposed. Soon it is possible to make out the texture of the ice revealing ravines, wrinkles which break into the white, carving it into dense blocks. At times, it is a mountain but it may also be an animal reclining on its side. And then, they appear: three men looking back at him. Three men who, soon, will be looking back at us.

These precise techniques, these hours of solitude, these measured gestures, all of it is necessary to render visible the traces of the way these bodies moved through the snow, of their energy, of the epic nature of the journey. Three men are returning to life, in silence, in darkness, reduced, like tribal shrunken heads, transformed into symbols on the paper.

Thirty years earlier they disappeared while trying to reach the North Pole in a balloon. Their names were Nils Strindberg, Knut Fraenkel and Salomon August Andrée.

Absence had made mythic creatures of these three men, phantom pirates, drowned mariners, whose ghosts had continued to sail the seas. Sweden had never recovered from it, nor had the rest of the world. For thirty-three years, hypotheses had proliferated much like the theories that flourish surrounding the disappearance of a plane from the radar.

So often we feel more curiosity about those who slip into obscurity than interest in those who return, especially when the place where they have disappeared is more like an absence turned landscape. It was precisely those men who had to disappear – some went so far as to say it had been intentional. There are always some, in every era, every century, those who feel compelled to cross frontiers and fall down on the other side, and as much as we praise their courage and acclaim their exploits, it is the reassuring confirmation that the limits are there for a reason, which we cling to above all else – the belief that those who breach them end up foundering in a place where they will never know rest as we will never cease to invent lives for them, or miraculous escapes.

Ocean currents were compared with air currents, the men were said to have been carried on the whims of the wind, towards Siberia and beyond, a floating buoy was discovered, a messenger pigeon intercepted, bones were unearthed, remains exhumed: a thousand times over they were killed and brought back to life, such was the reluctance to accept their death.

And now, here they are. Visible at last. Revealed.

Hertzberg re-creates the long process that saw the pack ice absorb their flesh and blood, strips back, like dead skin, the pallid, sapping days, the snow, the light that burns as does the ice – everything which masked their image as their bodies, slowly, disappeared.

The darkest shapes are the first to emerge in the developing baths – their own silhouettes, then those of the tent, an upturned boat, rocky outcrops and, every now and again, a third, more blurry, silhouette, darker still: the photographer who has hurriedly returned to position himself in the frame having set the self-timer.

They are caught in various poses, next to the grounded balloon then alone on the pack ice or prodding a bear's corpse with a rifle. Impossible to distinguish any one of them from their posture, from their way of holding themselves, from their faces devoured by the light. These shots seem to suggest they are interchangeable, that their individual existences are of no importance, straining as they are towards the goal they have set themselves.

In that same year of 1930, a certain Gunnar Hedrén will carry out the autopsy on what remains of their bodies, dispatched in crates to Tromsø in Norway's far north. For two days, in the basement of the town's only hospital, he will examine, with a small group of doctors, the bones barely covered by stiffened folds of clothes which always survive their owners, empty sacks aping their shape, barely distinguishable from a pile of rocks or sand. They will try to determine their cause of death, to decipher what remains.

Hertzberg, too, is occupied with a similar task. He is exposing the images just as the bodies are being opened up, exposing their insides. But the images will never again be closed up. Every day, every year, they will take on a different hue in the eyes of the men and women who come to look at them.

ANNA

Stockholm, September 1930

The images will come soon enough, will appear on the front page of the newspaper, but for the moment the words suffice, headlines which make her halt in her tracks.

She stops. Anna Charlier. Anna with her finely drawn, gently upturned mouth, hair curling about her face, the hint of locks behind her ears and at her neck, covered by the lace of her high collar. There is something in Anna of Kafka's impossible lover Milena Jesenská, Milena the feminist, the communist, the resistance fighter, who died in Ravensbrück in 1944 – same gentle, dark-eyed gaze, same precise, animal-like outline to her nose and mouth.

Anna seems wiser than Milena. Her eyes have always had a soft glow to them, which has slowly turned into a profound sadness despite the way she persists in holding herself, despite that unduly tight corset.

The sudden immobility of her body in the town, the brazen fluidity of life all about her while she herself is stricken. She stops. Legs suddenly cotton wool. Or perhaps she continues on her way, perhaps the words need to take root within her, to expand to allow her to grasp their meaning. Words which from now on will play on loop through her mind: the bodies of Nils Strindberg, Knut Frænkel and Salomon August Andrée have been found.

She stops, or perhaps she keeps walking. Perhaps it is the pain that allows Anna to walk the streets of Stockholm as if nothing has happened. In the eyes of passersby she's just one more woman, no longer so young, of cautious step, a heaviness to her limbs, her gaze.

Perhaps this pain has already taken on too many shapes to suffer yet another metamorphosis – in doubt, first of all, then in the waiting, the impatient pain, when everything is a sign, a stabbing, an impossible tingling that slowly, slowly accedes to the passing of time, every day distancing the likelihood of a happy outcome, then the pain of afterwards, when finally one relinquishes, without truly admitting it, without excusing it, pain that is ceaselessly rekindled by the sparks of interest fanned by the newspapers, kept alight by family and friends, fed by the compassionate looks of strangers.

Perhaps it no longer knows what form to take, this pain, Anna's body being already so accustomed to its every ruse, unless it were to avail itself of some crack, a release valve, a gap between her ribs and chest through which to flee, to escape.

When Anna sees the photographs, she will no doubt try to discern which of those two silhouettes might be Nils, before realising that most likely he was still standing behind the camera, the third man devoted to the glory of these other two, and perhaps her initial response to this further absence will be one of being twice robbed, before her desire, her acute focus, turns that absence somehow into a more intimate, more weighted presence: these images are his offering to her, by way of the intensity of his gaze, the position of his body, his talent for framing the shot, his endurance as he waits and the cold that penetrates his extremities in the time it takes to pose. She will sense his presence, more so even than the others, behind these staged settings where he is invisible, and the shadows where he is standing, where she imagines him to be, out of frame, will somehow draw in the expanse of those places conceived from loss, created from an absence.

If Anna did stop, how I would love to know where, in which street, on what island, at which intersection, if she stopped in Gamla Stan, Stockholm's old town, a maze of streets surrounding squares edged by the tall façades of soft-hued buildings – dusty rose, burnt sienna, pale green – at whose windows you can make out the waxy leaves of pot plants and the glow of chandeliers, or maybe she stopped in Södermalm, that island where the streets are steeper, more uneven, for Stockholm is a city still shot through by boulders and forest, grey rocks punctuating the edges of narrow streets and shadowy courtyards where, from time to time, a tiny wooden house might peer out from behind a dog-rose bush.

Taking Götgatan, the main artery through Södermalm, there comes a moment when suddenly you're looking out over the sea, slate-grey in autumn, and there in the middle of the view, wind whipping your face, are the islands. You can spend hours scrutinising the verdigris of the roofs and the squat silhouettes of the churches, marvelling at the manner in which those refined structures adorn a savage, shattered landscape, a chain of islands soldered in winter by the sea turned to ice. Oh yes, I would like to know when it was, wandering down which street, which view before her, that she experienced one of those peculiar moments that can happen on returning to a beloved place, a moment which seems only to discombobulate, to awaken what for so long has remained slumbering. To know where she was when she noticed, on the front page of a newspaper, the words she perhaps had ceased to dread.

When the balloon took flight, as she waited for news, when, little by little, she lost all hope, she did not allow herself to die, as perhaps she might have thought she would. She crossed the Atlantic, settling in America before returning to Europe, all at the side of Gilbert Henry Hawtrey, her new husband trying in vain to fill the absence of a man who would never be able to age, to grow heavier, to let himself sink into that easiness which transforms the most passionate love into a somewhat paler contentment for which Anna, however, I am certain, would have given her life, her youth.

*

She did not allow herself to die but neither, for all that, did she ever truly recover, appearing always to float above, or below, things, in her house at Torquay on the English coast, where Agatha Christie was born and whose languid palm trees, turquoise sea and Victorian homes appear as reassuring as they are conducive to crime.

Often, Anna would take the road to the sea, would feel the clarity of the air in the scent of the lush greenery, of the sand warmed by the sun, would walk to the jetty waiting for the clouds to clear, for that inhalation of blue, for the sea to expand, gripped by the illusion that all that is distant is drawing closer, the voyage and the nostalgia suddenly within reach: all she need do would be to snap her fingers and that expanse would be no more than a puddle to step over, as she lifted her dress, and Nils would return.

Only men feature in the family tree of the man who has disappeared. August, *the* August Strindberg, but also Nils' brothers, Tore, Sven, Erik. A few others: all of them engineers, musicians, artists. Of the women, it seems, we know nothing. While she never bore his name, while she remained Nils' eternal fiancée, Anna is the only woman not to have been entirely forgotten. Not because she was an engineer, an artist or a musician: because she had suffered a misfortune. If this is the only salient feature that remains of her, with what should we fill her body? How do we know who she was?

Perhaps by looking first for feelings, gestures, reminding ourselves of that strange solidification of air caused by the presence of a loved one, amplified further by their absence – at least, at the outset, for after a few months of feeling as though your heart has been exposed to the open air, then come the days where that heaviness of every limb, that colonisation of your chest, starts to be eroded by pockets of air, and even before the feelings grow weaker, the gaps between them start to appear, in increasing number, increasing size, and it's a relief, at the outset, to start to feel in control once more, right before the panic that the other may have just abandoned this body that shall be left alone to remember.

It was perhaps then that Anna took on the peculiarly fixed gaze we see in photographs of her, the corners of her lips hinting at a smile as her gleaming, dark irises betray no trace of shadow or emotion.

She became a piano teacher. She gave recitals. But her hands started to tremble, ever more violently, until she had no choice but to stop playing. There is a noticeable difference between two of her scores: an even, shapely script marks the first page of Verdi's *Aida*, where her maiden name, Anna Charlier, is easily made out. On the score of *Carmen*, acquired some years later, one can just decipher her married name in a jerky, angular and shaky hand: Anna Hawtrey.

Despite the quivering cursive letters, their awkwardness, there is a resoluteness that surges through the handwriting, through that imposing H, that T drawn with one vigorous motion, the Y which runs over the final letter of the title. The graceful and restrained script she used as a young woman followed, docilely, the edge of the page. That of later years lurches forward, scoring the paper, losing its way.

She may well have been a musician but of that there is little remaining. What has been written, what is retained, is the trembling of her hands.

Anna has come alone to Sweden, without the husband with whom she is now living in England. She has come to spend a few days in the city she left over thirty years ago. Stockholm has changed, of course, as cities do in our absence. Its familiar flow, sweeping through the places she recognises, the shops she used to frequent, has suddenly deviated and the city is a film in which she no longer has a role, a set whose doors have closed to her.

The city of her youth, henceforth shut off to her, rolls out its elegant arteries, its shiny cobblestones, in the chilly russet of the Swedish autumn. Anna is probably astonished at its modernity, at the number of automobiles and hurrying pedestrians, whereas the time she has spent away from Stockholm had preserved the city as if in a child's snow dome. The wind here is cruel, cutting, a bitter gusting reminder of all that has been lost.

The funeral is set for the 5th of October. A state funeral, which she will not attend. She will not see them turn Nils' death into a sacrifice. They will celebrate the macabre end to his mystery without her. She will escape the multitude of umbrellas sheltering the gawping onlookers, a black mass from which a handful of heads covered in light-coloured scarves will stand out, escape the dark light reflected from the cobblestones and façades of the official buildings, the ardour of the crowd, the borrowed suits of the curious lining the cut that opens as the bodies file by.

She will not drown in the crowd that is gathered to receive the heroes or rather what remains of them – nobody knows exactly what is contained within those coffins, or to whom the bones belong, but the essence of the veil of mystery has been lifted, the pebble has been dispelled from the shoe of a nation lacking a conquest and elegantly written histories. She will not hear the din of aeroplanes escorting the ships or the shots fired in their honour, nor will she watch from the bridges as the funerary wreaths are thrown into the water while the procession with great pomp ploughs the furrow of this story, etches it deeply into the public's imagination, those present, those absent, those who will read the newspaper and repeat the news, leaving its mark on the city to the military rhythm of countless steps so that it might be rewritten, rendered legible, this saga that in the end led nowhere – since it is always worth reminding people that there is a reason for one's demise.

She will not see the flags hanging in the wind, drenched.

She would prefer a wreath be sent bearing this simple inscription in elegantly slanting golden letters on a broad white ribbon: *En sista hälsning till Nils – från Anna.**

Once she has returned home, to her house whose walls are covered with photographs of the face of the man who disappeared, of his full cheeks, his clear eyes, his well-trimmed moustache, Anna will gradually form her own wish, will decide that her heart, at her death, will be

---

*To Nils with love one last time – Anna

extracted from her body and buried next to Nils' ashes, a decision her husband will be unable to sway, she has a will of iron, Anna, gentle-mannered though she is, and when she dies in Scania, at the end of the 1940s, her body will be opened, her heart removed from her chest and burnt, its ashes deposited in a silver urn right next to Nils' remains, in the same grave, in Stockholm's Northern Cemetery.

There will be no flags for her, no guard of honour. There will be only the smell of earth and old sap that impregnates cemeteries, hundred-year-old tree trunks and box hedges trimmed into a maze, there will be, just a few metres from Nils' tomb, the resting place of Salomon August Andrée who led them across the ice and the sky to this great cemetery which today is ringed by a motorway that emerges from an interchange as you leave the capital, where cars drive too quickly to allow you to make out what lies behind the screen of trees, which tombs, which porticos, which family vaults, which bodies in that dark mass at the heart of which you can make out, beyond the harsh headlights, the trembling glow of candle-lit offerings made to the dead, fleeting as will-o'-the-wisp.

EXHUMATION

Kvitøya,
5 August 1930

One month earlier, something happened on one of the pieces of land closest to the North Pole, one of the most remote islands of the Svalbard archipelago.

It all started with a flash of light striking metal as the sun hit it, an unusual brilliance which the animals have become used to, here where they have made their nests, where they have their routines.

Here, everything appears uniform, monochrome, and yet everything is more vivid, more astonishing than anywhere else. At the water's edge, on the last island, the rocks are black, damp. Further away, the grey takes over, pockmarked by the light. The stones are marked by pink halos. Moss makes the earth spongy. The flowers are a feathery blanket that might have been dropped by a gull on the wing.

A breach, a chasm, an anomaly: this is how they are selling it, the first travel agents to add the Arctic to their brochures. A voyage into oblivion. Here you will find yourself far from everyday cares. The white is a blindfold placed over your eyes. A sweeping landscape of suspended animation, of sleep, virgin territory that will assume the shape of those who are first to tread here, those who will name its river mouths, its gulfs, its mountains. It is a piece of clay to be moulded, its black riches lying beneath the whiteness, waiting to be extracted, for under the snow, there is coal.

*

What landscape would be revealed if the Arctic were stripped of snow?

In August 1930, nobody yet knows.

Yet the mountains have already been bored through, rigged out with wooden poles, cables dangle against the rock, black appearing through the sparse grass, but you need only head away from the mines, from their subterranean world, to discover a vast and virginal land, outliving those who surveyed it, a place that could bring you undone, and whose mere existence was enough to expand the world, out of the sheer ignorance that surrounded it.

To get there, you must leave behind roads as smooth as pumice stone, rubbed until they are white, or black, you must cross the sea, follow the paths that little by little rid themselves of everything you know: houses, passersby, familiar-looking animals, even the trees, the plants, the smallest blade of grass, all of it slowly but surely growing sparser.

You must uproot, renounce, strip away.

Olav Salen is seventeen years old. Nothing more is known of him, there is no photograph, not a word of a biography, except that, on this day, he sets off for the first time to the Pole on the *Bratvaag*, a vessel headed for Franz Josef Land, charged with a scientific mission and also on the hunt for walruses.

In the summer of 1930, the ice has started to melt unusually quickly – expanding, liquifying, like an ice cube warmed in a hand. Channels have formed, water is hurtling down treeless mountain sides, rushing from glaciers, little by little the white has turned first yellow, the colour of a bear's fur in the folds of its limbs, then tawny, brown, green.

It's the sort of day, perhaps, when the fog has disappeared.

Certainly, this summer, it will be possible to go further than ever before. The *Bratvaag* has been making good time for ten days across mirror-like seas, where the sun, barely, has just risen. Ahead of seventeen-year-old Olav Salen, the blue splits open. It is as if he is parting it himself, with a slice of his hand.

Maybe it is from Ålesund, home port of the *Bratvaag*, that he has put to sea, Ålesund which could already be said to be North, which is already at the northern tip of Norway, where already the unrivalled light lasts as long as the darkness, landscapes as reluctant to plunge into the night as they are to emerge from sleep, where the cold lingers long enough to make you despair, where the first warm days bring madness, and from your throat a great breath of air that passes through your body, and which certainly that summer, milder than any other, more charged with promise, must be rushing through Olav Salen, and all his seventeen years.

For him, such an expedition must be the adventure of a lifetime, heading places where few vessels have ever dropped anchor. Even without knowing his aspirations, without ever having seen his face in any image, you can perhaps guess his impatience and fear, the pride, the cold biting his hands and the crunch of salt on his fingers. You can imagine him, his face, still pale or already a little ruddy, hair hanging in a heavy fringe across his youthful high forehead.

There are only men aboard the vessel. Who knows what or whom Olav has left behind: parents, sisters, brothers, perhaps a sweetheart, whom he held tight to his chest, or perhaps someone he admired from afar, with just a glance or maybe a kiss. It is possible, too, that back onshore, Olav has left nothing but the most tedious of jobs and bad memories. Perhaps Ålesund, for him, is a sort of hell on earth as well as doubtless being the only place he knows. Let us wager that his eyes goggle and his hands grip the railings at the sight of the spectacle appearing at the prow of the *Bratvaag* should he be allowed the time on deck to do so. Directly ahead of the boat, a mountain of ice rises above an island resting on the blue and white. A translucent, sparkling summit resembling those unearthly glass domes which will adorn the cities of the new millennium.

It is another planet, this supposedly inaccessible island, which they are only able to approach due to the unusually mild weather, the glassy sea, the absence of ice.

*

White Island, Kvitøya. Whether you are seventeen or forty, it is a thing of wonder, a slap. They have all described it, those who have seen it, and those who have perished there – that moment of sudden shock.

Gunnar Horn, who is leading the scientific expedition aboard the *Bratvaag*, describes *a dazzling white shield which seemed to float on the mirror-flat sea from which it rose in precipitous walls of ice.*

Perhaps the sky has become pink, like blushing skin, like the pale rose of a fingernail, like an endless morning. And even if Olav has not the time to contemplate the island at his leisure, even if he does not so much as cast it a look, even if he is obeying orders, responding to shouts, already preparing the weapons for the hunt, even if he cares nothing for pack ice and mirages, let us wager that White Island will leave its mark somewhere, on his retina, and then in a corner of his memory.

That evening they will sleep on the boat. And on the morning of the 6th of August, under an unyielding sun, Gunnar Horn will write: *A most intense silence prevailed everywhere, broken only now and then by thunder from the glacier to our north ... produced by large masses of ice loosening and plunging into the water.*

The sealers head away from the island in their boat. Olav is among them. Quickly they come across a huddle of walruses which they pursue southwards. For centuries people have been hunting on Svalbard, for walruses and whales, vessels flocking there in the sixteenth and seventeenth centuries, plying these desolate coastlines, the sea blushing red, ice turning scarlet. By the seventeenth century, there's no longer even any need to head back to land before butchering the creatures, carved up there and then off the sides of the vessels, sliced up on the spot, transformed, blubber rendered to oil, whalebones saved to make umbrellas and fancy corsets, all done quickly and efficiently before even making it back to land. By 1930, there are scarcely any whales left in the archipelago, all of them slaughtered, trussed up, dragged across the decks, like the walruses, massacred.

But White Island is so far north that the creatures living there had forgotten their fear of men when they saw them appear out of nowhere. The memory had already been lost of the arrival, right there, of three men, silent from exhaustion and staggering, the animals having assimilated the foreign elements they left behind – canvas, fabrics, tin-plate, bones. It struck them, the fear, all of a sudden, hearing the vessel butting up against the shore, sending them scurrying into their lairs, disappearing in a flurry. Arctic foxes know how to melt away, how to vanish – in the blink of an eye, a breath, not even.

Soon, the birds will stop avoiding the area, will resume their former flight paths, will reunite with their flocks. For the moment, the she-bears take shelter far from the coast, their cubs at their heels, and the walruses dive deep, where the water turns black. Everything is waiting for the silence to return.

On tracking down a herd of walruses slumbering on a beach, hunters have always taken advantage of the number of beasts in slaughtering them, their numbers and their sleeping habits, for unlike seals, more aware, more vigilant, walruses abandon their great bodies entirely to sleep. The hunters would anchor their whaleboat at the beach. Soundlessly, they would then go ashore and spear to death the closest animals. Those further away would try to haul themselves towards the sea but would find themselves blocked by the carcasses of the others. Glistening, heavy bodies blocking other glistening, heavy bodies. The hunters had only to aim their lances.

With the decimation of their population, the walruses are no longer such easy prey. Olav and his companion, the twenty-four-year-old Karl Tusvik, already a seasoned hunter, will probably harpoon them from the sea before finishing them off with a rifle.

You have to approach from behind, the hunters say, cloak yourself in silence, so as to better surprise them. You have to catch the walruses unawares on the ice floes where they're slumbering and which are liable to sink along with them if care is not taken, then take aim with a harpoon gun before finishing them off with a bullet into the back of the neck, where the bone is more easily shattered. Importantly, it must be done before the beast, suddenly awake, hauls itself upright, threatening the boat, using the force of its weight, its tusks as weapons – many a vessel has been holed in this fashion, and has foundered.

For Olav Salen and Karl Tusvik, it is not the placid face of a walrus they see, not its great obsidian eyes, its thick whiskers, its tusks of precious ivory, rather it is a brown mound they see, lacking form, structure, a somnolent hunk of flesh, covered in shells and seaweed.

So they shoot – harpoon first, reverberating as it strikes into the flesh.

And, again, they shoot – an immense creature on the shore.

Soon they are carving up their first kills, taking a knife to the tough, fatty, pink-blotched skin, and then the blade penetrates deeper, underneath it is dense, thick, viscous, a gelatinous blue-ish white, full of blood and entrails. The blade slides, the skin escapes their grasp, they're growing weary, their hands are warm, red, and that smell. Perhaps they talk as they work, unless they're concentrating, hands sore from the effort of penetrating the skin with the blade, they're hot, even though they're so close to the Pole, so far North, and when they wipe their brow, they leave red marks at the roots of their hair.

Keen to clean their hands, their forearms sticky with blood, and because they are desperately thirsty, Karl and Olav hunt around for some fresh water. They find a stream, cross over it. And it is then that something catches their attention on the other side: a bright flash.

At first they think it might be a reflection on the water, a fish that has washed up, the blade of a knife, so many hours have they spent now digging into flesh with that implement. But it is a piece of round metal. Nobody else has yet passed by that spot, neither of them, nor any other crew member, so Olav, or Karl, astonished, pick up the object, weigh it in their hand, watch as it catches the sun: it is an aluminium lid that stands out, in this virgin place, like some object that has landed there from another planet.

And then, everything happens very quickly. Their eyes are soon struck by another flash of light, this time it is bouncing off a brass ring, then they see a dark mass which they hurry over to inspect: a small boat. They lean over to look into it, rummaging around. Inside, a jumble of objects and, on several of them, the inscription, *Andrée's pol. exp. 1896.*

Were it not for those items, were it not for those words, it is probable that nobody would have remembered Olav Salen or Karl Tusvik. Their names have endured, resurfacing from underwater like an inflated object, all because their eyes, for just a moment, fell on an inscription, a name, a path that was out of the ordinary. But the lighting was so poor, the spotlight so brief, that nothing more of them will be remembered. Their names will remain an insignificant footnote, will leave scarcely a trace. Olav and Karl pass the mantle over. They hurry off in search of the captain, and he will be the one to claim discovery, the role of spokesman, along with a semblance of glory, he will be the one to return to the boat to announce the news: he has discovered the remains of the men whose disappearance has haunted Sweden and Norway for thirty-three years.

They return, in greater number, armed with pickaxes, with shovels. Stripped bare of the snow that had concealed them for more than thirty years, snow that will become increasingly rare, in ever more meagre drifts, more objects appear: a boathook, a sledge, a rolled Swedish flag, ammunition, a barometer, fragments of sail, a paraffin stove, a cooking pot and cup, lanolin in ceramic jars, a bottle, tablets, a handkerchief embroidered with the letters "N.S."

Most importantly, what everybody both hopes for and fears: bodies. The first, next to the boat, is a sack of dark fabric punctured by bones. Kneecaps protrude from what remains of a pair of trousers. A ribcage pokes through remnants of material. The head is missing. Bears, think the crew members. In the right inside pocket of the jacket bearing a monogrammed "A," a notebook, a pencil, a heart-shaped locket concealing a photo of Anna. Next to the body, a rifle butt, its barrel buried in the snow. To the north of the camp, under a pile of stones, there is another body, an attempt having been made to bury it by whatever means available, to wedge it in between the rocks, to protect it, even if the head is to be found, separated from that makeshift grave. Poking out, feet clad in straw-lined boots.

They also find a book filled with notes, meteorological observations, astronomical calculations. The paper is damp, its pages stuck together, but the writing, so neat and regular, gives the impression, thinks Gunnar Horn, of having been written in some comfortable room and not at the end of the world.

The men of the *Bratvaag* wrap what remains of these other men in tarpaulins, trying to keep the bodies intact, trying not to lose anything, given they consist of nothing more than a fragile collection of bleached bones and shredded fabric. They carry them aboard.

But there is one they are missing, to whom no fragment can be said to belong.

Knut Frænkel has not been found.

There will be another ship, then, the *Isbjörn*, whose men will search through what remains of the snow, raking over every square centimetre, since driving the search now is no longer mere curiosity but the pull of the media, of every Swedish and Norwegian company, the desire for scoops, details, the appetite for legend.

The Andrée expedition has become a human-interest story. People already realise the interest their story is generating, the fascination it elicits, people are digging, scraping, photographing the scenes from every angle, creating inventories of the objects that are exhumed; it is a peculiar form of archaeology, seeking better to understand the life of these men just as one might hope to reveal an ancient civilisation.

One photographer picks up a bone, belonging to man or beast he doesn't know, and takes it away with him in secret, a curious predatory reflex or perhaps an act of remembrance, almost certainly a little of both, and maybe even he does not really know. He will keep that bone until his own death, a relic, a souvenir, as if his camera, just this once, had been inadequate.

From these remains, the journalists draw out the first accounts. One of them hypothesises that the three explorers' balloon must have come down on White Island or somewhere in its immediate proximity. It would have been impossible, he suggests in the *Dagens Nyheter* newspaper dated the 7th of September, to drag all of the objects discovered at the camp over such a long distance.

He couldn't be further from the truth.

They must act quickly, the pack ice is closing over again. Soon the island will be inaccessible once more and those gathering images, the treasure seekers, will be trapped in the interior. The sun has continued to shine, the snow has melted still further away, revealing layers that have never seen daylight. The third body has finally been discovered, buried deep under the ice. Not far from him are found the copper canisters containing rolls of film, and the loaded camera.

DIGGING

Heading into summer 1897

Wе are still in the 1930s. Not for much longer. The photographs draw us backwards, into the dense opacity of those greys and blacks, back through the years separating their discovery from the moments they were taken, the years that have witnessed, slowly, this century teeter on its foundations and collapse, already, even as it has barely started.

Let's rewind the tape, dig deeper into those thirty-three years, leave this world which has seen the remains of Andrée, Frænkel and Strindberg return to Tromsø, a world so different from the one they knew and yet so similar, a world that is hurtling ever forward, but still punctured by absences, expectant waiting, silent, unrecorded lives, by a blindness to what is coming.

The images are like staging points for a free dive, letting us sink down, catch our breath, clutch onto the details, to what little is visible and, as we shift our glance from one to the other, letting us peer into the chasms that separate them, from which there is only a whisper to be heard, barely a tremor.

1926, a Japanese woman in a periwinkle blue kimono emerges from the shadows of some foliage: Albert Kahn has sent photographers to the four corners of the earth to create what he is calling "The Archives of the Planet," in order to keep a record of the trees with hollow trunks and immense roots, of the horsemen of the steppes, of dachas and cathedrals, of Canada's deep lakes, of celebrations at a birth, of tears shed for the dead, of national dress, of ruddy faces caught on autochrome plates. Powdery, light, one breath and it all evaporates. Look harder, deeper, and there, in a ray of light, in 1924, nine exhausted men are staring out at us, sitting in front of their tent which is masking the summit of Everest, there is nothing to be seen of the slope soaring towards the sky, nothing of the violence that opens up the road through the landscape, which provides artists with oases and tropical beaches, everything is bathed in light, the colours disappear. In 1923 a native Selk'nam man of the Tierra del Fuego emerges, a giant with coal-coloured skin, striated with white, his face hidden behind a wooden mask that has no hole through which to meet our gaze, photographed by an Austrian missionary at the very moment his people are disappearing, and the image is the ash, the leftover traces of an extinguished fire.

1915, and it accelerates, a yawning gap haunts the portraits as it does the memories of the survivors, a missing jaw, a glass eye, from the black hole of a face emerges the deafening din of explosions reverberating endlessly in our ears and away from the trenches there is another battle, in which Anna has her role to play. The battle that took Nils from her started well before the one that is now rocking the world – a fight that stretches towards the Poles, more sprawling, more silent. And yet, it is the same.

1913, and in Alaska, four men open a path through the pack ice, using no machine, no icebreaker, equipped with poles and ropes, not looking at the camera, balancing on the shifting floes, they criss-cross the landscape, digging through the earth's white crust, finding a gap, a way through.

In 1912, Alfred Wegener expounds his theory on continental drift: the world must have shattered from a single bloc into a multitude of shards, lands are no longer butterflies pinned to a naturalist's board, they wander, drift, never stop changing shape.

1912 is unsettled by the start of the First Balkan War, compounded by the foundering of the *Titanic*, immense, unsinkable, yet whose gleaming hull crashes into an iceberg, shattering with it those monumental staircases, the crystal droplets and the lights, whether candle-flame or glowing chandeliers, an explosion of pearls and silks – all of it dissolving into the black night, the thick ink of the sea.

That same year, in his final film, *The Conquest of the Pole*, ageing director Georges Méliès glorifies the very dreams of conquest encountered by the ship's hull as it foundered against them. On screen we see men constructing magnificently absurd machines, ridding themselves *manu militari* of the suffragettes seeking to accompany them, waving their hats, splitting open a cardboard cosmos populated by reclining caryatids and fantastical creatures and machines, battling a giant before at last finding the magnetic needle, the axis around which we are all spinning. They were not vanquished as were the passengers on board the *Titanic*. They claimed their revenge over the ice.

While Méliès is staging his glorious misadventures, people are awaiting the return of Andrée's expedition: they imagine the marvellous lands which he and his crew may have reached, the lands they will safeguard for them, this North Pole which they are struggling, despite recent discoveries, to pinpoint to an abstract geographic location, from which they would like to carve a continent, possessing a shore, contours, perspective and, why not, inhabitants. They populate it as one might populate the moon or indeed the planet Mars, populate it with indigenous peoples clad in furs and armed with harpoons, able to reduce the most virtuous of explorers to a state of savagery. And if the rigours of the climate have the good taste to shield the explorers from the sight of women's flat breasts and from genitalia poorly disguised by palm leaves, there is no doubt the heathens of the North are fierce, have a ferocious appetite and, one might say, have assumed their brutality from the bears.

This is what people have imagined ever since the disappearance of Andrée's expedition, this is how they must be living, amid imaginary tribes, or indeed entirely alone, reigning over an impenetrable kingdom, at the centre of the earth, accessed only through the gateways, the secret portals at the Poles.

*

In 1911, Roald Amundsen reaches the South Pole. Perhaps the earth is not so hollow, its openings are plugged, the notion of a subterranean kingdom loses its credibility. But then, what has become of Andrée?

1910 is marked by the passage of Halley's comet streaking by, flooded by unusually high waters of the Seine.

In 1900, at the Paris Exposition, indigenous peoples are exhibited, villages are re-created, people are fearful, they marvel, there is no doubt, the world is expanding.

In any event, the world is going through a period of introspection, rousing itself.

There is a better view from up above, one discovers things, has an overview.

Imperceptibly, people are already learning to detach themselves.

The image is a veil, a long march, an enigma, a door which keeps constantly closing, before our very eyes.

We must forget the others, all the images we know, that have made us who we are, so we can return to the cusp of the twentieth century, ignorant of what lies ahead.

We must plunge in our hand and dig around in order to grasp a moment, just one, and reimagine it unscathed.

II
THE EXPLORERS

SKETCH

Spring 1897

*J*ag kan ej följa dig.

"I can't go with you."

At the end of this sentence which Anna has written on a piece of paper stuck to a notebook which will accompany Nils on his expedition, a well-drawn, nicely rounded full stop. Above it, a carefully sketched drawing in black ink: a balloon that resembles a fat lolly, a flag on either side of the basket and, on the ground, a small figure, her hair in a bun, waving.

There is the balloon, and the men one imagines to be in it.

There is the nation, the flags, the country.

There she is, destined to remain on the ground.

There is nothing more to say.

I can't go with you. When did she give him this drawing? Let's try amid the greenery, in the garden: there they are, in the sun, which at first is lighting up their faces too brightly for us to make out their features. It is April or May, there are bright patches on the cast-iron table and at the bottom of Anna's dress, red spots at her décolletage, it is warm, she is perspiring, something is gripping her, as it is him in his suit, you have to look hard to see any rift, adjust the light, wait for the picture to reveal itself.

There you are. She's stretched out. It's a photograph, another one, found in tatters among the vestiges of the camp, Anna is lying there in the centre, smiling, in the grass, arms crossed behind her head, puffy sleeves, playful look, a dark skirt – is it black?

Something is missing in this image, perhaps the frisson that precedes desire, signals its presence. They left too long ago for it still to be possible to grasp the link, the one that is passed from one hand to another, from the hands of a parent to their child by way of the slow thread of gestures and family photos. To bring it to life, it must be rubbed up against something else, the colour brought out, or the trace of some movement, and to do that we could look, let's say, at Edvard Munch's 1895 painting, *The Day After*, in which a young woman is lying asleep on a white bed, hair spread out over the pillow, her blouse almost entirely undone, exposing her chest, and yet there is not the slightest suggestion of lasciviousness, rather a peculiar sort of solitude. There are bottles of alcohol on the table. Her skirt is brown and flecked with dark spots, perhaps flowers. Her very pale arm stretches out into the void towards the edge of the painting. The inside of her wrist is exposed. Her head appears to tilt backwards, as if she had collapsed, as if her sleep were a relinquishment. And yet, she has strength. A Madonna with her eyes closed, destroyed but peaceful, a Madonna who will offer a different hue to Anna's ferocious joy, her sparkling smile.

Perhaps this is what is needed: the medium of painting, the memory of a life that still eludes photography in order to give flesh once more to Anna, to Nils, who suddenly leans in. He too has skin there to be grasped under his starched shirt, a shirt secured by the same bow tie from the pictures taken before his departure, Nils, the one who always gazes directly into the lens while his companions look to an invisible vanishing point, already playing at conquerors.

Suddenly Nils' body bends in the declining light, his shoulders are round and smooth underneath his shirt, there is something crystalline and moist about his gaze, and on his skin is the scent of those who blush easily, a sweeter whiff of youth about the nape of his neck where Anna rests her cheek, and then her open hand on his broad back. She takes his face in her hands, certainly. He is incapable of lying, so what then? What acceptable version do they invent together?

Maybe there are no patches of sunlight, no cast-iron table on the grass, just tall windows, a small room, a white bed where Nils' hand now wanders over the pale flesh of the inside of Anna's wrist.

She would be lying down, then, stretched out like Munch's young woman, no more posed, no more stiffness, a devastation linking the hollow in her belly to the tightness in her chest. A devastation. Nils, again, leans in, and there is a throbbing in his neck, in his loins, at their temples pressed together, and their ears are humming, they are deaf, and blind, their pulse forcing their lips apart, and together they rise, and she presses herself more deliberately against his body, buries her face into his taut neck, her hands descend towards his lower back, there where the flesh curves, feeling him renounce one thing entirely so that he might accept another, unreservedly, until he lets out a sigh, scarcely audible, for her ears only, and she holds him tighter, still, and the pressure brings their bellies together, one into the other, taut, pulsating, indivisible, and to let him go is a suffering, forever put off until tomorrow.

In the beginning, she was astonished at the power she wielded over this boy, so tall and so serious, who from the moment they first laid eyes on each other would lose all composure. In the beginning, it was almost a game, it was enough that she drew closer to him, barely half a step forwards, having first ascertained there would be no witness to their mutual stumbling in a world more confused, more silent, more weighted, it was enough that her breasts touched his chest and pressed gently against him for his eyes to lose themselves somewhere in a place that had nothing to do with calculations, flight plans, pleasantries or any of his other daily preoccupations, and that made her laugh on the inside, a silent, knowing laugh that she held deep within herself, without moving away from him at all, without taking so much as the slightest step backwards, and it was enough that she take his generous, full lip between her white teeth, and that she bite it, barely, for his eyes to close almost painfully and for him to move closer still, as warm and smooth now as his sex was hard against her belly, no longer able to control his hands or the expression on his face.

There is something about the sudden weakness of this otherwise sturdy body that undoes her, this body no longer governed by anything but desire for her, and whatever it is that renders him weak when he now holds her tight, there is nothing she can do, it unanchors her, more than all the charm and appeal of others she has known, this avowal of abandonment, this defenceless, hungry body, this lost gaze, as if constantly astonished to discover she is precisely as she is, this face which she takes in her hands, again, which she caresses, leaving no hollow, no relief, tracing with her fingers, her lips, every last gentle contour, she no longer feels like laughing now, not at all, they share the same anxious gravity, attentive only to that which is breaking apart within them.

Around his neck he wears a thin chain with three charms hanging from it – a cross, an anchor, a heart. The light catches the metal and Anna's hair, which the photos never show her wearing loose but one imagines to be thick, difficult to comb. Her chest deflates abruptly and he holds her tighter still.

His tongue in her mouth. What does that do? Has she had time to know? Her skin which quivers when she lies down, when she dreams of his trembling hand slipping along her belly. She is alone.

There it is, the roles have been handed out. *I can't go with you.* What words does he find to tell her? Words of consolation, a tender confirmation of the place where each one of them has accepted they shall remain? Or perhaps a promise, even if in vain, so barely credible: one day perhaps, together, in the Great North. Maybe she pretends to believe it.

She does not know the name of this place where she is unable to accompany him, she probably still believes it is about the pack ice, the adventure, unless somewhere within herself, buried deep, where tears are formed, she already has a notion of what it might be like.

What she does know, what she has been taught since childhood, is that the decision is not hers to make, that it is possible to bind her life to that of a man without having one single word to say should he decide to take off to the Great North and leave her behind, earthbound, and she should already be considered fortunate to have been able to choose him, this man, with as consolation prize this desire so rarely issued with convenient arrangements of marriage. Are these the beginnings of anger already or might we still believe a sense of pride?

What will it look like, for her, the day after, the day when she gets up alone, with not even a cross marked in the diary, no end to the waiting, the endless expanse of that first day without him?

Nils, too, could say the words she has so carefully written, could rule a black line between earth and sky, or he will be no more capable of following her into those infinite hours that are already amassing, following the meaningless gestures she is steeling herself to enact, in the familiar places where he no longer is, on the chair which is no longer bathed in patches of sunlight, that chair which, probably, never existed.

It is evening. He rises. The drawing is miniscule in his clenched hand.

For her, the day after has already begun.

CROSSING

May 1897

From afar, it resembles a long, nocturnal journey stretching into the hesitant start of day. Their lasting impression is of a gradual sinking as they make their way towards a growing light, the light of endless days – the polar summer will last for more than three months, three months of brightness, day and night, which they will have to take advantage of before they experience the flip side of the coin, the darkness of the months which will follow.

They leave separately, Frænkel and Andrée together, then Strindberg accompanying Swedenborg, the man who will serve as replacement in the event one of them must stand down.

Lulled by the regular rhythm of the train, Frænkel and Andrée doze on their seats, anonymous travellers, or almost. They have been given some flowers, anemones and carnations, and they are at a loss as to what to do with them; the men find them a nuisance as they look out the window, watching the passing parade of lakes and forest. They let them wilt on the wool of their dark suits. The light fades, heralding nightfall.

Every stage of their journey reminds them of the same journey made the previous year: every silence brings back the shouts of the crowd that had gathered to wish them well at every port, every station, the women, the men in their Sunday best, the young children with arms full of flowers, the little girl who had handed Andrée a rose bush from which he had been supposed to toss a bud over the Pole, and whose tiny roses had ended up withering as they had waited for the winds. Since the winds had not seen fit to blow in the right direction, they had had to wait another year before trying again, before repacking their bags and preparing body and spirit once more. To be ready, no matter what.

In their luggage there are starched ties, elegant gloves. They have in mind their departure, but also their return, so they might be presentable for the crowd who will soon be cheering them on once more. Between the two, departure and return, their adventure will last just a few days, a brief episode when they will have to grit their teeth, suffer the cold, endure without complaint, but it will be nothing more than a parenthesis in anticipation of the triumph to come.

Andrée nods off, he's snoring, mouth ajar. Frænkel watches him. It's warm in the train, muggy, the spring sunshine lingers in the heavy curtains, soaking into their jackets and bringing out the scent of the flowers. Frænkel looks at the man he will have to follow, with no regrets, unquestioning, with whom he will take off over the ice, and it seems hard to comprehend, in this comfortable compartment, this long, russet twilight.

Andrée cuts a fine figure, even asleep, his posture proudly upright, it seems he never lets his guard down. He has anticipated everything, prepared everything, chosen the members of his expedition carefully – cut from the same cloth, just younger, less experienced, engineers, indoor types, more used to smooth wooden desks than wild expanses, dependable fellows, neither particularly fearful nor too demanding, motivated by the exploit itself rather than being avid for glory, reasonable men who will know how to rise to the occasion, without ever treading on his toes.

Frænkel has recently qualified from Stockholm's Royal Institute of Technology. Strindberg, who is only twenty-four years old, has an assistant teaching position there. The former is to be entrusted with the meteorological observations. They will rely on the latter's scientific skills – in astronomy, physics, mathematics and, in particular, photography.

Andrée is ambitious and clear-sighted. The attempt to reach the North Pole by balloon, in addition to being unprecedented, has the advantage of elegance. No more exhausting processions on skis across white expanses, no more howling dogs, or labouring vessels. They will not even need to set foot on that inhospitable land. Andrée's pledge is to fly over it and toss over a buoy which will be the marker of all humanity that is gathered behind his balloon, sharing his dream of painless conquests.

At that very moment, there are many alarmed by his apparent lack of professionalism. His knowledge of the Arctic is vague, his predictions seem fanciful, but there is a general sense of excitement in the air. Financial backers and scientists rush headlong into the ever-gaping breaches in the whirring progress of the world, there is a will to conquer, to discover, to map. And then Andrée is persuasive, impassioned, he inspires confidence with his stature, his moustache, his calm and superior manner, the flood of details with which he inundates his audience – it's a tune one can listen to, take at face value.

This man, with his fancy words, in his stylish suit, accompanied by two strapping chaps who, like him, are not some small-time adventurers, but civilised men, whose lack of experience in the terrain will be compensated for by the reassuring extent of their knowledge, this man is going to clear a path without fuss through the air.

For a long time now, from the warmth of his office at the Stockholm Patent Office, where he is an engineer, Andrée has been plotting, planning routes, maps, hot-air balloons. Down here, at eye-level, all that can ever be seen are the imperfections, the clumsy, rough plans, the peeling paint on the window woodwork, the mess on the workbench, the piles of papers, the cobblestones below, still wet with rain. From up in the sky, he would no longer see any such annoying details, everything would suddenly make sense, like a message from which you need some distance in order to be able to read the whole thing.

So Andrée paid for his own balloon, the *Svea*. His first trips were short, windy, poorly controlled, local flights around Stockholm and Gothenburg. From his gondola he saw shimmering towns reflected in his astonished eye, only then to see them bury themselves deep in the forests, and their myriad lights drown among the trees. That extraordinary panorama of western Sweden – lake, forest, lakes, forests, so rarely interrupted by the blonde patches of summer fields – turned blue, turned black, as he rose, a landscape exaggerated, mirrored, that never seemed to end. But the maps of his flight paths were not quite up to the task. The slightest fog, the slightest cloud and he was disoriented, lost his sense of direction. From lake to lake, from forest to forest, Andrée battled the sensation of reliving the same moment, again and again, so much so that as he approached the island of Öland, spotting a lighthouse and hearing the crash of the tide on the shore, he took the sea for yet another lake. As he floated higher, everything became hazy, it all looked the same: he was lost, in mid-air.

He needed another balloon, more reliable, more responsive. Its name, *The North Pole*, not being in his opinion sufficiently triumphant; he chose instead *Örnen* – Swedish for "eagle." Perhaps he knew the story of the alchemist John Damian who, in the sixteenth century, made a madcap attempt to reach France by air, departing from Stirling Castle in Scotland, with wings of eagle feathers affixed to his arms, and who excused his failure on the grounds that a few chicken's feathers had unintentionally slipped into the mix. That flightless fowl, that earth-bound bird must have sabotaged the eagle's flight: a modicum of humility, a recollection of domesticity would have been sufficient to bring him down.

No chicken's feather will spoil Andrée's flight. Eagle-like, his balloon will cast its piercing gaze over the outer limits of the world, note them with the precision, the clear-sightedness which the sky permits, and set about embracing them.

Frænkel looks at Andrée's luxuriant moustache which almost entirely conceals his lips, scrutinises his prominent nose, the cross-hatching at the corner of his eyelids lending a hint of mischief to an otherwise severe aspect, as if he himself were not entirely convinced by his own gravitas. It all appears to be there, already, in his face, his unwavering will, his faith in the clear and straightforward virtues of science but also his quiet folly, blind to the prospect of failure, like the almost childish way in which he will insist to the very end upon apparently trivial matters – a good meal, a pleasantry, the curved outline of an island.

Frænkel does not manage to sleep. At twenty-seven years of age he could be taken for thirty-five. Dimple in his chin, a small, elegant mouth, tautly drawn and with an arch as distinct as the sharp V of his hairline: it would have suited him, too, to be known as the eagle.

Just prior to leaving for the North, he accompanied Swedenborg, the understudy, on a trip to Paris. While overseeing the construction of the balloon, entrusted to one Henri Lachambre, they tried to anticipate the events to come, as if they were preparing for a performance without knowing anything about the theatre in which it would be produced or the public they were likely to receive, a performance like one of those nightmares in which you find yourself on stage without knowing a single line of the role you are supposed to play.

In Paris, they discovered another atmosphere, there was something different in the air, other faces, too – the Parisians, the women in particular, including their landladies, fussed over them, in spite of the fact that they were hardly explorers yet. The aura surrounding them was one of exploits to come, more dazzling, perhaps, than that of exploits already accomplished. They had done nothing yet, but they would, that much was certain, wearing halos already of the snow that would cover their shoulders, in the landscape they had never seen.

They visited workshops, learned about the technical specifications, and most of all they wandered, along the Seine, faces shaded by the tall trees lining the stone embankments, at night making the most of the cafés, the little backstreets. Paris, for them, was the South, a Latin land as remote as the one where they were to come to grief, a mild and welcoming fork in the road. Once forced from one's comfort zone, it is less painful to envisage the wrench of a new separation. Paris was the first stop, the deceptive antechamber for what was to come.

*

Frænkel leans his head against the windowpane. If he opens the window, an odour of hay and pine resin wafts into the carriage. He could get off at the next station. Andrée would barely open an eye and would probably fall straight back to sleep. He is not particularly old, only just forty, but already, when he sleeps, his face sags, no longer as taut as at the start of the journey and his body, tensed at the effort and the dream of taking flight, appears to lean stiffly, as though cast from a single piece.

The train makes frequent stops. Frænkel would only have to step over the running board in order to jump onto the platform. He could stretch out his legs in the tall grass and slip away, unnoticed. By the time he returned, the train would be long gone, Andrée still fast asleep on board, heading off to this solitary venture which has always been his alone. Train journeys allow for such passing reveries but, of course, Frænkel does not stand up, a dash through the tall grass is for madmen or poets, and he is a man of honour, serious and trustworthy as only the truly insane perhaps are.

When the train reaches its destination, it will be necessary to meet up with the others, take the boat to Norway, shut themselves away in the cramped cabins or take some air up on deck, stare at the vessel's foaming wake into the night, dine in Gothenburg, then in Bergen where it is already colder, where more and more alcohol is consumed, where they watch the mountains carve trenches into the sea.

They will sail between the islands, at North Cape. They'll try to get their bearings in the fog then make their way again along the vivid green, vertical coast, where red wooden houses perch along the clifftops. They'll cross the Arctic Circle, feel the first snowfalls on their skin. They'll eat berries, salmon and reindeer meat.

They are almost at the end of their journey. Once past Tromsø, the landscape becomes increasingly inaccessible, increasingly distant as the notion settles in their mind of a whiteness that will erase everything around them. Nothing remains but this goal of theirs which feels like an abyss, and through the clamour of drunken evenings – the animated dinners on sailing ship decks or, during the brief stopovers, through the speeches, the toasts, the garlands of lights, through the inebriated nights that lay waste to them – the whiteness continues its relentless expansion, cutting them off from their dining companions, their drinking partners, swathing them in their own particular aura. Other people talk to them respectfully, awkwardly, as you might address those preparing to leave the earth when you have your own two feet firmly anchored to the ground – they barely dare to shake their hand.

So, of course, there is to be no question of retreating like the previous year, impossible to make the journey back in the opposite direction, to hear the clamour dwindle, along with the number of bouquets. Once they have reached Svalbard, they must resolve to depart, whatever it takes, for as is quite evident, they already have.

They had already left when each of them lying in their bed, in the warmth of their sheets or indeed of another body, listened to the noise of the town as if it no longer quite concerned them, unwittingly ridding themselves already of the voices and presence of others.

They had already left when the balloon's gondola took off from Parisian soil for the first time, when Frænkel felt the air grow heavy and slip past his body, when he saw the layout of the French capital grow sharper as they rose, then dissipate once more into the urban fabric, punctuated by the silhouettes of her mythical monuments – Sacré-Cœur, Notre-Dame, the Eiffel Tower – the layering of the centuries, the geometric shapes assumed by the slightest filthy little courtyard and undesirable neighbourhoods when seen from the sky, the lacework suddenly disclosing the architects' visions. How he appreciated the calm as the contraption gained altitude, as the noise faded, as the wind fell, and the rhythm of his heart finally settled, when a bottle was then opened, the landscape admired, when you could laugh at your own fear.

It seemed as if he could see the true face of the world, uncluttered, stripped back, known to so few men, a vision that succeeded in convincing him of the necessity of their own undertaking which, ultimately, would mean placing at the North Pole the first stones of this civilisation, whose crowning glory was laid out beneath him and which, by dint of their own straining efforts, of whose excesses they were as yet unaware, would lead to the unveiling of the world's pole from its icy sheath, so that it too might one day be offered up to their fellow men as Paris had just been offered up to him.

They have all already left when the desire to go conceals everything else, and so Nils, Salomon August and Knut were looking out the window, drinking tea, kissing a cheek, an eyelid, and already they were elsewhere.

They slip across the open sea. The occasional translucent block of ice floats on the calm water. There are many of them, only men, gathered on the deck of the boat, watching the last archipelago come into view, watching Danes Island take shape.

Where they drop anchor, the way is blocked by immaculate ramparts, their gunboat, the *Svensksund*, in whose hold the balloon is resting – deflated, flaccid, a suit waiting to be filled with a body – breaks through the ice while the carrying vessel, the *Virgo*, which is following them with the remaining equipment, slips through in its wake.

Inching forward, they force their way through Svalbard's barriers. Metal strikes and grinds against the solid blocks, darkened by the sombre colours stretching from sea to rock. What you see is a long, silent ribbon, what you hear is a silence punctuated by a tear, a crash, by the screech of birds who every now and again swoop down towards you, a flash of fear and incomprehension in their eye – they have never seen any human, no, or anything that might resemble one.

In order to unload the *Virgo*, they must explode the remaining ice with dynamite: a muffled noise, liquid, immediately swallowed up, ice crushed and submerged, the path is clear.

ROCKS

Two long months

There is a slight sense of déjà vu to the landscape. Nothing has changed in the intervening year, except perhaps the light, which changes so quickly so far north, as well as a few minor details which they are amused to point out. Notwithstanding the almost intimidating grandeur of their surrounds, Andrée enjoys finding himself on familiar territory.

Further on from the shore on Danes Island, where the snow thickens, there is a small house which they name "Pike's House." Nearby, the balloon hangar constructed the previous year is waiting for them, an impressive construction erected on the shore, a spider's web of wooden planks and canvas, housing for the balloon.

Andrée is reassured, it has scarcely been damaged by ill weather: all they need do now is wait for favourable winds. He raises his hand in the clean air. He remains like that for some time, a stiff scarecrow warning off the Arctic terns. He's trying to get a sense of the wind, thrilling to the slightest gust. Then he lets his hand drop once again.

He would have liked to have been able to anticipate everything but, of course, it's impossible, their journey resembles nothing that has gone before, it was absurd to sketch out a plan. They will have to improvise in order to avoid the thing he most fears: having to return home once more empty-handed.

Days go by. As the winds, evidently, are taking their time to appear, they do all they can to stave off the unpleasant premonition of some sort of persistent curse. They pretend not to notice time passing, the days mounting up, spring heading towards the light of summer. Instead, they spend time sorting themselves out, turning this shingle beach facing the open sea, this pebble strip overwhelmed by enormous mountains, into their base camp, their testing ground, their playground. There is an entire team of technicians, scientists, mechanics, some of them very young, posing proudly in their work gear, faces blackened, hands hanging at their sides, and then there are the curious, the journalists and the public figures drawn by the scent of adventure and success.

Here on this lost island, they organise their social rules of engagement from scratch, based on that other society, the more extensive one waiting for them back in Stockholm, and elsewhere. Same hierarchies, same humiliations, same amusements – caps and white tablecloths, ice buckets, reclining chairs and elegant music in the evenings at supper time, a society of men in their own company, consisting of manly games and tasks, a society identical to their own and yet at the same time losing the memory of what has been left behind.

Nils is already taking photographs. A little off to the side, a little removed, he then returns to his companions, smiling, after having slipped away, revealing nothing of his premature regrets which are still made easier by the frisson of adventure.

Just imagine the music resonating between the mountains, in the endless daylight. Just imagine the luxury on display in the white light that highlights every detail of the setting – a table, a chair, a jacket, the elegance of a cufflink.

Nils presses the shutter release as if it were a trigger. In the evenings, if he is asked, apparently he plays the violin.

Andrée has itchy feet. He goes back and forth in the rowing boat, spruces up the balloon house, clears away the snow, draws up lists, measures depths, writes secret missives. I can see him heading off, already a little stooped, along the grey shore, I can see him nodding his head, reviewing his calculations and, already, his failures, resolutely contesting the landscape's recalcitrance – it will prove more stubborn than himself.

To keep himself busy he keeps a log of the numerous delicate species of vegetation, even if their growth is slow and their size diminutive. There is the Alpine rock-cress with its four white petals and golden-yellow heart; the dwarf birch, relic from the ice age, which seems only to share its name and the shape of its leaf with those species growing in milder latitudes; the polar willow which grows to only 5 centimetres and spreads, creeping, over the rocky ground, creating patient Lilliputian forests which Andrée steps over, cautiously, every now and again managing to flatten them. There is the Arctic harebell and its little purple corolla; the Svalbard poppy, its leaves and stalk cloaked in a fine down to protect it from the wind; the widespread pillows of rockfoils seeking out the sun's weak rays; and the black crowberry, whose succulent berries are like birds' eyes hiding in its foliage.

And many more still, he loses himself among them on his tireless walks along the shore. He gathers, keeps an eye on the vegetation and other signs: harbingers of their departure. The waiting seems to seep out of the landscape itself. It moves, changes, breathes to its own rhythm. If the cold returns, the ice will close up. If the weather remains fine, the sea will open. They are reliant on it, the weather, so there is always a point to his observations. To observe is always to hope, to be afraid. At night, Andrée dreams that the wind rises, he feels it take his body, whip his cheeks, bring tears to his eyes. On waking, the air is still against the disappointed skin of his hand.

All, or almost all of them, suffer in silence. Some of the journalists, some of the notable types, weary of the polar drizzle that makes their whiskers curl, have decided to do an about-face, drawn by the prospects of more accommodating lands or of following more fortunate explorers. But the imagination and enthusiasm of those who remain is redoubled. They make merry out in the open, in shirtsleeves if the sun is beating down, they have ski races, at the edge of the glaciers they gather larvae and insects entrapped in the ice. They are like an army with no adversary that ends up wishing for the enemy, listening, at night, for illusory signs of its presence. They put their nose to the wind, kill time as best they can.

They pace the shore, the beach, the rocks: the slightest fragment of stone contains a world in miniature. The colours, just to start – the smooth shapes of obsidian black outcrops, relics of lava, as if harbouring the vestiges of heat at its heart, and then that other black which is only surface deep on the rougher, dryer rocks, a stain that crumbles under the lichen's flamboyant bite. It seems as brittle as ash but it is hard, coloured through, stained in patches like hand-blown glass, bright orange or anemone-red, alabaster powder of shellfish in the glass paperweights shaped, like ink blotches, by the puddles punctuating the rock.

Honeycomb rocks, cavities reflecting every variation in the light, creating transparent pools between two anthracite faces, cave-like, rusty brown, pools sheltering slippery organisms which they poke at with their fingertips, grottos where the water shimmers, icy cold, leaving sulphurous halos on their clothes and dangling hands – they leap from one rock to another, rediscovering old reflexes, bodies cast into the void, feet which find their footing at the last instant. Rectilinear blocks, split into geometric fragments, piled one on top of the other, prove convenient stairs which they never tire of scaling.

It's as if nature is slipping a foothold under each of their steps at the very moment they are about to fall, slicing sheer rock faces into smooth, horizontal plates, shot through by karstic faults, a pale pink that looks almost malleable, soft, alive, yet is harder still than the stone encasing it, quartz-like in its translucency.

Other rocks, close to the shore, are gently curved, almost liquid, and already the sea is there, those hillocks rubbed by the emery board of the waves, the blue of a hollow cheek, a pulsing temple, veined yellow and grainier than the sand itself, milkier than the reflection of the sky in the basins carved out by the tide.

All day they inhale to the rhythm of the sea, insistent, omnipresent, blending with their own breath which dissolves in the receding tide, grating at their chest as it scrapes away at the shore, they revel in the light. They are far away.

One of these men waits with greater apprehension than the others, observes the landscape quite differently. It is Vilhelm Swedenborg, the replacement, the reserve. In a few days, a few weeks at worst, he will head home or take off towards the North Pole, resume life as it was or cover himself in glory – does it make a difference, whether or not it is posthumous? Should it make a difference? Should he be hopeful or afraid? Swedenborg no longer knows.

Andrée seems, first and foremost, to have his heart set on him by virtue of his name, since his family, which numbers no fewer than five explorers, turns out to include the inventor Emmanuel Swedenborg, the Swedish Leonardo da Vinci, known for his studies on the Milky Way, the solar system and even for having met God in person, who is said to have shown him the heavens, the angels, an entire distant world he was then duty-bound to share with ordinary mortals. The replacement's reputation is further enhanced by that of his father-in-law, Adolf Erik Nordenskjöld, the first explorer to be correct about the Northeast Passage. Such pedigree is not to be sniffed at: the prestige of all these great men will certainly reflect on the expedition as a whole by virtue of the presence of their descendant.

For the time being, Lieutenant-Colonel Vilhelm Swedenborg has not, however, done much exploring. He has a rudimentary knowledge of the mechanics of the balloon, watched the streets of Paris grow smaller in the distance from its basket, alongside Frænkel, tried to overcome his cold sweats and his motion sickness.

Doubtless he is watching Frænkel and Strindberg closely, on the lookout for any sign of weakness, of having caught a chill, a fever, or for any shift in mood. His life depends on these men, on their physical strength, on their moral steadfastness.

As the days pass, he sizes up the balloon as one might an enemy, a hope, watching it slowly inflate, in the balloon house, until it assumes, as if by miracle, its perfectly round shape. He crawls, with the others, across its smooth surface, right over the delicate fabric, in order to caulk any leaks as they are revealed and seal them with varnish, endless coats of varnish which will soon enough prove insufficient to prevent it deflating, imperceptibly but undoubtedly, as their wait continues.

At the start of June, there they still are, fabricating toboggans from animal pelts, hurling themselves full speed across the snow, laughing like children.

LEGEND

1839

More than fifty years earlier, she is waiting on a similar beach, looking out to a similar sea, in a cold even more biting.

Léonie d'Aunet is nineteen years old, has dark-blue eyes, smooth, black hair that falls in ribbons at her temples. She, too, has seen the coast take shape at the prow of the vessel where she had been sleeping for months in her cabin lined with reindeer skins: a line, a pale shape, scarcely different from the floating blocks of ice, a land of *trompe-l'oeil*, as if fashioned from the same materials as the sea.

There are so few ever to have reached this place that it might suffice to link them, to draw the contours of a small community unaware of its own existence. *As for female explorers*, she wrote, she has the honour of being *the first such specimen*.

In order to make it this far, she has had to convince her future husband, the painter Auguste Biard, to participate in a scientific expedition – from which he will return with sketches, paintings – and, on top of that, to agree to her accompanying him.

Then, she has had to survive an accident in a horse-drawn carriage, slice through the snow on a sleigh pulled by reindeers, swallow down akvavit and soups in which she feared gunpowder had been sprinkled, tumble into icy water, suffer seasickness and the jibes of crew members who called her the "thin, peaky, skinny woman, with feet like sponge-finger biscuits and hands that had never lifted an oar; a woman to be snapped over your knee and stuffed into your pocket in pieces."

She encountered peculiar customs in Belgium and Holland, then the red houses of Norway, the sepulchral panoramas of the Lofoten Islands and the lost town of Tromsø where *most of the houses are set on wooden piles and hang in the air like coffee tables*, and whose only street, the Canebière of Marseille of the place, comes out at *an enormous green and blue glacier, perfectly capable of swallowing you under an avalanche, if you were curious enough to observe it at close quarters.*

Ultimately, she will spend only a short time in Spitzbergen, the main island of the Svalbard archipelago. She will only glimpse it. The place will, above all else, remain illuminated by the path towards it, that slow climb towards magnetic north where every estuary, every rock, every variation in temperature hints at its contours.

As she waits for the boat to depart once more, Léonie walks the 100 paces along the bay facing the open sea, a bay licked by the dark waters leaching from the blocks of ice. She peers at the bones that litter the shore, hunches over those of walruses and seals left by fishermen but also those of men who have not survived the wintering, exposed now to the air amid the worm-eaten planks of their coffins. The ice was probably too hard to allow their exhausted companions to dig through it in order to bury them, unless the humidity of the permafrost has brought the bodies back to the surface.

It is still a delicate matter in Svalbard, even today, to bury the dead. As the frozen earth preserves the cadavers intact, and with them any illnesses, viruses, contagious remains from the past, local laws prohibit anybody dying there. The elderly, the unwell, all those who do not appear fit for that harsh, glittering, ephemeral life, are advised to end their days elsewhere.

Nor is it advised to give birth in that place, which bears so little resemblance to any other: owing to a lack of infrastructure to accommodate them, pregnant women who are approaching term are dispatched to the mainland.

*

Léonie knelt down, as she tells it, hunched over the bones. She picked up those she was able to pick up, placed them into the gaping coffins. She read the dates, the places inscribed on the graves, attempted to decipher the names. In two of the coffins, the bodies, clothed, were still almost intact. She realised she may never see soil again, never see France, her home, she sensed that she was at the very end of the world and that it was perfectly possible she might share their fate, caught here forever by the winter.

She felt miniscule, then. She has written as much. She did not seek to conceal her fear. She wondered how they died, imagined their final moments, their last fires, their final meals. By way of another grave for them, she drew the peninsula where the graveyard was, that had never before been mapped.

Upon her return, she is pregnant. She will soon give birth to a daughter conceived somewhere in the Great North, a child of Spitzbergen, who will answer to the curious name of Madame la Baronne Double and who will write several books under the pseudonym Sparkle before dying in 1897, precisely the year when Strindberg, Andrée and Frænkel will themselves arrive at the archipelago.

The story of Léonie d'Aunet could stop there. Perhaps we might have remembered her, perhaps not, but there would have been some hope that she remain, in our memories, *the first specimen of a female explorer*, had she not been stripped of her feat in the same way as the suffragette tossed from the basket of the hot-air balloon in Méliès' film: expelled from the sky much like being written out of the expedition.

The mark that Léonie d'Aunet is to leave in the annals of history will not be the traces of her footsteps in the snow, or that peninsula which she was the first to sketch, but the more bitter mark of another sort – the sort which turns a life into some minor news item.

A poet has been seduced by *her gaze so filled with shadow*. He has just lost his daughter, drowned in the Seine one day when there was not a breath of wind before a strong gust picked up, capsizing the boat she was on. He is no longer able to write, he is looking for something to cling to. She will be that something, this woman so full of energy, irony and drive, only four years older than the daughter who has disappeared, bearing an astonishing resemblance to her. They commence a liaison which will never truly finish, despite everything which is to come. He writes to her – he is a poet, he knows the words to use. His name is Victor Hugo.

Caught in the act of adultery by her husband who has had her followed, Léonie is sent first to a prison for "fallen women," then to a convent, losing custody of her two children, while Hugo, protected by his parliamentarian's privilege, resumes his life as a poet and statesman. He will maintain contact with her until the very end, helping her as he is able, but nothing will breach the divide that has opened between them – he is on a pedestal, she is beneath him, impossible to come together again, to extend a hand.

Many years after her journey, left alone with her wavering explorer's memories, she will continue to write books which various people persist in attributing to her lover. *A Woman's Voyage to Spitzberg* will be all that survives of her work, just as she will retain the jagged form of that island in one corner of her mind, in prison, at the convent, then through the poverty of her final years, that island where she spent so little time, gathering the bones of the dead, fearful of the ice closing over, not considering, perhaps, that this hostile place was providing her all the latitude that would ever be offered to her, a reservoir of space she would forever draw upon, fighting for the fact that her name might be associated with this image of a polar landscape and not that of an adultery, miserably established, in a small bedchamber, by a police superintendent.

She was left with the shape of an island and the persistent echo of a legend, told to her by a German shopkeeper as the two women sailed along the coast of the little island of Falster. A rich woman, the shopkeeper told her, had ordered a church to be built and had vowed to live for as long as the structure remained standing. That was three centuries ago, she added, the church is still there, the woman too, unable to speak or even to move, just a body lying in a wooden box, watched over by a priest.

Upon every one of her birthdays, the woman gathers her strength to ask if the church is still standing, then lapses back into her lethargy, hoping in her innermost being for the destruction of her life's work, reminding us that the places to which we choose to link our lives can sometimes have the power to bend them, that endeavours which were supposed to render us immortal may ultimately weigh us down, making us regret the hours when nothing had as yet been started, when we would rise in the morning with the simple desire for love, adventure and that immense desire, which the brevity of Léonie d'Aunet's journey will have served only to nourish, becoming ever keener as the journey itself grew distant, so vast as to cradle her entire life.

WHITE NIGHT

June 1897

Nils is on night duty. This evening, he is the one to keep watch in the balloon house. The balloon hangs over him, enfolding him in its webbing which is covered in the cursed snow that continues to fall despite Andrée insisting so vehemently that the sun is supposed to shine at this time of year, this snow which is making a liar of him, undermining Nils' trust, the blind faith he had, until now, in the expedition's leader.

He no longer really knows from whom or from what he is supposed to be guarding the balloon – from the bears or from the sharp beaks of the petrel birds, or perhaps it's from a member of the expedition, tempted to sneak out of bed and try to sabotage their attempt, while there is still time.

By the end of spring, there is no longer any real night to speak of. The never-ending daylight has already leached into the night. There is barely any darkness left, where you might conceal yourself. Nils probably quite likes it, the darkness, for it allows him to be alone. The night is never black, never silent. There is the screech of birds in the distance, some of which will follow the balloon's ascent into the sky, and then the long periods of heavy silence, offering remote companionship to the others' breathing.

The smells of the open sea and of the water trapped in the ice, denser, in some strange way more liquid, catch on the tongue. Nils is alone and yet not entirely, so he may choose who to invite into this half-somnolence, this languid vigil, under the fragments of sky that escape the reach of the balloon's glowing cupola.

By day, increasingly, he finds himself shut away in the darkroom he has set up on the gunboat, *Svensksund*. There he experiments with photographic techniques. He's studying, developing, creating. He is learning, already, how to transform their life into evidence, into memory. There is the time he takes for the shot, wedging his tripod into the snow and allowing his companions to perform the ballet of their daily routines or rather, to mimic it, again, for the camera's slow, fixed eye. Frozen by the exposure, each of them proffers their best angle, there in the middle of a snowscape turned theatre set.

The pictures which show them in motion are those that require the greatest effort: they stand observing a mountain ridge, lined up like toy soldiers, faces serious, hands on hips, one of them lifting an arm to point something out – he must have held it aloft for quite some time, waiting for Strindberg to immortalise him. To see them now, it is hard to say whether they are wanting to fix these lived moments in time or if they are merely acting them out for show.

In one of the photographs, they are standing in the balloon house. The balloon makes a lightweight, bright roof overhead, a circus big top. A sort of cloud, a mist, filters through an opening: is it vapour or a failing of the camera unable to adequately capture the light, transforming it into this milky halo and casting a veil over some of the faces? It's as if it is heralding the start of a performance. There they are, ready to take their bows. They're proud, all of them, laughing, animated and yet at a loose end.

In other images, some of them are perched on the balloon's fabric, sitting on the great, supple dome, blurring all notion of space – they could be atop a stationary flying saucer or perhaps some space station intended to capture messages from outer space.

There is the time when the shot is taken and then the time spent in the darkroom where Nils is now alone, coaxing out all that took place out in the open air. All that remains, already, of the shouts, the bravado, the gesturing, is the hollow darkness.

He seems to have more need for a bit of distance than the others –
a need to cut himself off, to carve out his own space, in the darkroom
aboard the *Svensksund* or under the tent, on the beach, or by night
under the balloon's nocturnal dome. Once they take off, they will be
sleeping huddled up against each other, there will be no more solitude,
or anything like it, so he takes advantage of these final moments. He creates his own reserves of silence, his own cave-like space. Photography
has always offered him that possibility; since adolescence he has never
grown weary of the withdrawal required by the world in order to allow
its transformation into images. To document this voyage he has the
best material at his disposal, the technical innovation which, in 1897,
roll film still is – so much easier to handle than glass plates. He plays at
being the sorcerer's apprentice, revelling in the miracle of reproduction.

When he looks at the silhouettes starting to emerge, just before they
take on human form, perhaps he is mindful, initially, of the abstract
outline traced by the light, of those moments when inanimate matter
is suddenly transformed into something tangible and just as quickly
disappears again – only a few seconds of overexposure and the image
dissolves back into darkness.

Even before the expedition begins, he is already documenting its
traces. He will no doubt wonder, again and again, what his photographs
will look like, once they have taken off, once they have been developed.
Will they be legible? Will there be sufficient contrast? Will they not risk
being overexposed in that endless daylight? Technician that he is, he
will doubtless try to anticipate the quality of the blacks and the softness
of the greys, and he will despair at all the white which risks chewing its
way into those living forms. And doubtless, he will end up growing used
to the idea that he will not develop them himself, that if they ever come
to life, it will be in a stranger's hands.

In the artificial shadows of the darkroom, perhaps Nils also sees the
contrasts in his own life growing sharper, sees the guiding principles of

61

his own existence more clearly, with their ridgelines and boundaries, and perhaps he is astonished at not having known how better to distinguish them when he was still able to.

Seen from here, from the top of the world, his life resembles yet one more photograph, smooth, flat, its composition perfect, allowing him to identify every salient element, every precious moment which at the time he was incapable of recognising, such as the circumstances that had brought him to this point without his ever noticing how each step had led to the next. That innocuous comment made to Andrée in his office in Stockholm, that evasive answer which had nonetheless led to his unwitting involvement in this folly of a plan that initially had only been alluded to indirectly.

He suddenly hears them differently, the pleasantries bandied about at soirées of the well-to-do, a small glass of port held between two fingers, little by little their playful conversations settling into this peculiar complicity that acknowledges neither distance nor hierarchy but that permits slightly firmer handshakes, slightly more open smiles, a complicity that transforms into an ever more binding agreement. He recognises those moments well, now, those interlocking instances that traced out his trajectory, remembers the tracks which he himself assembled, blindly, one by one, and onto which he then slipped.

We seize on one moment among others, without knowing immediately what makes it unique, significant, something that will only be understood going forward, like an image appearing in the chemical baths well after the moment it was taken, like the expression on some faces that will belatedly be illuminated.

Nils learns to extract the crucial scenes, to transform the years lived into a succession of moments, one linked to the next according to a logic that is suddenly clear; it is as if he is leafing through the album in which his entire life is brought together to be displayed and, from this distance, it seems to him that everything which amounted to fat, to excess, all those impatient hours lived without ever identifying a purpose, were there only to serve as the cement for these essential moments which suddenly are materialising before his very eyes.

Thus, when he met Anna, he did not identify immediately what was transpiring between them. Maybe, initially, they were content to throw each other polite looks as he left the house where he taught violin, and where she was responsible for looking after the children, sensing unspoken affinities – both straightforward young people, but well-educated and enjoying a shared love of music.

Perhaps they spoke of composers they admired, notes they stumble on, and maybe one of these confidences led to the first stirrings of their emotions, their first smiles. Perhaps, then, after a day filled with wrong notes and children's cries, they found themselves one evening boarding the boat from Johannesdal to Stockholm, the boat which soon enough Nils would take every weekend in order to join her at the residential accommodation where she would be studying music, since Anna had no wish to remain a governess the rest of her days, but instead wanted to appear on stage, to make a living from what she was teaching.

Perhaps they walked, that evening or another, along the edge of the road, not too far, not too close to one another, savouring the incongruity of that first rapprochement, being next to a man, a woman, out in public, when one is neither brother, nor sister, nor even related, the strangeness one seeks to pass off as routine, the steps that are shared, bodies adopting a stance they have never before adopted, and while they were slow to realise how close they were already to one another, that a flush was mounting in their cheeks, a tension within, perhaps Nils and Anna spoke of violin bowing, or one's touch on a piano, and maybe he invited her to a restaurant in Stockholm, under snow, expecting a first fleeting touch of her hand, unless it was she, Anna, who sought him out, Anna who one day would demand that her heart be torn from her.

Perhaps they laughed at the curious coincidence of her name which struck them like a portent, Anna Charlier, the word *charlière* in French meaning precisely the sort of gas balloon in which Nils was about to take off. A name like an omen which neither of them would have noticed, an omen by which, on the contrary, they would have been subsumed, as if sealing a sort of pact, as if her very name were an encouragement, giving way to some weakness.

Perhaps, so newly betrothed, they had no time to know the effect of their skin, one against the other, what torture, what friction, what desires spurred on by the slightest approach, absent those clothes which concealed Anna's breasts from Nils just as they hid from her that broad chest, that tender sex, those rounded shoulders.

Had all this not yet allowed her to experience pleasure, perhaps Anna never knew what she was already missing, a void all the more poignant for not ever knowing what might have satisfied it, forever compelling her to conjure up Nils' skin at the touch of her English husband, to seek, in that body, the forms that had taken flight.

Or perhaps they had, before the marriage, moved further along than propriety might have required, heightened by the imminence of the departure or by the small hope of a return, perhaps the prospect of separation pushed them more quickly towards each other, made them search under clothes with eager hands to discover the contours of their bodies, made them bury their faces against skin, go deeper, to discover, with an intensity which subsequently, in the loneliness of their memories, would have them transform their awkwardness into passion, what ordinarily would only transpire during the course of a wedding night.

Perhaps it is that which Anna will have such difficulty forgetting, the urgency which causes a hollowness in the belly, which has one breathing at the other's ear, because that is enough, a breath, that, and the heat of one's lips. But maybe they were happy enough to talk, in that Stockholm restaurant, candles and white tablecloths, windows open to the night, perhaps, without admitting so much, they were a little bored in each other's company – perhaps absence was the grand story of their love, opening it up like a wound.

*

From here, these questions no longer have any meaning. All that remains are the images. They are enough, for Nils, who lets them slowly file past into the night. He is not at sea, he is not up in the sky, it would not be so bad if he were to fall asleep, so he lets sleep come, he remains on the brink, on the verge of foundering, in that place which still belongs to him and where everything, at times, is still able to co-exist, the candle flame, the weight of the night sky and always that photograph found in pieces in the remains of the camp, always Anna, lying in the spring-time grass, her hands hidden in the mass of her hair, her smile that knows what is coming.

As he falls asleep it all blends together, the sphere overhead, that taut skin quivering in the night, and the skin of the girl who is breathing so far away, in the distant warmth of his deep sleep – growing large, in his dreams, like a giantess.

Perhaps, too, he is able to visualise the snapshots he might take of the future – the crossing and the return, their plans, a wedding, maybe he is already able to transform them into memories, to choose the lighting, the composition, as if he had already passed through to the other side, a lifeless observer, calm, able to see himself walking to the altar, Anna's skin against his, in his impossible memory.

What beautiful memories they will be, whispering into the soft auricle of her ear, telling her of these nights when he was thinking of her, tiny beneath the giant orb of the balloon where he is able to imagine himself in mid-air, already in the gondola and, still on the threshold of sleep, telling himself that they are controlling the pitching and tossing, that they are almost there.

ASCENT

11 July 1897

I t is departure day.

The final day on the ground.

The day whose every minute they will have the chance to run through, replaying every moment, revisiting every image, over and over again. The leaden grey of the sky and the faces of those gathering to see them off. The looks that lock with theirs just for a moment. The handkerchiefs. And the panic that makes the heart race.

It is a majestic presence there in the hangar, surrounded by miniscule men. The sandbags, their ballast, are still resting on the ground, white sacks linked to a multitude of ropes. It seems immense, stable, the material incarnation of the most considerable expertise – ergonomic, and skin tautly stretched; the Svalbard wind snarls around it.

They can wait no longer. The wind has arrived at last and they must seize it, as the balloon's thick, diamond-scored fabric quivers, they must leap into the gondola, hurry to send final telegrams. Not to leave now, when the opportunity is finally presenting itself, would be to admit that they would never leave, that the whole enterprise, from the outset, was doomed to fail, so notwithstanding doubts and premonitions, the lines binding them to the earth must be cut.

The haste of these final hours is matched inversely by the languor of those hours that preceded them, time that had stretched out is recaptured, tightened, there are regrets perhaps for having allowed it to slip by,

66

for not having done more, not having done it faster, now all the technical adjustments, the written farewells, must be squeezed into the remaining moments, and it's creaking, breathing, finally they will be leaving.

There are dozens of them, all busying themselves, coordinated, a true ballet. Were one to gain a little height, to rise above to have an overview, what a peculiar spectacle it would be, all these tiny men dismantling the wall of the balloon house, pushing carrier pigeons into their baskets, making final adjustments, pulling, cutting, climbing, polishing, repairing, shouting, steadying, stumbling, bustling. The balloon is battered by the violence of the wind, its calotte, stretched to breaking point, makes muffled sounds – the sandbags are not enough to hold it in place. The aeronauts try to boost each other's courage by opening one final bottle of champagne.

They climb into the basket.

Together they raise a toast, lift their glass to the sky.

The final ropes are cut through with a sword.

The balloon does not ascend immediately. For a moment it remains almost immobile. All three of them are suffering a sense of disbelief, overwhelmed by the apparatus now containing them, directing them. In the photographs taken just prior to take-off, they are squeezed into the car and, all of a sudden, you might say here are three men who are play-acting, and you might think to yourself, they will come back down, they are going to laugh and return to earth, but they do not come back down, they remain in the wicker basket which, having just been released, is swung abruptly against the balloon house walls by that much vaunted, long-awaited southerly.

They must find a way to cushion the shock, deal with the most pressing matters first. They have no time to see anything, to observe anything, to make any announcements. They must take the wind and rise up, too high, too quickly, stomachs drop, hearts rise to the mouth, the balloon dips in an air pocket and down plunge their hearts once more.

*

Some years later, in 1912, in a glacial February that has Paris feeling almost like Svalbard, Franz Reichelt, a ladies' tailor originally from Austria, will undertake the first flight from the Eiffel Tower.

The skies are in fashion. Aircraft have just started criss-crossing the sky. Everybody is designing parachutes. None of Reichelt's test runs have, for the moment, proven successful, but perhaps he is counting on that mythical place that is the Eiffel Tower, on that iron *grande dame*, or on a unique juncture of time and luck for this particular flight to succeed, despite everything. He refuses to carry out trials with a dummy and appears empty-handed, proud, dressed in the outfit which he has been working on for two years, a design inspired by the morphology of the bat, fervently hoping to prove its efficacy.

It is 8:22 in the morning. The cold is piercing. Reichelt has been filmed and one can still see him today, standing at precisely that point where it is just as possible either to jump or to head back down, to resume his life once more or to launch it into the void.

His supposed wings have not yet been unfurled, you can just make them out around him, in sooty black and white, a cumbersome framework of fabric which gives him the look of a child in fancy dress. He is wearing a sort of cap, which he removes for a brief wave, and baggy trousers. He spins around, as if at the circus, or in an arena, so he might be immortalised from every angle by the camera. All you can see of his face are the brown tips of his moustache.

And then, he is up, at the guardrail of the first level, 57 metres above the ground, he has climbed up onto a rudimentary scaffold – a stool balancing on a low table. His wings, now, are unfurled, black, thick, constructed entirely of starched fabric. He waves his arms about furiously.

This is the point when time suddenly coagulates: these thirty seconds when he hesitates before leaping.

The two men who were there to assist him are now out of the field of vision. He is alone, facing the void. The panels of fabric making his trousers billow around his ankles, probably some laboriously conceived technical detail that serves only to lend him a bulkier appearance.

He does exactly what individuals who suffer from vertigo are coun-selled against doing, he looks down, tips his head, lifts it back up, the sky, the earth, now he has one foot on the stool and the other on the guardrail, it is increasingly difficult to retreat, he shifts himself forwards in little jolts, never truly upright, never truly immobile, destabilised by his own body's disarray and by the gusts of wind which unbalance him, precipitating his fall, much as the favourable winds determined the timing of the Andrée expedition's departure.

All at once, the images of Reichelt and those of the balloon about to lift off seem to be inverse reflections of the same trajectory: just as they rose upwards, he is about to leap into the void, as if, in the space of an instant, heaven and earth had been inverted.

We see almost nothing, of the sky, nothing of his face nor the sen-timents that pass across it, we see only his moustache, a feature that conceals everything else – emotions and regrets, anguish and courage; it reduces him to a symbol, a toy model, a minor character from another era, gesturing ludicrously, when in fact what we are witnessing is a man about to send himself to his death.

Now Reichelt is just looking down. He is still making minor adjust-ments, his body tilts forwards, we will never know if the defining moments of his life flashed before him, images, perhaps, from his childhood in that part of Austria which now forms part of the Czech Republic, from his Parisian life – Franz is now known as François, one year earlier he obtained his French citizenship and it is from the iconic monument of his host country that he is choosing to leap, small-time immigrant tailor that he is, who has left, by way of last will and tes-tament, a letter riddled with spelling errors, perhaps, but written in French, in which he bequeaths to his employee the benefit of his unpaid invoices and, to his father, his jewellery and watches.

He will jump from atop the structure which is France's pride and joy, as Andrée, Strindberg and Frænkel took off for the glory of Sweden. But we are no longer in 1897, we are in 1912 and the world has changed, the First World War is not far off and, while technological advances are allowing men to be sent into the sky, many, too, find themselves on the roads and many, like Reichelt, are no longer keen to insist upon belonging to their country of birth but rather their desire, at any cost, is to be adopted, to be recognised.

It is a long time, thirty seconds, when one is struggling to decide whether or not to die. Reichelt leans forward on the foot resting on the guardrail, he loses his balance, his face contorts, the fabric behind his head unfurls a little further in the wind, an immense monk's hood which conceals his face. Instead of displaying their wingspan, his wings fold back in and surround him as he drops like a stone. Later, they will measure the depth of the hole left by his body in the frozen ground.

ANDRÉE'S JOURNAL

11–12 July 1897

No land in sight. The horizon is not clear however. It is indeed a wonderful journey …

… a fulmar visible quite near the car
Coffee made in 18 min.
Sucking the claw-wrench
fulmar   rain of pease

WEIGHTLESSNESS

11 July 1897

It is only when he sees the balloon lift off, that broad cupola of cross-hatched pink silk, hanging over the mist, that Swedenborg realises that he is still on the ground, a replacement who has not had to replace anybody, a spectator among spectators, and we will never know if he was champing at the bit, cursing their good spirits and their cast-iron constitutions, or indeed if he thanked his lucky stars along with theirs.

As the balloon becomes a tiny dot over the sea, Swedenborg's own journey diminishes also to the point where it leaves that peculiar impression left by certain dreams, certain endlessly revisited fantasies. He was physically and mentally prepared, he was ready for anything. A thousand times he saw himself leave, a thousand times he saw himself fly off. From this point onwards he will live with the weight of this journey that was never undertaken, the details of which, for more than thirty years, he will never be able to imagine. And in 1930, when the bodies of Strindberg, Frænkel and Andrée are repatriated to Sweden, Swedenborg – an ageing, retired colonel – will be one of the party escorting them, parting the black-clad crowd to bring them back to their tomb.

A drop in temperature. A drop in morale. The reading of a wind. A hydrogen leak. Had one of them renounced, Swedenborg would have climbed into the basket in his place and one day his body would have been found under the snow, and it would be Strindberg, or perhaps Frænkel, accompanying his coffin.

He looks skyward for a long time, until the balloon disappears into the fog.

They are alone now. Far from onlookers and hurrahs, with no more witnesses, apart from the camera's eye which will make an appearance soon enough, and despite every attempt to rely on it to fill the void, everything which escapes its gaze will remain theirs alone.

For the time being, it must be said, there is not much to see. Even though Nils has the camera glued to his wide-open eye, everything is blurry, everything is white, an opaque sky, dense, criss-crossed by fulmars and ivory gulls, damp from the squally fog.

"Look! Down there!" cries one of them, finger pointing: curious creatures diving and re-emerging through the distant waves.

"Sea serpents!" They exclaim, laughing.

They could almost believe they are weightless, these men, elegant explorers rising above the melee, even if they must quickly acknowledge, as Andrée described, that the balloon is a little *depressed*. Its skin, it is true, already seems not as taut as it was upon departure. Something is subsiding before their helpless eyes.

Not much being known of the climate in this part of the world, Andrée thought that summer would see constant and glorious sunshine. The sun is not shining. And the fog is descending. The balloon is growing heavier. Suddenly, there is panic: they are sinking, it is as abrupt as in those dreams where one misses a step, cries out, wakes up covered in sweat, but they do not wake up, they cling on, busy themselves. Frænkel hastily clears the sails with which the balloon is equipped, hunched against the gusts of wind he burns his palms on the rough rope but to no avail, they are losing ever more altitude, dropping towards the sea in sudden jerky motions.

The draglines, ballast ropes intended to facilitate steering, detached themselves shortly after departure. Without them, their balloon is nothing more than a wisp of straw subject to the whims of the wind, the density of the air – impossible to steer.

*

73

At that precise moment, it is still possible to send a signal, to make an emergency landing on the last spit of land still visible, an island by the lofty name of Vogelsang. But they send no signal, clinging on to their balloon which is already unable to be controlled.

In the panic, Nils forgets to throw over the final message which their companions who had remained on Danes Island were later supposed to convey to Anna for her birthday. The farewell gift, with which he had wanted to mark his departure, remains in the basket until it springs to mind once again during a brief moment of calm and he tosses it overboard, but too late, over the wrong island, where nobody will ever set foot.

The sea draws closer, they can now make out every quicksilver crest carving out the back of the waves, they hold on tightly, shouting orders, inaudible questions, but in the fog that muffles it all, in the din of the cursed southerly wind now blowing so hard having had them wait so long, all they can make out are snatches of each other's voices, calling, continuously, for more ballast to be released. They throw overboard what remains of the sand, empty cans, soon it will be provisions bags, instantly devoured by the fog. How many days' survival does each of these bags represent? How many renunciations, each pot of cranberry jam? They end up deciding to offload the cork buoy which was to mark their triumphant arrival at the North Pole, and watch as it falls.

Suddenly, the wind dies. They stop moving. They hold themselves still, soon they are holding their breath: any gesture may mean losing their precarious balance, plunging them into the void. There is a moment of complete stillness. The balloon is stable. Even the birds are quiet. Their voices resonate, strangely, in the icy silence. They cannot see past 2 metres. All they can make out is the pink of the canvas and the silhouettes of their companions, busying themselves with something or nestled into the car when, taking turns, they allow themselves a few minutes' rest. Everything is calm, then, so white, suspended. Their contraption, with its increasingly pointless technology, is the only evidence of mankind for kilometres around.

They appear to have reached their cruising speed. They slide the spirit stove down using a rope, well away from the fabric to avoid it catching fire, and heat up some soup and hot chocolate. They are thirsty, all the time. They breathe, they look, they test the wind. Above the clouds, the sun burns more brightly. The earth stretches out beneath a sky that is finally blue.

There is a moment when Frænkel, Strindberg and Andrée, between jolts, can relax, when time suddenly condenses, when the months of waiting, hesitation, anxiety, suddenly seem laughable. Seen from the skies, they are compressed, these months, into a moment that is pure present, heightened by adrenaline, they need only ascend and everything becomes concrete, sharp, simple in a way which allows them to forget the damage to and inadequacy of the balloon's functioning. Everything dissolves into this dense new sense of time, each second weighted with new sensations, far removed from the rambling days they have left behind them.

Despite every attempt to anticipate the slightest detail, to expect the worst, that moment always arrives, no matter how brief it is, when it is all happening, when you are right in the very heart of things, when the wind is blowing, when the cold is biting, when you wish for nothing more than to be borne away.

Their enthusiasm is short lived: all of a sudden, they are light, too light. The ascent is almost as abrupt as the drop, not the slightest item of waste can be discarded, not a single gram lost, they risk being sucked up by this entirely new lightness. They tense themselves, refrain even from sprinkling the pack ice with their burning piss until once again, slowly at first, they start to fall.

The carrier pigeons are growing impatient in their cage. These birds who find themselves in mid-air, prevented from flying, have been

provided by the Swedish daily newspaper, *Aftonbladet* – much like
Nils' camera, the birds' little round eyes, panic-stricken at every jolt,
are supposed to bear witness to the grand adventure, to be the bear-
ers of good news. Each one is provided with a message intended to be
sent back to the newspaper's premises, in Stockholm, but there had
not been enough time to train them to find the correct building in the
maze of cobble-stoned streets: even were they to extricate themselves
from the mists of the Great North by some miracle, they would run
the risk of losing their way in the sinuous streets of the city among all
the other birds, without anybody ever noticing the little roll attached
to their feathers, or the words stencilled under their wings: ANDRÉE
ANDRÉE ANDRÉE.

Trying to keep their balance in the pitching basket, one of them,
Frænkel, Strindberg, perhaps Andrée, opens the cage and releases
several birds who bat at his frantic hands with their wings, pecking,
panicking, before dispersing in every direction. Quickly, the cage is
closed back up on the remaining birds.

Carrier pigeons match their flight to the paths taken by humans,
they too are subject to the grid-like division of territory. Like us, they
fall victim to Svalbard's monochromatic landscape, its infuriating
characteristics of repetition and reflection. Three of them, however,
manage to make their way clear of the fog.

The first will find its way to Iceland, the second, towards the north
of Norway, where its message will be discovered three years later. The
third penetrates the mist before disappearing over the sea. Something
bright appears as the water approaches, the shades of grey harden, and
out of the smooth expanse forming the backdrop of its flight, the bird
spies a dot from which is rising a plume of smoke: a steamboat. Two
ivory gulls appear from the fog and harry it, hastening it away before
finally it comes to land on the deck. The captain, taking it for a ptar-
migan and no doubt imagining the subtle taste of its flesh, perfectly
roasted in his kitchens, drops it with one shot. Its journey is at an end.

*

What message were the explorers able to entrust to the stubborn bird? What appeal for help, what admission of failure could have been worth attaching to the neck of a poorly trained bird released in mid-air only to land, by some miracle, in the hands of a curious sailor who unfolds the paper, sticky with the creature's blood?

A few words, neatly written, no wavering. Everything is well in the best of all worlds. They content themselves with noting their position. Already, they are writing their own legend. Thumbing their nose at misfortune, at the poor winds and at failure, a lie or a talisman.

Perhaps the sailors give a few hurrahs in honour of the explorers, unaware they are losing their way, alone, barely a few kilometres away, proudly and in silence.

HÉLÈNE GAUDY

MESSAGE FROM A CARRIER PIGEON INTERCEPTED IN NORTHERN ICELAND

Dated 11 July 1897
Found in 1899

The mood is excellent.

ICARUS

12 July 1897

In one of the rare introspective passages in his diary, Andrée wonders, in a reflective mood, if he and his companions will be considered mad or if somebody, someday, may attempt to imitate them, tacitly admitting that the whole enterprise is above all motivated by a desire not to remain *a man in the ranks*, a link in the commonplace chain, not to be forgotten. To which he adds, quite explicitly: *We think we can well face death, having done what we have done.*

To rise above the ranks, leave that common chain behind and take the King's highway, that is what they all want, thereby leading them to another, glittering, less ordinary route, a chain whose interlocking links will lead them, step by step, up the ladder to the heavens.

In 1872, following in the footsteps of Portuguese inventor Bartolomeu Lourenço de Gusmão, who seventy-three years earlier saw the first balloon lift off the ground, the Montgolfier brothers try to capture the clouds in a cloth envelope in order to fly. Seeing the fabric of a shirt rise over a fire in their chimney, they ponder, repeat the experiment and end up understanding: it is not clouds which permit flight, but the heat caused by combustion.

They burn everything they can lay their hands on, they try hay and manure, old shoes, rotten meat, and, on the 4th of June 1783, the first hot-air balloon is launched. Learning from their progress, a Frenchman by the name of Jacques Charles, known for having captured on paper the image of a silhouette taken over the space of a few moments prior to the invention of photography, attempts to make a hydrogen balloon fly. Photography, aeronautics: the struggle is the same. Always a matter of seizing, capturing, contracting, possessing.

On the 27th of August 1783, Charles launches the first gas balloon which he christens the *charlière*, the name whose similarity to Anna's will resonate like an omen. A few weeks later, the Montgolfier brothers' contraption will lift off before Louis XVI at Versailles, with Laika the dog's predecessors on board – a duck, a rooster and a sheep who glide at over 500 metres before descending once again. The rooster's beak is damaged by the hindquarters of the sheep who, for its troubles, is allowed to see out the end of its days grazing in the royal menagerie, carrying with it, in its impenetrable eyes, the memory of a sky still beyond the reach of man, while it continues peacefully to chew its preferred choice of straw.

Then, there is the first man to fly: Pilâtre de Rozier, proud, in his elegant cloth globe, with its ribbons and Prussian blue trim, Pilâtre who will subsequently resolve to cross the Channel, contrary to the direction of prevailing winds, seeking to accomplish a feat that still has never been achieved. He will set off, regardless, despite the absurdity of his plan, because the financiers are waiting, because he can no longer pull out, because the reputation of the king, who, in five years, will be guillotined, could do with such an achievement – so it goes when the money of others finances the dreams that one believed, once, to be one's own.

Pilâtre and his companion, who goes by the angelic predestined name of Pierre-Ange, take off in their repeatedly patched balloon, and are brought crashing back to earth shortly after the launch by an ill wind from the west. Doubtless, a simple tear brought it all undone, the fabric, their lives, the crossing. Pilâtre will lend his name to one of the meteoric craters on the moon, a hole of 50 kilometres diameter, roughly the distance between Chartres and Rambouillet, a black spot in the vicinity of the Newton, Drygalsky and Pingre craters, not far from

the Mare Humorum, since setting foot on the moon has allowed us to
name its every nook and cranny, as we do with everything we own.

There is the first female aeronaut, Élisabeth Thible, who rose into the
sky singing an opera aria, then there followed many more manned
flights, until we come to the great aeronautical festival of Versailles,
where Étienne Montgolfier flies his new balloon to the astonishment
of the King of Sweden, whipping up an almost religious fervour,
embodying in his flight the dreams of a technical revolution, and the
almost supernatural fantasy of a monarch capable of reaching the fir-
mament from the heights of his palace. Artisans, linen manufacturers,
labourers mix with the elegant company of the court. None of them
share this belief but they are all looking up to the sky. Part of the balloon's fabric catches fire: the crowd, chasing the balloon, tear off the
charred fragments.

No sooner has one flying machine crashed than another is there to take
its place, a new link in the chain that little by little is lifting off from the
earth. For so long people have had their noses buried in the landscape,
we were such a small part of it, buried in it, blind, we did not even recognise it as a landscape, the nature that we sensed before even seeing
it – the hostility of the heat and the cold, foreign cultures to be domi-
nated by the use of force, the darkness of forests spun into fairytales.

In order to transform it into a landscape, we had to step back, find
the perspective offered by a painting as much as by a map, recognise the
nobility of places we had not yet tamed – the Poles, the seas, the jagged mountains – we had to classify the world, and to do that, rise ever
upwards, in balloons, then aeroplanes, and then one day, space stations.
Holding fast the chain, we gained height, we extricated ourselves from
the green, the blue, from the earth's depths we have seen, we created
order, disjuncture, learned how to name countries and plains, oceans
and ice and distant moraines, learned how to hold the most hostile
expanses in the palm of our hand, until the green, the blue, the earth's

depths we have seen are nothing more than memories, objects lost along the way.

Almost forty years before Nils captures, through the fog, an almost invisible glimpse of the pack ice seen from the sky, before he sketches a map indicating the balloon's successive positions, the photographer Nadar is attempting to take the first aerial shots of Paris. To see it is not enough: it must be transformed, into proof, into something useful.

It is, at the outset, a fiasco. High above the interlacing streets, from the basket of his balloon, Nadar takes marvellous shots, but on his return to earth, everything is black. The city, invisible. He has often failed to capture a scene he was after, spoiled by too feeble a light, too fidgety a subject. He is used to finding technical solutions, to adapting to obstacles. He has had such success, capturing fleeting expressions, the absinthe-fuelled looks of poets, and should be able to immortalise Paris. But the city will not easily surrender. On the plate, there is nothing.

He starts over, is doggedly persistent. The city is fickle and its new forms impossible to capture. So, he moves away, attempts other flights, this time in the country. From a balloon tethered to an apple tree, he overlooks pale expanses, gentle slopes, and it is here, now that there is nothing left of what he was hoping to see, that something works. The reflection of the world, this time, will leave its shadow on the paper, he can feel it: this time it will work. Once back on the ground, he hurries to an inn. He cannot risk losing a single detail, details which may well have seemed insignificant were they not the first to be captured: a farm, an inn, a gendarmerie, the tiles on the roofs and, on the road, an upholsterer, running, terrified, perhaps, by the curious contraption gliding overhead.

In 1868, Nadar, whose peregrinations will inspire Jules Verne in his *Five Weeks in a Balloon*, finally captures some photographs of Paris. He can provide the chance to see what he himself is one of the few people to have witnessed: the over-arching order of the world, its very structure revealed. But his images are not destined solely to be admired, to inspire works of fiction; they will be used primarily for the purposes of mapmaking and military strategies. All that effort, those attempts, the taming of light and air, the artistic ambition, the nights of insomnia, the races against the clock, all to facilitate the work of military personnel, to improve performance on the battlefield.

Nadar is not naive and is doubtless sufficiently patriotic to take pleasure in it all, much like Strindberg, Frænkel and Andrée, who also know they are there to advance their nation's interests on this great chess board, to annex virgin territory, to bring water to the mill of discovery and domination. In addition, they probably feel a sense of pride. And then there is probably some other part of them that is knocked askew when the balloon brushes dangerously over the first slabs of pack ice, grazing the ice and propelling them briefly back into the air: soon the reasons they are there will be meaningless. They will never see, from up high, the patterns created by the pack ice at the edge of the North Pole. Their pictures will not allow them to trace the shape of the furthest islands and the last pockets of open sea, their maps will remain too imprecise to permit even the slightest conquest, the most modest land-grab. They will have to find other purposes, other reasons, other hopes, they will have to renounce grandiose titles and spectacular exploits, they will have to survive, it stops here and it is immense, the pack ice beneath them has devoured the sea, there is no more water, there are no more islands, no more homeland, or possible illusion. This is where it starts, now.

ANDRÉE'S JOURNAL

12–13 July 1897

Not a living thing has been seen all the night, no bird, seal, walrus or bear.

Strindberg seasick.
Through the fog the ice and water are visible lifted up along the line of vision and the water is consequently bewilderingly like land.
It has deceived me several times.

Monotonous touch new touch
another touch

LIMBO

14 July 1897

They jettisoned some sand to slow the fall. The balloon lost what little altitude it still enjoyed. They saw the whiteness, below them, approaching. They absorbed the shock. The basket was dragged along at full tilt for a few metres, and then everything came to a halt. Even the messenger pigeons still shut up in their cage survived unscathed.

They extricate themselves from the wicker basket with some difficulty, finding their feet on the ice. Their legs tremble, their hands shake. All about them, the pack ice is immense, but they give it scarcely a glance: they are at work, hard at it. For seven long hours, they set up camp, erect their tent, organise themselves, check their equipment is functioning, ensure their supplies are appropriately stored, raise the flag of the United Kingdoms of Norway and Sweden, an attempt to persuade themselves that they are indeed somewhere.

This landscape: never have they seen anything like it. While Strindberg and Andrée have previously been to Svalbard, they know only terra firma, the mountains, the shoreline, and the long stony beaches. This – the white, the ice – they are seeing for the first time. And yet, in their journals, they describe nothing initially of their surrounds. It is too soon, too new, it is overwhelming and impenetrable, resembles nothing, comes at them from all sides. This place, they scarcely dare look at it and for a long time they hold it at bay behind their lowered eyes, like shadows we might sense behind us, quietly threatening.

*

They throw themselves into their work, as if nothing has changed, as if this were yet one more harmless stage of their adventure. Probably better not to stop too quickly, not to cool down, not to think too much, not to look around.

When they finally do so, they are utterly spent. Tomorrow, they will be stiff, they will move more slowly, feel discouraged, but for the time being, something is burning within. Andrée clambers on top of the basket. It is not particularly high, he can see that now it has fallen from the sky, but the landscape is so unrelieved that it allows him a little height all the same. Strindberg takes a photograph of him: Frænkel is also in the field, looking at Andrée. They both have their backs turned, one behind the other. Andrée, atop his perch, is upright, the conqueror, legs apart, one hand in the air as if wrestling the sky. Directly behind him, the cross of the flag would make the perfect background had the photographer focussed on his face but from where he is standing when he presses the shutter release, there is just a very small man and a very small flag. Frænkel, hands apparently in his pockets, seems to be observing the scene, phlegmatic but amused.

Nonetheless, Andrée is indeed able to see: a hectoring brightness that sets off explosions behind their eyelids in every absent colour, this place where every relief in the landscape seems to repeat itself. Everything they know, everything they're used to – mountains, hills, ravines and streams, dales and plains – all of it seems to have been reduced, eroded, filed away with an emery board and glazed in white.

Here, it is all the more intense, more radiant, impenetrable, like petrified desert forests, and where once there were trees, plants, now there is nothing more than ill-defined rubble veined with ancient markings, a dizzying array of collapsed bridges, fossilised riverbeds, and all of it covered in this glittering substance which is neither ice, nor truly snow but somehow both at once, paste jewellery, the same dazzling effect.

Andrée rubs his tired eyes with the back of his hand. So this is where they find themselves, from here they will march.

They lie down to sleep, around the burning camp stove. They watch the smoke from their pipes, their cigars, mixing with the drizzling mist which cloaks the landscape. What landscape? There is nothing but white to nestle into.

The place where they find themselves does not feature on any map, it is not even a place, just an endless, edgeless expanse. They have no notion of which direction to take. Viewed from the sky, the landscape appeared flat, no nuance to the immensity; there are protrusions now, they discover. They sense the presence of animals they can no longer keep watch for, quietly, from high up in their basket. The bears have altered in scale. The men know this, and hatch their strategies, plan their weapons, manage their fears. Soon, they will be butchering their first cadavers.

In their journals, they write several times that no land is visible, but they never lose hope of seeing it appear, of making out some fissure, a feature, a darker crest. They blink their eyes. When they reopen them, still blinding light, still ice as far as the eye can see and not a thing to relieve it.

They start by waiting, a long time, several days, next to the stranded balloon, not really sure what might eventuate. While they wait, the snow falls on the sagging fabric. They watch it disappear, slowly, beneath the whiteness.

They know they must set off once more, contend on foot with this pack ice they had reckoned to float over, but still they find reasons to delay their departure. They must plot out a route, determine which supplies to bring with them, grow used to their sleepless nights. So they grant themselves this time, this extended period. The world has forgotten them, that much is certain, during those long hours, and it is almost good, their eyes suddenly closing, this sleep which they welcome, finally, without resistance. It is like playing truant, taking the exit ramp. They reheat some hot chocolate, into which they dunk little cookies with butter and cranberry jam. They are in limbo, they are invisible. Perhaps they have already disappeared, chuckling behind their curtain of mist, chuckling at still being there at all.

By drifting on their ice floe, it could well be that they end up somewhere, end up colliding with some form of land, filthy and hirsute, having managed to drain their final can of beer. There would be nothing more to do but to step over a lead of seawater and set foot on terra incognita, to plant their flag. And that would be that.

Yes, they could settle themselves down to wait, it is a possibility that is no more unhinged, at that particular moment, no more cowardly than to get up and set off on foot. Perhaps this is it, this is what they must do, they toss it out there like some sort of provocation, a joke: just stretch out, doze off, turn into armchair explorers, immobile travellers at the mercy of the landscape, nonchalant, enjoying a lark. Now that would be novel, a veritable feat. Not to resist. To offer themselves up entirely to the pack ice, because movement is fear, they could tell themselves, a little drunk, a little tipsy, yes, moving means being afraid of all this white, all this emptiness, it means imbuing it with life no matter the cost. Let us remain lying here while we are no longer afraid. Let us remain lying here, drinking, eating, examining our past, turning things over, perhaps this is the ultimate show of courage, an expedition never so much as attempted.

But they will pay dearly for this respite. When they decide they are ready, when they set off, nine days after landing, the ice floe on which they have settled will have drifted so far they will find themselves already more than 30 kilometres further from their goal.

ANDRÉE'S JOURNAL

14 July 1897

[Pages 20 to 23 have been left blank.]

SPERM WHALE

15 July 1897?

The photographs of the grounded balloon were probably taken during those first days, in the first hours, just after the landing, when they were still stunned by the shockwave of the descent, or else a short while later, perhaps on the 15th of July, after they had collected themselves, taken hold again of their hopes.

They would not speak to us in quite the same way had they been taken in the rush, in the urgency to bear witness, or even in the period that followed, with the desire to leave some record.

As the camera will not now be used to take aerial photographs nor for mapping the territory, they will give it a quite different role, and it is evident here, in these first images. Henceforth, it will document their daily life, attest to their continued existence, give them reason to maintain their bearing. This piece of equipment, weighing 7 kilograms, fragile and unwieldly, which Nils will drag about with him everywhere and which he will need to set up on an imposing tripod for every shot, will become a companion, a third party, an ever-ready eye requiring a dignified demeanour, creating by its mere presence that dissociation permitted by photography as much as by the act of writing: carving out a distance which leads to each man being his own witness.

In this first image, Frænkel and Andrée are standing next to the balloon. One of them is looking at the lens. All that can be made out beneath his

90

headgear are the black holes of his eyes and the shadows weighing on his face. He's posing, without bothering to give an impression of haste, of anxiety. If it is difficult to recognise him, the contrast between his posture and that of the other figure – moving, shielding his face from the camera – might lead us to suspect that it is Andrée, who will never abandon his position as leader, who will, in every situation, pose for posterity, but perhaps I'm mistaken, perhaps Andrée is driven by matters which escape me, perhaps he is the one who is heading over to the balloon while Frænkel, already, is feeling discouraged.

On the shot which appears to follow this one, they are both immobile. Completely still. In the interval between those two photographs, the brutal precognition has probably already lodged itself in their consciousness that they might never return home. More than a fissure: a chasm, which they must grow accustomed to living with, striving to fill it with their words, their images, soon, with their bear skins, their beer and their soups – a void is no longer so visible if it is filled with all you have, if buried within is your own happiness and courage.

They look at it, this chasm in the shape of a balloon, they photograph it, pose next to it, accept it, immortalise it, because that is all they can now do. For a while, they would stroke its cloth flanks, watch over its death throes until it disappears – whale, sperm whale, immense sea elephant, phantom boat much like the one Ernest Shackleton will one day watch as it sinks beneath the waves.

Shackleton's odyssey will commence in 1914 – a trans-Antarctic expedition involving two vessels, the *Endurance* and the *Aurora*.

Anna will no doubt follow, with the preoccupied attention which she will make her own, the departure of these mariners who are allowed to slip away in the middle of a war. They have suggested delaying their departure in order to fulfil their soldierly duties, but they will be more useful down there, they are repeatedly told, on the sea: they will better serve England by navigating their way across the high seas.

They, too, will fight their battles, wage war against the pack ice, against themselves.

On the 19th of January 1915, the ship is gripped by the ice. Shackleton prepares to winter there, without struggling to free themselves, or sending his men in search of assistance. He does not wish to take pointless risks; his goal is not to lose a single human life. He turns the marvellous conquering instrument that is his vessel into a stationary refuge.

All about the boat is a landscape of ice. This shifting place, these tall waves, this raging sea, it's as if they have all been rendered solid. As if a picture taken in error has fixed the surroundings as well as the crew members, caught in too lengthy a pose. It's not just that they have made landfall: the entire landscape, and time along with it, has stopped around them.

The boat is encircled by frozen hills and cliffs, hummocks whose contours they are only able to make out with the aid of a lamp, which projects yellow tongues into the endless night. They are jammed in the cold, in time, in the blackness, months of polar night still ahead of them, months which, one might say, will never end. Around them, almost everything has been erased. And yet, they experience the ease with which, on the smallest plot of land, in the darkest, smallest cell, you can so rapidly feel at home. How quickly they come to know the slightest fissure, the slightest protrusion. A minuscule kingdom, their kingdom, dark as a cavern, restricted to what little can be made out, where, behind those initial blocks of ice illuminated like a theatrical set, there stretches a vastness of which they know nothing.

Shackleton's men, who had been keen for discovery and adventure, find themselves recounting their life story playing cards in the dry warmth of their cabins, drinking more than is wise, sharing their sleepless nights. They had forgotten, no doubt, the game-playing that populates the boredom of childhood, the hours filled rubbing along with others, inventing challenges, whole worlds, those times that divert them from their desires while never ceasing to arouse them. Every now and again they bicker, often they grow bored, but generally they settle in. This could last months, years. These men know how to adapt.

But they have underestimated the sapping work done by the ice. While a new sort of egalitarian society is forming on board – even renowned scientists perform the most unedifying tasks, as they throw themselves into frenzied football matches and thrill to the sound of musical instruments on the 'tween deck, otherwise known as *The Ritz* – the ice continues to apply its pressure to the hull. The boat tilts, cracks, lists. Soon, they must resolve to abandon it.

Suddenly they are hastily gathering their belongings, once again the cold feels impossible. Everything that was weighing upon them when on board the vessel now assumes the caustic flavour of nostalgia as they are plunged into the darkness. The majestic sailing boat that has for months towered, stationary, between blocks of ice, becomes a ghost ship abandoned by its crew, crushed, engulfed by the deep waters. They see it disappear, little by little, they photograph its death throes: the hull, first, swallowed up, then the dense interlacing of masts, then rigging and sails, all rolled away – a great spider crushed in a hand.

A sailor had thought it better to leave his guitar on board: Shackleton insists he return to fetch it. There is no matter too small, as far as he's concerned, when it's a matter of survival. Or rather: it is precisely in the details that their survival will occur. On the 21st of November 1915, the vessel disappears altogether.

They march, heading across the pack ice, scaling hummocks standing several metres tall, every moment at risk of being separated by the fissures splitting apart the ice floes over which they haul themselves. The drift ought to have led them towards an island but, in this regard too, nothing is as they expect. If the ice has an infuriating tendency of never drifting in the right direction, Shackleton will prove more stubborn still. He is in no hurry, he wants to live, to save his men, no matter how long it might take, or the sacrifices to be made. Their new camp will be called Patience Camp.

He has a good head, Shackleton, both before, during and after the expedition, the same broad, gentle face that invites confidences, in whom you might confide your fears, the same frank gaze, the same furrowed brow. Whether he is wearing shirt and tie, dark hair gleaming with pomade or sporting a small sailor's beard, chewing on a pipe, his skin weather-beaten as he puts to sea, emphasising his anxious eyes, it is the same attentive face, the same honest demeanour, open to others, even if from time to time he is known abruptly to retreat, seeking the solitude required by the keen sensitivity that governs his spirits, his moods. He always returns to play cards with his men, listen to their grievances, be generous with provisions and a word. He inspires respect in the sailors who affectionately call him the Boss, and who, for the most part, will follow him wherever he may lead them, even long after this hell where they find themselves trapped.

They drift northwards, in the direction of the Drake Passage. Are they still playing cards? Are they singing themselves hoarse to the strumming of the guitar? Is Shackleton still reciting the verse of Browning or Yeats as he is wont to do? How long can one continue to play cards, to recite poetry, to strum a guitar in the face of such deprivation, such despair? The ice floe on which they have sought refuge is their new ship, exposed to the wind from all directions, fragile enough to break under the weight of their patience. They manage to clamber into the dinghies they had been dragging behind them just before the ground beneath their feet dissolves entirely.

At first, they try to reach the aptly named Deception Island, where there is a provisions depot and a small wooden church which they are hoping to pull apart in order to shore up their boats. But the only land they manage to reach is Elephant Island, which is quickly revealed to be a frightful place: a mass of icy slabs, peaks, ravines, stalactites and caverns, of crags and needles – a glacial island, cursed.

They extricate themselves as best they can from the raging sea, catch their breath on terra firma. They are overcome, exhausted, spent. In the black-and-white photographs, their faces are black.

They are like the others, they look the same: an army of dark-faced men, in heavy clothing, who continue to pose to the very end because they are constantly mindful that the only thing that still justifies this suffering is these images which render them links in a chain and not merely some castaways, alone, on death's doorstep.

Many have died, who were part of that chain, a whole army of phantoms crushed by the ice, finished off by the cold or malnourishment, unfortunate sailors emerging from a pirate movie, skeletons devoured by scurvy and deep-sea fish.

So, to be upright, able to bear witness, that is still something to justify turning your face to the camera, proud – Shackleton's own fingers will suffer frostbite after donating his mittens to the expedition's photographer.

Elephant Island is too isolated, too inhospitable. If they remain there, they will die, and quickly, they must set off once more. Accompanied by five others, Shackleton takes to the sea again in one of the lifeboats, the *James Caird*, after the carpenter has done his best to caulk the leaks with oil paint and seal blood.

They must reach South Georgia, but the surrounding waters are known as the most treacherous in the world, battered by unimaginably wild winds. What Shackleton takes to be the white edge of clouds is the crest of a rogue wave, falling from the heavens to crash over them, violently tossing the boat about, before spitting it back out, as it waits for the next gaping abyss.

When they at last draw up to South Georgia Island, it takes them several days to recuperate. King Haakon Bay is despairingly deserted, and the sailors are in a terribly weakened state. Shackleton decides, then, to traverse the island on foot with two of his companions – although it would be more accurate to say that they would be scaling the island's mountains. They climb, hustle, crawl, drag their broken bodies along the peaked mountain ridges. Increasingly, their journey comes to resemble a truly nightmarish sequence of hostile, desolate places, with no hope of salvation. Upon finally reaching the other side of the island, they discover whalers who congratulate them on their courage. Shackleton lends them only half an ear, distracted: what he wants is to retrieve his men who were left behind.

After several fruitless attempts, assisted by local fishermen, several crossings where once again he hurls his exhaustion at the crest of the waves, Shackleton decides to send a telegram to London to ask for assistance, to which the King himself replies in amiable fashion that he is delighted to hear he is safe and sound and hopes that his men, too, will be rescued just as quickly as possible. England is in the midst of fighting a war and has other fish to fry. Shackleton will have to handle the matter on his own.

Yet again, he sets off, this time aboard a Chilean vessel, and manages to recover his fellow adventurers.

All of them.

As help arrives, the men of the *Endurance* raise their arms, facing the open sea, they wave everything they can lay their hands on, caps, even cans of food. They are saved.

Later still, Shackleton will find the crew of the second boat, the *Aurora*, at the end of no less epic a journey, during which three men will have lost their lives.

Upon their arrival home, the survivors are greeted by a world of gunfire and bloodshed. Had they been dreaming of respite on their return, of peace and quiet, they are greeted with nothing of the kind. They head off to the trenches. Several of them will die on the fields of honour.

Shackleton will lead other expeditions, will perform other feats of arms. He is best suited to the sea, in other areas his life turns to disaster, he accumulates debts and affairs, businesses doomed to failure, and in 1922, he will return to South Georgia to die of a heart attack – so keen was he to set off that he neglected to have himself examined despite his waning health.

It is there on that island, too, that his wife will have him buried, where he saved his men, where he let his goal be transformed, putting up no resistance, the simple continuation of their existence more precious now than that much longed for conquest. *We have failed*, he wrote, by way of introduction to his memoirs. *The story of our attempt is the subject of these pages.*

On the evening of the 20th of July, Andrée notes in his diary that the balloon's netting strings have sunk 132 millimetres into the snow and ice.

How many weeks will it take for the fabric of the balloon to be buried entirely in the snow?

How many days for this fully inflated contraption to leak out onto the ice?

How long to realise that everything you have prepared for, dreamed of for years, is similarly in the process of disintegrating?

Once this moment has passed, when they have come to terms with their failure, they will set off on foot, unaware at times whether they are moving with the drift of the pack ice or fighting against it, hauling their loads, arguing over the subject of seals, admiring the landscape.

Bright sunshine. Smooth ice, writes Andrée.

ANDRÉE'S JOURNAL

18–20 July 1897

Morning of the 18th, seals and fulmars pretty long sight but no land visible in any direction.

In the morning all the pigeons had flown away.

INVENTORIES

21 July 1897

They are not keen to see their ice floe shrink to the point where they must cling to each other on just a few metres of pack ice, and they probably realise that to remain stationary will ultimately signal their end, which is already much what these curious days feel like, it's true, as they wait under a dome of white clouds, in a world with no shadows, no contrasts, no shore.

They will head for a supply depot, towards Franz Josef Land. They could have chosen to aim for Sjuøyane, the "Seven Islands," marginally easier to access, but that is territory which has already been mapped out. Franz Josef Land is more mysterious, more untouched. Even though Julius von Payer discovered it in 1873, its mapped outline remains approximate and there are islands en route which they hope they might be able to name. This is how they are still thinking at the start of summer.

Before leaving, they carry out an inventory of their materials. They still have three sledges and a boat, hardly suitable for a long march as they were intended only to be used at the end of their journey, to cover the final kilometres which were to have separated their landing spot from a triumphant arrival in Siberia, in Canada or in Alaska.

They take out the cans, the medications, the firearms, the whisky, the champagne. They attempt to sort the items, they keep almost everything. They keep neckties, padlocks, drawing pins, a pink silk scarf. They keep a large white embroidered tablecloth. They keep a whole host of useless items. They do not have the maps we have. They do not yet have an account of their own story. So then, any of it may prove useful, any of it may provide some hope. The silk scarf as much as Anna's portrait.

They are hardly dressed for the situation – bespoke outfits created by accomplished tailors, pocket handkerchiefs but no furs, oilskins, both checked and striped, dark glasses. Andrée does not bother to don the glasses that might protect him from the white glare, from the notorious snow blindness which slowly but surely works its damage.

In order to get a more specific idea of the clothes they are wearing, we must refer to the inventory drawn up after the discovery of their bodies, after the long hours spent restoring the scraps of fabric covered in seaweed and shellfish, unfurling the material that had set hard as stone, separating fibres compacted by the ice, polishing, drying, assembling, even creating an identical copy at times in order to make a reconstruction of their elegant attire, more reminiscent of a spread from the fashion pages than an image of explorers of the Great North.

It is a list of their personal effects which offers us the most vivid insight into their appearance, their bearing as much as the sensation of wool on skin, of a linen shirt against the chest, of a gold chain knocking against the carotid artery. The material of their old clothes relegates to the background the images in their bleached black and white, renders them three-dimensional, and here they are, risen from the dead.

They are standing on the pack ice, dressed in woollen coats, blue-and-white striped jerseys over flannel shirts, hands encased in mittens.

Andrée is wearing a hat, which will still be covering his skull when he is pulled from the ice. Strindberg, a hunting jacket with slanting pockets across his chest, black puttees decorated with pompoms, boots, a woollen beanie or a checked hat. Against his chest, the chain with its three charms – cross, anchor, small gold heart.

Andrée is wearing a ring, a heart and a locket containing a photograph of his parents around his neck, and Frænkel has a costly pocket-knife with a mother-of-pearl handle in his jacket pocket. His pullover was knitted in Iceland, his undershirt made of finely striped linen. He, too, is wearing boots and hat.

Here they are, all three of them, less warmly dressed than any tourist attempting to climb the most insignificant mountain. They are considering it now, the landscape, and starting to appreciate the dangers it might conceal, as much as its marvels and curiosities.

Their knowledge of the Arctic is not so thorough as to know exactly what has already been recorded, and so anything might prove useful, anything might constitute a notable event – that bird brought down by a gunshot, that seaweed with the acrid smell, a precise description of the composition of the snow.

As if they were not already sufficiently loaded down, they cram into the sleds a veritable travelling cabinet of curiosities, each relic carefully bundled up with the means to hand. In precisely numbered tubes, Andrée stores samples of plankton and algae, clay, the rare leaves to be found in the ice, most likely carried by the wind from distant Siberian forests.

The world feels within reach, it is an era of accessibility, they feel duty bound to seize the smallest of atoms, the slightest speck of dust, this is why it is here, the world, to be discovered, they are a long way yet from a time when children will be forbidden from picking flowers or killing insects, this still feels like progress, a form of courage, to unearth, to extract, to remove, it serves only to increase the sum of knowledge, to encourage the easy belief of being surrounded by an inexhaustible bounty, and how unfortunate it would be not to avail yourself of it.

Today, post-2000, an era which for them is still so distant, we are busy taking samples from the great glaciers to ensure their silent narrative does not disappear with them, tonnes of core samples from the ice carried down by hand from the white walls, then labelled, dated, transported by boat in order to create a gigantic library, a digest of geological, climatic, even cultural memory, for the ice carries records of our modes of agriculture, preserving unbeknownst to us, the most prosaic traces of our existence.

There is an attempt to save some of it in the hope that, in a few hundred years' time, these containers may be opened, these archives unveiled, and our invisible memories will not have disappeared entirely, just as in Svalbard, photo-sensitive films are being stored in a bunker, fragments of the world's memory – texts, photographs, artworks, an ultra-modern version of the explorers' buried images.

In another bunker, carved into a sandstone mountain 130 metres below sea level, the global seed vault was established in 2008, where seeds of every subsistence crop on the planet are being stored, waiting to be sown in a place where that species might have become extinct – corn, rice, barley and wheat, sorghum, soya or sunflower and, in seed form, the shade offered by foliage, the woody tangle of roots, all of it invisible but present, stored in containers for the long haul, for the catastrophic event so often imagined, for that unfurling wave, or the inescapable sun.

Global warming has seen the permafrost melt faster than anticipated, water has penetrated the vault, not yet causing damage, not this time, but it seems change is more rapid, is having a greater impact than what has been implemented in the hope of resisting it. The landscape eludes representation, predictions, plans, in short, it eludes everything, it is slipping through our fingers.

They, too, take samples, create archives, start turning circles, find it impossible to stop, and the appetite for hunting and gathering will become an attempt at saving themselves, and the landscape, so crushingly powerful, will become so fragile that only fragments will be saved, witness to all the rest, to be removed from the ice before it disappears.

Andrée prises open the skulls of gulls to examine their eyes, trying to understand what mysterious mechanism allows them to escape the effects of snow blindness. He walks, eyes glued to the ground, a little hunched, looking for the slightest breach in the landscape that he might scrape away with his nails, stuff into his jacket pocket.

He heads off into the distance, under the watchful gaze of the others. He is already old, it strikes them now after seeing him endure sleepless nights and this bitter disappointment which renders him strangely more voluble, more impassioned. He speaks far too loudly for their own liking, gestures far too grandiosely. So, to shield him from their own despair, Frænkel and Strindberg start adopting the same tone, the same gestures, the same enthusiasm. They are going to scrape away at the pack ice, make scientific discoveries, bring back specimens – but to where? Nobody asks that question.

Despite everything, they are all clinging to the notion of a return, of there being a shore. If they themselves do not have the materials or adequate knowledge, somebody, somewhere, will have it for them. They are gathering reminders of the world, mute specimens to be given voice by somebody else. This, surely, is what they are thinking about as they add a new stone to the pile, another piece of driftwood. About that distant person who, at some point, will know how to read the signs which they themselves are gathering in their ignorance.

If they are embracing their roles as conservationists on the pack ice, as gatherers of bones and seaweed, photographers of distant lands and the most minor details of their daily life, it is because there is something more fragile still which they probably wish to preserve. Not just this place where they find themselves but the belief in a return – the bustling city, the distant home, the link to those who are waiting for them. By taking those pictures, gathering that moss, they are looking at us, already, looking at them, and they are no longer quite so alone.

ANDRÉE'S JOURNAL

21 July 1897

Test of level-sextant with exc. result.
We managed to get some things dry.
21/7 Loading the sledges.

Nisse fried the bear's meat excellently on "Primus."

CARAVAN

The approaching summer

For three months they will march. The pictures say nothing of the time that accumulates between them, nothing of the long, empty periods between the rare moments where they pose for the camera. They march, and they don't hear the sound of their steps. The snow absorbs, moulds itself, fickle, working its way into the space between sock and shoe, into ears, down necks, it seems soft, it bites.

They march today as they did yesterday, no matter the hour, whether night or day, regardless, when they have had a chance to sleep a little they get up and march until it is again time to rest, to chew on some meat, hold their hands close to the camp stove, sleep, find a little warmth huddled one up against the other, then extract themselves once more, walking until it is again time to sleep.

Waking each day is shattering, an utter loss of their bearings. They no longer know what hour it is, what day, no longer have any idea where they are.

They march, but it is not a straight march, it is not linear, no, what they are forced to do is together drag the first sledge a few metres forwards, sliding at times more effectively than at others, depending on the quality of the snow under the runners, then they must return and start over with the second, with the third, this one laden with the dinghy, their march involving a constant back and forth, to drag their sledges and boat forwards, one by one.

They are each hauling over 100 kilos, there are too many things they are still unable to decide to rid themselves of, a whole host of useless items which they continue, day after day, to drag behind them, joining forces, tensing their muscles, and returning again to drag the next one – they have, however, relieved themselves of one portion of their load, have left behind some supplies after gorging themselves on the things they were unable to bring with them, have then fallen asleep, bellies swollen with corned beef, pigs' trotters, tinned sardines and preserved fruits in syrup, washed down with champagne.

They march, keep their flag close – much like they keep their meat, directly against their body in order to defrost it – so they have it to hand should they finally have the opportunity to raise it, in a place further north than any other has been. It is a parallel war, Shackleton called it the "white battle," played out at a distance, in space and time, between packs of exhausted, frozen men, each for their part seeking to outstrip their invisible adversaries, by a few kilometres, a few metres even, a test of endurance that unfolds over years, staked out by each of them, and for those who come after them, by paltry indicators: a cairn, a bottle in the ocean, maps to delineate a desert and prove that somebody has made it so far.

It is only having passed these markers, when there is no longer anything to cling to, when you can be certain of walking on terra incognita, that you feel the real achievement begins. And so, the flag, carried against their torso, may fly where no flag has ever been displayed.

Nisse fell in the water and was in imminent danger of drowning. He was dried and wrung out and dressed in knickerbockers, writes Andrée, who calls Nils by the diminutive, Nisse, and describes his misadventure like that of a comic-book action hero.

Indeed, there's something of the characters from the *Nickel-Plated Feet* comics about them, which is admirable because nothing seems that serious, nothing seems likely to happen to them.

Their equipment is pitiful and yet they persist, they joke about, poke fun at the old bear killed by Andrée, whose teeth are so broken, whose flesh is so tough that he must certainly be the oldest resident on the pack ice or perhaps a defector from some European menagerie, he is so old, so decrepit, he must have had ten lives at least before finishing up on their plates. They experiment on the culinary front, seal blood crêpes or perhaps seaweed soup, do things without complaint that no other has done, as lighthearted as amateurs and as solid as heroes. There are only three of them, where so many expeditions consist of dozens of men. Three of them, as if from a storybook, three cheerful chaps who've washed up on the pack ice, going nowhere, but marching ever onwards.

It's as if they are weightless, these men, who keep gazing at the hues in the sky and the colours of the birds, who continue to walk, with no expectations, at least, nothing rational. Well may they march, but they will never arrive anywhere and even were they, by some miracle, to reach one of the supply depots left by some previous expedition, all they could do would be to finish off the remains. Then wait.

Strindberg's observations of the moon's position indicates we have indeed gone west, further than we had thought, writes Andrée.

They march, for days that never end, one single interminable day as if time is no longer leaving its mark, their bodies the only barometer, increasingly unreliable as they struggle to remain deaf to its appeals, so there are hours, whole days, where they too lose sight of their limits, their borders, where, in unison with the polar day, they are nothing more than a march in the light.

They march, in that steady brightness, their whiskers a constellation of ever-present snow, checking on each other, always verifying that they are there, all three of them, each one a bearing and a marker for the others, watching over each other as you might scan for a child whose hand you have just released, they mustn't stray, mustn't flag, they know that the one who flags will bring the others down – three, it is not a number able to be reduced, divided, should one of them waver, the triangle flattens, disappears.

They march, and although the snow is silent, all about are cries and cracking. Here, there is no such thing as silence, something is always screeching in their ears, birds flying past, the ice as it cracks and, over the top of it all, the wind, deafening as it rises, vicious as it dies, the rare periods of peace serving only to sharpen the gusts as they pick up, turning it, the wind, into a gong, a blade, a butcher's knife honed on the ice, and then they no longer hear each other, can no longer speak nor laugh nor even cry out in despair.

If one of them should fall into the water or lose their way, in those impenetrable days when the wind hurtles the snow into the crevices of their faces, they have a whistle, a feeble whistle, the sort used by police-men and children playing, a whistle which they blow should something happen to them, to alert the others, carving a hole in the din with the reedy sound of their instrument.

Sometimes, they hack away at the ice with their axe to check its thickness, to clamber over a hummock that is too high, too sharp, but more than anything, probably, to attack it, this landscape, shatter it with their own sharp implements.

When the silence returns, they listen. They keep an eye out. They listen for the slapping of waves, the sound of open water which would allow them to travel by boat, to put an end to this marching and to hope for solid ground, on the other side. They are listening out, through these brief silences. They want to believe it is there, the sea, just ahead of them, only a few more metres, they can hear it, see it already like the mirage of an island in the desert, but it is only the wind taking on its shape, its smell, mimicking its song.

And always, it is there, the pack ice, stretching out before them.

*

Soon, they will start dosing themselves up on morphine, on opium, to relieve the diarrhoea, the cramps and pain, to settle the coughing although they do not believe any germ could exist there, in the ice. They allow the heat of their bodies to dry their clothes while they wear them, legs covered by knickerbockers stiffened by a thick layer of snow, buttocks steaming, constantly wiping their noses, now streaming fountains as a result of their endless colds.

I washed my face for the first time since the 11 July, Andrée will write on the 2nd of August. They eat more than a kilo of meat each every day, deal with problems as they arise, they persist, they march. They never stop marching.

At times they must support each other, one of them almost carrying another, clutching onto a pair of shoulders, a waist, a painful foot to be dragged along, much like they drag their sledges, the breath of one man in another's ear, their matching skin turning to black.

Their bodies are furrowed by the landscape, marked by everything about them, they melt into it, lose themselves in it, they take on its features.

ANDRÉE'S JOURNAL

21 July 1897

Do you want to wash yourself, Nisse?
Wash myself? No, I washed myself the day before yesterday. The dirt
that is left is of such good quality that it is impossible to remove.

COMPLEXION

1882

Fifteen years earlier, Andrée sets foot on the Svalbard archipelago for the first time. He is obsessed by one question: what does the cold do to men, to their skin, to their organs, and what of the harshness of the Arctic, and the ice, and the darkness? It is winter, so it is dark. He settles in with a group of scientists, into the Svenskehuset station – a wooden hut, its timber planks abraded by the salt, standing on the shore like a house in a horror movie, where seventeen Norwegian hunters have previously succumbed to lead poisoning.

They are a little bored, not that they ever admit it, they are still young, impatient, full of plans, they discover the searing cold, which draws them around the fire in the evenings, has them reminiscing about the good food they would eat back home, the beautiful girls back home, the bright sun back home, a sun so warm that gilds the countryside. They play at imagining they will never return and wonder at how their absence will be overcome, that ever-so-short absence, the insignificance of which Andrée will measure only by the yardstick of an absence that will leave him with no words to describe it. The muffled sound of the grey waves can be heard on the beach.

What effect do these extreme conditions have on the human skin? Andrée wants to find out, to confirm if the greenish tinge taken on by faces in the polar night is a result of the darkness on the skin itself or an optical effect caused by the return of the light.

He shuts himself away in a darkened room for an entire month.

He remains there alone, in the darkness.

When he emerges from his confinement, when he looks in the mirror, he observes at length his skin which has changed colour, which no longer resembles human skin but rather that of some unknown species that lives in darkness underground. A greenish-yellow skin, a skin which is no longer his own.

This hue, then, was not just an illusion created by the workings of the retina, the eye's mysterious mechanism: it is something real. He is the living proof, he will be the record – his own skin has become the photo-sensitive surface, man turned guinea pig, man turned image.

He feels the texture of his skin: it has the complexion of an ancient painting, of the skin of the dead fallen at the foot of the cross. He observes what the North is doing to him, how he is taking on its hue, becoming part of it, already.

Often, it seems, the peoples living in far northern parts, those who live in Svalbard, in Greenland, in the Faroes, in Alaska, will tattoo a map of their territory onto their very skin, an outline of their landscape, a form of refuge, a flag. Andrée has tattooed onto his skin the very essence of the night.

He probably celebrates the fact with a schnapps.

Yet he underestimates the strength of the connection which links them, himself and this Great North, that he has not yet truly explored, like his own destructive power, which he shares with those who will follow in his footsteps.

Andrée cannot imagine that one day the ice will not be rock solid, that the panorama will dislocate, causing rockslides and rivers of mud, a collapsing of the blue, white walls, straight into the grey waters, and it will not simply fall, it will crash, with the roar of a storm, a tempest, a multitude of explosions, one merging into the next.

He cannot believe that the pack ice will disintegrate, that the fossilised bones of prehistoric creatures will emerge, from the Antarctic to Siberia, gaping-mouthed time bombs with ivory teeth, strains of anthrax emerging from the cadavers of reindeer, methane, carbon heating an atmosphere already unusually warm, forming pockets that extend beneath the green grasses where, under the phosphorescent sky glowing over the Siberian tundra, reindeer farmers will discover chasms, rifts and black holes that open up overnight. A landscape of living matter, releasing mysteries and creatures, as unpredictable as a wild beast and equally lethal.

Andrée is still observing, somewhere, in the mirror, his yellow-ish green face. Marching across the pack ice, he is probably scrutinising the effect of the Great North on himself, unaware that the landscape is just as capable of transforming itself, that even the ice is forming channels, that it, too, is disappearing.

Their sledges draw tattoos of pale lines on the icy surface, wavering like the tracings of rivers on ancient maps, where each outline mimics the successive watermarks left behind on the earth, where the lines tangle like locks of hair. They hold the cold barrel of their shotguns in their cloth-wrapped hands and let them drag behind them – one more track, providing an outline of their steps. But they cannot make out the pattern of their journey in the snow, the fissures left by their bodies, the deeper, flowing wake of the boat behind them and the lines they leave behind in the pools of mint-green water.

It is a collection of markings they could only ever have deciphered from the basket of their balloon, from where they could have observed their doubles carving out a path, might have guessed at their future. Perhaps they could have detected in this unpredictable mapping, in these curves, these dots, these dashes, a sort of hieroglyphics from which they could draw a meaning, a design, a direction.

But they fell out of the sky. They are unable to see anything. They must march in ignorance, much as they are limited to seeing the ruin of their own face in the damaged skin of the others. They have no choice but to continue blindly to trace their passage across the pack ice, sketching out its missing borders, drawing lines on the space, ever ignorant of the neat circles being drawn with their bodies by the drifting, shifting landscape, the mark they are leaving on it, like the imprint left by the light on the sensitive gelatine of their photographs.

NEW YORK TIMES

23 July 1897

Has Andrée crossed the Pole?

CHICAGO NEWS

30 July 1897

He may be in Alaska.

LAKMÉ

25 July 1897

It's a black-and-white family photo, the sort you find by the thousands these days at secondhand dealers' stalls. The Strindberg family are posing outdoors, in front of some tall trees. Standing in the centre is the father, Occa, imposing and rotund, sporting a mischievous smile, and a jacket cinching in his solid torso. He's holding a walking stick in one hand and in his other appears to be a cigar.

To his right is Anna, her white arm slipped through his dark one. She has just a hint of a smile, is wearing a curious pale-coloured hat, set at a jaunty angle. A corset is cinching in her chest, which is concealed by rows of lace. I don't know who the others are. Five women of various ages, one of whom, wearing a severe expression, could well be a man, an androgynous figure with broad shoulders and sparse hair. The gaze of an adolescent girl creates a distant vanishing point in the second background to the image.

Their clothes are lightweight, they remain at the table for some considerable time after the meal, intoxicated by the sound of the sea, a little sand still in their shoes. A Swedish island presents an ever-changing face. In winter, fault lines of pale rocks mimic cracks in the ice, blackening in autumn and in summer they dry out, suddenly covered in the maquis scrub reminiscent of southern France when the water takes on a turquoise glint reflecting branches of pine.

This brilliant green, this blue translucence, the quiet ennui of conversations preceding the siesta, all very likely images to populate Nils' dreams, which themselves grow increasingly vivid as sleep grows ever rarer. Images which probably end up superimposing themselves on the monotony of the snow, which itself will preoccupy Anna, the snow that will cover those sunny beaches with its whiteness – both of them, Nils and Anna, at times reunited by this impossible layering of landscapes.

Anna waits, during the long lunches which flow over into the afternoons, just as there is always waiting at a family meal, limp in the languorous summer weather, arms in the cool shade of the parasol, the scratchiness of grass on the skin of her knees, but her waiting is not governed by quite the same rhythm as the others.

Nils' relatives are waiting, behind the four walls of their homes or in the shade of their gardens, surrounded by their gilt frames and their fresh flowers on their blonde wooden side-tables, they are waiting, together, for their son, their brother, to return to fill the hole around which they are gathered, while Anna, orphaned young and one of eleven siblings, is the one displaced, emerging utterly alone from her youth to follow a mirage, a memory.

Under the veranda, the bird given to her by Nils is brooding in its cage – a messenger pigeon with nowhere to fly, serving only as an endless reminder of the journeys she will never make.

They called it Lakmé, after their favourite opera, the story of a young Hindu woman who falls in love with an English officer, unbeknownst to her father. She tries to protect him, hiding him in the forest and caring for his wounds before taking her own life when she realises that the man she loves, for whom she has cared, plans to abandon her and go to war.

Lakmé puffs herself up, coos, the bird's beady eyes stabbing at her own.

A pigeon instead of a heart, a flustered pigeon to be held tightly in her gloved hand so it might settle.

It is her birthday. She is twenty-six years old. She is no longer a child, not at all. She may no longer take the liberty of casting a sidelong glance, of fleeing like the other young woman already almost out of the camera's field.

She holds herself upright, her arm slipped through her father-in-law's.

She has no other choice, no other possible role, she has not even had time to marry and already she is widowed or almost, worse than widowed, a Penelope with neither shroud nor suitors, whose image reveals nothing of what she is holding within. Perhaps nothing appropriate, nothing you might imagine. Perhaps there is a laugh which grips her belly, like the creaking of a door between body and soul, or a hunger for some other love. Perhaps the gap between this place where she is confined and the immensity of her longing is making her ironic and unapproachable. Perhaps she is growing increasingly absent, for longer and longer periods at a time, forgetting to reply should somebody ask her to pass a dish or share a confidence. Perhaps she only remains attached to members of the family for the morsels of Nils they unwittingly offer her, when the same dimple flashes across their face, the same smile, and perhaps she struggles to calm an unjustifiable fury when faced with the bodies of these strangers in whom flows even just a little of his own blood.

Perhaps this photograph is just as deceptive as those of the explorers, a white lie, told out of consideration, the sort told to children so as not to hurt them, concealing out of politeness, pity, whatever it is that passes across her eyes, those great, dark eyes with their hint of quiet turmoil. Her hands are flat against his lower back. The pressure is building. Ears humming. Eyes closing. Her body giving way.

Wait for one year, before starting to worry.

That is what Occa said to her when they went by boat to the little island of Vänö to collect the telegram containing the news that the balloon had just taken off.

As if it were possible, for one whole year, to keep the anguish at bay, as it expands, makes itself at home, as the boat draws away from the island. As if it were possible to keep from her mind the balloon and the men it contains, to force her thoughts to remain at the gates to her consciousness, for a few minutes, a few seconds – for a year.

Does Occa, his father, truly think that is possible? Or is he too an expert in the art of the white lies told to children?

If Nils had been there, where would he have been standing in the photograph? Would his presence have altered any part of the rigid family arrangements in front of the lens?

He would probably have taken Anna's arm, breaking up the unnatural couple she makes there with her father-in-law, and around whom they are all gathered, with him trying as he might to fill the absence of his son with his broad body, trying to re-establish the central focus on the men in the family, a task which falls to him alone, given how few men there are.

Nils, however, does have three brothers, but Tore, Sven and Erik are still boys, visible in the foreground, sitting on the ground, one of them sprawled in the grass, body slouching, folded awkwardly, a look of doleful provocation on his face. His air of casual indifference is evident. You can't help but wonder why he has not been reprimanded – presumably an indulgence permitted by their worry. The boy next to him, a little older, is sitting up straight but his expression is darker still, and his large hands are those of a man.

Erik will become an architect, Sven, the curator of an art gallery, Tore, a sculptor. He will be the one to design the funerary monument of the expedition in the Stockholm cemetery, a great stone needle symbolising the ice whose modernist design will cause a scandal.

He will be the one to identify Nils' body by its chipped tooth in the hospital at Tromsø.

Again, he will be the one to send Anna the letters discovered at Kvitøya.

Later, Tore will have a son, Göran, who as director of photography on various Ingmar Bergman films, will re-create that same implacable summer light on those Swedish islands, who will illuminate the faces of those finally able to divulge their stories and their secrets.

Sometimes it takes years, it requires children to be born and to grow up, requires entire generations to interpret a look, so that a whole life of waiting and pent-up desire might emerge, so a braggart of a boy, trapped in mourning for his brother much as he is cornered in the thin frame of family photos, ends up producing the child who will in time know how to widen the focus, how to disrupt the pose, how to render the scene fictional – for the better.

ANDRÉE'S JOURNAL

25 July 1897

*Fourfold hurrah for N's sweetheart when the 25 July broke.
Gull with red belly. Wings blue underneath and above. Dark ring
around neck.*

FALL

In the space of a moment

When he falls, the others barely hear him go down. They could almost continue on their way as if nothing had happened, so unreal it all seems, and the pack ice as unchanged as ever.

But Nils shouts, waves his arms about. Knut and Salomon turn around. The water snatches away his breath, paralyses his limbs, it's a matter of seconds. They leave the sleds, run, grab his already stiff body and haul it onto the ice – it seems you summon an unexpected strength in such situations, that you can retrieve somebody who has just fallen off an ice shelf, grab him by the hair with the tips of your fingers before reviving him.

They lay him out, coax him back, rub him down.

Nils has lost his voice, his eyes are wide open, his wan colouring brings out the patches of grime on his skin, they probably shake him with an energy intensified by the fear of being the next to fall in, and he revives in their hands, his voice slowly finding its way back to his throat. He swears. He spits. They make him drink some schnapps, then some coffee.

Where did he go, in that livid moment when he was unable to see nor speak?

Perhaps he was resuming his position, that vacant spot, on a Swedish island, at the centre of a family photo, on the empty arm of his fiancée.

LETTERS FROM NILS TO ANNA

Extracts
24–25 July 1897

I am really rather tired, but must first write you a few words. First and foremost I must congratulate you, for today is your birthday. Oh, how I wish I could tell you now that I am in excellent health and that you need not fear anything for us. We are sure to come home by and by ...

... yes, how very much all this occupies my thoughts during the day, for I have plenty of time to think, and it is so delightful to have such pleasant memories and such happy prospects for the future as I have, to think about!

... Just now we are putting up the tent and Frænkel is making the meteorological observations. Just now we are enjoying a caramel, it is a real luxury. As you might imagine, we do not stand much on ceremony here. Yesterday evening I gave them soup (as I am the one who attends to the housekeeping) which was really not good, for that Rousseau meat-powder tastes rather bad, one soon becomes tired of it. But we managed to eat it in any case.

... round about there is ice, ice in every direction. You saw from Nansen's pictures how such ice looks. Hummocks, walls and fissures in the sea alternating with melted ice, everlastingly the same. For the moment it is snowing a little, but it is calm at least and not especially cold. At home I think you have nicer summer weather.

Yes, it is strange to think that not even for your next birthday will it be possible for us to be at home. And perhaps we must winter here for another year more. We do not know yet. Now we are moving onwards so slowly that perhaps we shall not reach Cape Flora this winter, but, like Nansen, we shall be obliged to pass the winter in a cellar in the earth. Poor little Anna, in what despair you will be if we should not come home next autumn. And you can think that I am tortured by the thought of it, too, not for my own sake, for now I do not mind if I suffer hardships as long as I can come home at last.

… Now the tent is in order and we are going to our berths … We discuss our mental characteristics and our faults, a very educative … I chat with …

… Andrée has spoken about his life, how he entered the Patent Bureau.

Frænkel and Andrée have gone forwards on a reconnoitring tour. I stayed with the sledges, and now I am sitting writing to you. Yes, now you have evening at home and you, like I, have had a very jolly and pleasant day.

ERASURE

25 July 1897

They watch him write. They have set up their camp on a large, open, snow-covered area, without many undulations or irregularities. They observe as Nils carefully works on his letters, chewing on his soft caramel, covering the paper in ink like a diligent schoolboy, taking care to set everything down, doing his best to ensure that his missives, although impossible to send, have a conversational air to them.

Salomon August and Knut exchange conspiratorial glances. They are not mocking him, they feel as protective of Anna's presence, somewhere in Sweden, as they would a flame; she is a moral anchor for them all.

Andrée has left no love behind. His aged mother, Mina, at first counselled him against leaving, before then feeling bad about depriving her son of a heroic destiny and encouraging him to fly off with her blessing. She will be spared the news of his death: she will die shortly prior to the start of the expedition, in that period when the waiting for their departure has not yet turned to disquiet, and she is able to cling to the very end to the image of her son's triumphant taking off over the sea, to the crowd's rapturous applause.

Perhaps the sight of Nils' serious face bowed over his letter, and the sense of Anna's presence it creates when, caught up in their imaginary conversation, he allows a smile to escape, perhaps all this brings to mind, too, the face of this mother or some other unknown woman, or maybe a man, whose lives might have intersected with those of Salomon August or Knut, leaving an impression which suddenly, against the white background of their march, reveals just how deep an impression they left.

In any event, they cling to it, encourage his attachment, this thread which links them to the earth, without suspecting perhaps the object of their envy already no longer quite exists. There is no sign of an issue which nonetheless persists: how to preserve Anna's face intact. Nils probably feels he must try to stop himself thinking about it, this face, the sharpness of the image catching him by surprise when it appears unbidden but which is proving increasingly elusive when he tries to summon it. He may well from time to time even seek to deny himself the pleasure so as not to wear it thin, or scrape it away, bleach it, so as not to make it fade away.

Often faces that have been lost are revived by people we encounter, even if they bear only a fleeting resemblance. You might see a child in the street and it is your own that rushes forth, caught in the same fit of laughter or the same fit of tears, a stranger lends his face to that of somebody you have lost and suddenly they are there, present, and you're transfixed on the footpath, watching them pass by.

Here, there is no fleeting silhouette, no gaze to reflect Anna's own and bring it to life. He does not rely on the gaze of his companions, quite the contrary, he thinks instead of how one day he will try to rid himself of the memory of their faces if ever they return home, of the time it will take to forget the features he has had to look at for too long, the red patches on their flesh, the watery eyes, the cracked lips which he will perhaps be forced to summon up endlessly, in his memory, so as finally to wear them out, turn them into shadows, black holes. How he longs for a different face, somebody, anybody, a new face that might, for a moment, bring Anna's back.

Of course, there are still the keepsakes, the pictures. His companions sometimes see him bring out a photograph or a scrap of paper which he pores over with an intensity that is a little forced, as you might rub a magic lantern, trying to make the features of his fiancée appear from it. When he catches their looks, he puts away the tickets to the exhibition which they saw together before he left and which he carefully keeps to hand, he closes up the locket where her portrait is hidden, he will open it again later, in the tent, when he is alone, and then he will try once again to jog his memory, but every evening it will be harder to bring her back, every evening she will lose something, a detail, several, and they accumulate, these absences, turning her face into some tenuous composition, lacking form and vitality, reduced to what he remembers of her – that she has brown eyes, straight eyebrows, that there is something about the arch of her eyelids which falls and rights itself just as quickly when she laughs, when she pouts, and her mouth eludes him, her elegant lips with their deep corners disappear into a line which is no longer able to open at the warmth of a breath, and her little round nose, pale, nothing more than an indistinct area, a void in the picture, features that are no longer connected, which he realises are no longer reflecting what he is feeling, he would have to stop thinking about her for days, weeks, and only then would she reappear before him, but what else should he think about?

He raises his eyes to look at his companions. It is time to eat, they didn't dare interrupt him, they're hungry, waiting for him. Nils carefully puts away the letter he has started, he stands up, goes over to join them, perches on the photographic apparatus, the box containing matches or the medicine chest – one of the three seats they have at their disposal, each no doubt having their nominated favourite, that evening they drink some coffee and a bottle of fruit juice, which prompts Knut to move away from the others so he can enjoy the last drops, hidden from their view, they have a laugh, toast each other, one of them might lay a hand on Nils' shoulder to comfort him or to share whatever recollections of her remain.

Scarcely a week later, Nils will stop writing. He will remain silent so as not to lie or have to conceal Anna's presence in a conversation that is increasingly solitary, artificial, so that her mouth might still open into a laugh or a kiss, so he can continue to hear the fresh sound of her voice in the depths of his ear.

For now though, they head to bed, all three of them huddled into their reindeer skin sleeping bag, and probably he hopes that before morning dawns she will be reborn from his dreams, vibrant and alive.

ANDRÉE'S JOURNAL

30 July 1897

But don't worry.
Joking about reindeer hair everywhere. Lose one you find a thousand.
Silver-fork.
The Polar dist. is certainly the birthplace of the principle of the
greatest stumbling-blocks.

REED

A detour

The pictures taken by Fridtjof Nansen in the year prior to their expedition, the pictures Nils mentions in his letter to give Anna an idea of the landscape surrounding him, gave them a foretaste of their adventure, along with a persistent feeling that everything they would see had already been seen, that they were already too late to be the first.

In those photographs, there are other men posing on the pack ice. Other men who, from a distance, look very much the same – from a distance only, though, for on peering closer you can see how covered in hair they are, beards long, haunted looks on their faces, as damaged as Strindberg, Frænkel and Andrée still appear vigorous and intact, as if nothing could dent them.

The spark for Nansen's adventure came from a pile of dead wood: fragments of the vessel from the *Jeannette* expedition, crushed by the ice not far from the New Siberian Islands, debris from the hull and stem that had drifted so far from there, all the way to Greenland. If these paltry remains had made it so far, why would not he? Nansen had wondered.

The year is 1884 and suddenly, everything becomes clear: the drift will provide the path and all he will have to do is follow it. He will allow his own movements to be directed by that of the pack ice in the mad hope of reaching along the way the inaccessible North Pole.

Nansen works on the design for a unique vessel, the *Fram*, which, instead of being crushed by the ice, will allow itself to be led along by it. He will calmly turn the harshness of that icy landscape to his advantage. Resistance is the key, he is convinced of it, as well as a certain flexibility, which his expedition will come to embody.

Unlike Andrée, Nansen has been broken in to survive in a hostile environment. His childhood was spent running around, swimming, his adolescence spent fishing, hunting, sleeping next to a campfire high in the Norwegian forests. He has become familiar with every leaf, every insect, the taste of every plant and also the danger they might pose. Having been put on skis at the age of two, he took out the national cross-country championship at a very young age. He is as talented at sports as he is at science: a crack ice-skater, an expert in the nervous systems of marine life and a formidable hunter of seals. He has already led an expedition on a traverse of Greenland, revolutionary for the modesty of its means and its few men, all of whom returned alive and in good health thanks to their lightweight equipment and their appreciation of Inuit and Sami survival techniques. Furthermore, his countless successes have made him a star attraction in social circles and have led to his being awarded several medals: the least one can say is that he has all the qualifications.

The *Fram* leaves port on the 24th of June 1893. As expected, he finds himself caught in the ice, but its revolutionary design means they are able to withstand the pressure for some considerable time. Despite this initial technical success, the vessel advances far too slowly for Nansen's liking; he has no intention of passing the time playing cards and drinking litres of rum as Shackleton's men will subsequently do.

So, he makes the rather questionable decision to allow the crew to continue their drift and to launch himself on his attempt to conquer the Pole by dog sled, alone, or almost. From his crew he chooses an accomplice, a certain Hjalmar Johansen, who was so desperately keen to participate in the expedition that he accepted a position bearing no relation to his numerous qualifications: stoker in the ship's boiler room. Nansen most likely values his enthusiasm, his impeccable physical conditioning along with his selflessness, which will certainly render him the perfect companion.

In March 1895, two years after their departure, Nansen and Johansen, along with their twenty-seven dogs, disembark from the *Fram*. Following an endless journey across the pack ice, they make it to the northernmost point ever reached, at a latitude of 86°13.6'N.

But they remain unsatisfied. They are keen to reach the Pole, despite increasingly rough terrain that is strewn with great chunks of ice. On the 13th of April, their watches stop abruptly – doubtless their complicated mechanisms have suffered at the hands of the cold. Without knowing the time, it is impossible to work out their longitudinal position and thus the direction in which they must head. With no marker in time, they have lost any marker in space.

They finally decide to set up camp on an ice floe that is more or less stable, and from where they can make out an island on the other side of the open water – a possible refuge.

One by one they slaughter the weaker of the dogs in order to feed the stronger ones.

By the 6th of August, they have killed the last remaining animals.

Using their two kayaks and a sail, they cobble together a makeshift catamaran in an attempt to make the crossing. There is every likelihood it will prove their final effort. But if fairies exist, or angels or any other heavenly being likely to be watching over audacious explorers, they must all have been leaning over Nansen's cradle at the same time, so often was he miraculously saved. Not only do the two companions arrive at the island, but they manage to construct a solid shelter for themselves, dug out of the snow, reinforced by stone walls and protected by walrus skins. There they fall sleep. There they wake up. And life continues on its round.

They remain in their hole throughout the winter, waiting for more favourable conditions to return, together keeping watch over the fragile flame of their life, exposed to wind, snow, and so fearfully cold that even men such as they cannot poke their nose outside without risk of it falling off. There they remain, each getting in each other's way, each indispensable to the other, each tiptoeing around the other before daring to use a familiar form of address, eating preserves from back home by the light of a whale oil lamp, reading and re-reading their almanacs, waiting.

To mark the New Year, they start to fashion themselves clothes out of an old sleeping bag, and in May, wearing the new outfits they have so patiently sewn, they set off once more, with their skis and kayaks.

Of course, none of the territory they cross bears any resemblance to the map supposed to represent it. They recognise nothing, constantly lose their way, are attacked by fierce walruses who damage their boats, repair the boats as best they can, wonder if they haven't mistaken which island it is, are on the verge of losing hope when Nansen, who has headed off alone on a reconnaissance sortie after thinking he has heard something that sounds like barking, ends up encountering, miraculously, another explorer.

Just picture the scene: Nansen is tramping across a white land, under a white sky. He has not spoken to a soul other than Johansen for months, on the assumption they are still speaking at all. He has seen only bears, arctic foxes, walruses and ivory gulls, he is utterly exhausted, and there, against that pale immensity, he makes out in the distance a black dot, it is moving, no question, undeniably alive, walking on two legs, it does not appear to be threatening, and soon it becomes clear that it is sporting a moustache and a rather endearing little hat.

ANDRÉE'S JOURNAL

1 August 1897

This evening we have seen the back of a new animal which looked like a long snake 10–12 meters ... a dirty yellow colour and, in my opinion with black stripes running from the back for some distance down the sides.

It breathed heavily almost like a whale which I suppose it really was.

Stockings are dried best by putting them on over the feet.

MIRACLE

1896

Nansen isn't dreaming, it is indeed a man, like him, although one may have doubted at that moment that they belonged to the same species, so different does this new person look – with his elegant clothes, his appropriate footwear and well-shaven cheeks – compared to the bear Nansen has become, cinched into his sleeping bag, his face black, hair indistinguishable from his beard, and an unpleasant odour of grease and whale fat trailing in his wake.

And yet, after a few moments' hesitation, the stranger extends his hand, asking: "You're Nansen, aren't you?" "Yes, I am Nansen," he replies.

And that is that.

If all that is not sufficiently surreal, Nansen and this stranger, another explorer by the name of Frederik George Jackson, decide, a few hours later, to immortalise their meeting and dutifully re-enact it for the camera.

In the image we thus have, we see Nansen from behind, doubtless judging that his face was insufficiently presentable to be captured for posterity prior to the bath that awaited him at the camp. His tailoring skills could nonetheless be appreciated by the way his thick clothes enveloped his massive frame – Nansen and Johansen had put on 10 and 6 kilos respectively during their winter hibernation, probably a result of too much bear fat.

The man facing him is shaking his hand courteously, for a long time, too long a time, because of how long it takes to pose for the camera – one imagines it is Johansen, numb, exhausted, who has had to remain still that whole time, his finger frozen to the shutter release, immortalising his companion.

In the background a mountain can be made out, striated with snow, along with a little black dog, probably the one whose barking has just saved his life. As a way of thanking Jackson, Nansen will name the island after him, the island they have at last managed to escape, once and for all.

Jackson leads them to Cape Flora, where he has set up camp. This is where the other photographs were taken, the ones where we see Nansen and Johansen staring into the lens – the two of them like celestial vagrants, their faces serious, brown, reticent.

There has always been an intensity to Nansen's gaze, even in the shots from his youth in which he resembles a sort of Norwegian Rimbaud, aloof and proud, his eyes ablaze, incandescent. Here, in these pictures of a man at his limit, his irises are so pale as to seem white, and the void they carve into his face is almost disconcerting as his beard is illuminated by their unearthly light, the visage of a deposed king.

In order to recast him in human form, he has been decked out with a curious hat which seems ill-suited to the polar climate. He holds himself upright, despite, you might imagine, his aching muscles, frostbite, suffering, ever mindful that somewhere, lying in wait behind the camera, posterity awaits.

Johansen has recounted in his diary that during their forced hibernation on the island, his companion, once the authoritarian leader, had ultimately been replaced by a *taciturn and courteous man, determined never again to undertake such an expedition.* The reticence is there, written on his face, along with the firm resolution never again to have to experience what they have just survived.

As for Johansen, he has a somewhat disillusioned look about him. The ski stock he is holding in his hand diminishes his presence, it is longer, disproportionate in comparison to his tall body. His clothes are more shapeless, and a sort of hood lends him a vagabond's appearance. A less celestial vagrant, an even more defeated monarch. He has not been granted the backdrop which gave Nansen's figure a vanishing point worthy of a Romantic landscape painting. If each of them is represented by their own symbol, Johansen's is the humbler wall of the hut, with its stubby chimneys, its basic door and windows, a miserly pile of wooden planks.

After all that time spent suffering the other's smell, enduring the emanations of their bodily functions, a peaceful hierarchy has been re-established. Once more returned to the company of men, each resumes his assigned role. Some resume their place with the elegance of those who have always known that somewhere waiting for them is a position by the hearth, and it sustains them, even when they have suffered as Nansen has, when he has believed himself broken. There is something about other men, like Johansen, that bends – their body weakened by the dreary return of things, the brutal reappearance of everything he had thought to have escaped.

While Nansen and Johansen were waiting it out in their hole, the crew members of the *Fram*, still gripped by the ice, killed time as best they could. But with summer approaching, the sailors were able to reach open waters and succeeded in making it to Norway, years after their departure.

They first fetched up in the small port of Vardø – houses on stilts, wood, lots of wood, water – where they encountered, in their own miraculous turn of events, Professor Mohn, the man responsible for the very theory of transpolar drift that had inspired Nansen, as if the Great North had just been reduced to no more than a single block of ice, where a handful of explorers might afford themselves the luxury of encountering each other by chance, exchanging a handshake and sharing, for a few hours, their preposterous plans before setting off once again as if nothing had happened.

Nansen is fretting about the *Fram* and on the *Fram* they are fretting about Nansen, and yet all of them are drifting, without knowing it, in the same direction. It is aboard George Baden-Powell's yacht, where they are celebrating his success, that the new polar hero receives a telegram announcing that his vessel is heading straight for them. Nansen and Johansen meet up with the crew at the port of Tromsø. There are shouts, hugs. They no longer believed it possible, nobody believed it, how could anyone have believed it?

They are feted everywhere they go. The story of their exploits, their survival, their subsequent reunion, ignites the whole country. They are met in every town with jubilation, cheers, lights, banquets. Thanks to these men, we now know that the North Pole is not located on terra firma but on the floating pack ice, even if many refuse to acknowledge the fact. If it has not yet been reached, one might henceforth at least imagine it – one of the world's final frontiers is starting to take form.

In Oslo, still known as Christiania, King Oscar organises a spectacular reception in their honour. Somewhat incredulous, they walk through a human archway of 200 gymnasts. Johansen notes in his diary: *It turns out, real life is not as dreadful as I imagined.*

Nansen is to keep his promise: he never sets off again. He will be satisfied publishing the account of his voyage which, like everything he undertakes, will be a great success. Later, he will devote himself to those with no choice but to be on the move: as the first High Commissioner for Refugees, he will establish the passport which will bear his name and give those who are not yet called migrants international protection, allowing stateless persons, also, to cross borders. It is no longer a question of making the world larger but of making it more permeable, more welcoming. Much as he availed himself of the ice to make his name, Nansen uses the light kindled by his expedition to illuminate the way for others, those suffering the most, those in their thousands, who are in greatest need.

Johansen's own descent into hell begins on their return. Drowning in debt, incapacitated by alcohol, he struggles to re-adapt to this real life that bears so little resemblance to the life he was dreaming of from that frozen den.

Years later, Nansen uses his influence to have his former companion engaged on Amundsen's expedition, leading him to attempt another adventure to the Pole, this time to the Antarctic. Johansen, however, struggles to follow orders. He has seen too much, endured too much. Something within him is obstinate, resists. He would like Amundsen to have the benefit of his experience, but Amundsen chooses not to listen to him, he is stubborn, and has his men take risks, Johansen being one of the first to fall victim. The conflicts between them grow so violent that he ends up being ousted from the expedition.

When Amundsen sets off once again, Johansen will remain at base camp, contemplating the catastrophe which so certainly awaits this new crew, imagining the hardships and the hostility of the ice, congratulating himself on resisting the temptation to be swept up in another voyage which in his eyes is already doomed to failure, to disappointment.

But this expedition will succeed. Amundsen will be the first to reach the South Pole.

Less than a year later, Johansen will take his own life.

ANDRÉE'S JOURNAL

2 August 1897

I do not think we made 2km in 10 hours.
Axe destroyed.
1 skua visible and 2 gulls circling around the body of the bear.

It seems as if good country was more fatiguing than half-good.

RELICS

A Future

In Oslo, where Johansen died, on the Bygdøy peninsula which looks back to the city from the far side of the fjord, there's a museum these days dedicated to the *Fram*. The boat is still there, preserved in a carefully lit building, a vast jewel in its vast setting, surrounded by the galleries where the sailors' relics are exhibited. You can stand on the bridge, duck into the cabins where clothes have been flung onto the bunks and left there as if their owners might, at any moment, burst into the room in their shirtsleeves, to eye one over. Outside, where bronze statues of the triumphant explorers stand gazing out to sea, you are met with the full brunt of the wind as it blasts from the Baltic.

The museum that traces the wanderings of Andrée's expedition is far from impressive. From Gothenburg, a train ride of a few hours brings you to central Sweden, to a place called Jönköping, where you wait on a deserted railway platform alongside an enormous lake, and the only demarcation between water and sky is the line traced by the next train to Gränna.

Andrée's birthplace is a little old-fashioned picture-postcard town, its wooden façades a parade of pastel colours. The rock candy for which the town is renowned spreads into the small streets the smell of hot sugar mixed with stagnant water as you approach the lake. Behind shopfront windows and watched on by tourists, artisans stretch the sugar, rolling up great translucent threads that resemble the serpentine glass of their Venetian counterparts. They twist it and turn it, blending the colours, until they are left with the tiny treats to be handed out to wide-eyed children.

No need here to wind back the clock: you might as well be in a protected enclave, bordered pleasantly by the shore, decidedly out of step with the outside world. The air of unreality is accentuated by the radiant summer sunshine, so that the white fibre-glass polar bears adorning the surrounds of the Andrée museum appear perfectly bizarre.

On the lawn, a panel where you can be photographed poking your head through the hole where the explorers' own heads should be. In the adjoining shop, *I Love Andrée* badges are sold alongside little hanging balloons.

This is where their clothes are to be found, displayed behind glass, where the photographs can be seen. The relics exhibited here are simple items – jackets, shoes, their everyday utensils – some almost intact, banishing time and distance as effectively as the atmosphere of the town, yet one more reminder of how brazenly we are survived by objects, and of the significance they assume when life slips away and they are accorded once more the weight they enjoyed in our childhood, their power as a viaticum, as talismans, to offer us comfort.

There is an emphasis on the whimsical details of their saga, the margin-notes of the story, like the locket next to which Nils and Anna's love story, which has been left in the original Swedish, is described on an information panel.

These fragile vestiges of the everyday in the Grenna Museum provide a welcome contrast with the pomp of the *Fram* museum, from its ode to heroes who, here in this place, still resemble men, tangible and imperfect.

Had they returned, had they achieved their goal, what sort of a museum would have been built in their honour, what story would have replaced the one by which they are defined today, comprised of scraps of their daily life, their untarnished good humour, their falls in the snow, their wanderings across the ice? Those men would not have existed. There would have been others constructed, glory filling the gaps, offering another side to their faces. Even their silhouettes in the images would have appeared more upright, more deliberate, and not as lost in the immensity.

Would Andrée have garnered that glory for himself alone? Would he have relinquished any to the other men, allowed them their memories, to enjoy in their golden years?

Which of his companions would have suffered the most from the world awaiting his return? Strindberg, perhaps, had *real life* not lived up to the heights of the life to which he had clung, or perhaps Frænkel, the one who without a doubt has most evaded description, whose edges are most blurred, whose presence is the most unresolved?

The one of whom we know nothing, or almost nothing.

The one still to be imagined.

ANDRÉE'S JOURNAL

3 August 1897

"Is it easy to get across? Very easy once it is done."

I made a fork for Frænkel. The forks photographed.

PORTRAITS

Just thirty years old

Knut Frænkel was born in Karlstad on the 14th of February 1870. His childhood in the untamed landscape of Jämtland – a mountainous region punctuated by lakes, forests and moors – saw him develop a marked interest in outdoor activities and a robust physique, well suited to extreme climates.

As a result of his father's job with the railways, from a very young age he grew accustomed to a life on the move which nurtured his taste for discovery as well as an unusual aptitude for sport. He is a less exemplary scholar – he fails his first attempt at the baccalaureate, is awarded it the following year, an outcome which he accepts with equanimity: it is not about to stop him discovering the world. The sedentary life, comfortable in front of the hearth, is not for him.

Neuralgia forces him to abandon a military career: he turns to engineering instead. He is utterly focussed on success, achievement, progress. Curious about every sort of innovation, he puts himself forward to Andrée, who realises quickly that here is a man who is not himself ambitious, but a man of consistent character, harbouring neither secrets nor duplicity, an audacious soul who would be indispensable to his expedition.

From the moment they depart, Frænkel takes all the risks: he is constantly out front, weathering snow and wind, hauling more than his due share. Committed to recording his meteorological notes, efficient when erecting the tent, he carries out his tasks without complaint, is ever-present when his companions require a shoulder to lean on. He buries himself in silence, everything straining towards the goal on which he is focussed. Through to the end, he will be the scout, the first. Reticent because he has no energy to waste on idle chatter, efficient and endowed with a somewhat severe common sense, he can be relied upon.

Or this, perhaps, instead: Knut Frænkel was born in Karlstad on the 14th of February 1870. His childhood in the untamed landscape of Jämtland saw him develop a taste for achievement and solitude, honed by a lack of tolerance for others. As a result of his father's job with the railways, from a very young age he was forced to move from one place to another, preventing him from forming attachments, resulting in feelings of insecurity and impatience, constantly driving him to seek out ever more extreme experiences that always leave him dissatisfied.

He fails his first attempt at the baccalaureate and, as a result, harbours a deep sense of failure that his success the following year will never quite erase. Neuralgia forces him to abandon a military career. After falling into engineering, almost by default, he volunteers with Andrée, who is well aware that only the most hot-headed of men would risk following him.

From the moment they depart, Frænkel is keen to demonstrate that he is the hardiest, the most audacious. He is constantly out front, never sparing himself. But his companions' tendency to rely on him is constantly gnawing away at him. His irritable temperament turns quickly to violence. He would not survive two days alone, so he must continue to put up with the others, avoid any outbursts, swallow his bile. Through to the end, he will be the scout, the first. Reticent because there is nothing to say, he strides ahead so as to hear the others no longer, hoping to be the first to lose himself.

There is something of Knut Frænkel that lies perhaps between these two portraits. Something that allows us just a glimpse of the man, allows us to draw closer to some understanding of him by the casual contact, the uncertain combination of a number of hypotheses.

He manages, though, still, to fall into the interstices between the gaps which have opened up between these suppositions.

No sooner does he come within reach, than already he has slipped away.

ANDRÉE'S JOURNAL

5 August 1897

On all fours today as in the spring of our youth.
A rafting of more than 1 kilometre.

MUNCHAUSEN

At the beginning of the month of August

Sometimes they look at each other as if they were perfect strangers. They are constantly approaching each other, then drawing apart, joined by an invisible thread which, like mountaineers' rope, slackens when they stop marching. In those moments, each of them grasps once more what remains of his personality, for a few hours they cease to form part of this many-limbed monster governed by a single mind, this beast they have become in order to survive.

They detach themselves, like overripe fruit, each of them landing on their square of snow, their few centimetres of fabric or sky, in those rare moments when they are once again themselves. What remains of yourself when you have become a link in a chain, an atom with no distinguishing features? They would have to remind themselves once more what they look like, have to know how to reactivate those distinctive features that have been part of their identity since childhood, and whose rough edges they have been trying their whole life to smooth away.

They cling to what people used to say about them in their youth, repeat to themselves the few comments which, without even being aware of giving them any weight, somehow came to define them. Alone now, they chew over episodes which made them stand out. Anything to find a distinguishing feature, anything which might identify the guiding principles of what you might call a personality.

*

At the society dinners which Andrée attended mainly to ingratiate himself with his financial backers, he was accustomed to impressing his audience with his witticisms, his swagger and relaxed sense of humour. Conscious of the significance it assumed along the path to success – this ability to distinguish himself from others – he had done his utmost to adopt the character which his moustache, his stature, his smile, tended to imply.

He threw himself into heated discussions, was a passionate advocate for technological, political and social progress, and for the rights of women and workers. "Now that is a committed man," people would murmur in the corridors, "a man with a clear vision and an ability to speak his mind."

All of which was true, and it counted for nothing, as he had quickly come to understand, in that vipers' nest of high society. He who had come from that small town with its permanent odour of rock candy and stagnant water, descended on his mother's side from a longstanding and respectable family of clergymen, had quickly learned to make himself heard among his six brothers and sisters. Science had set him apart, had given him the marbles with which he now entertained himself, rolling them across his hosts' waxed parquetry floors.

Science: the lofty ideals which Andrée would constantly brandish when discussions would become controversial, when faced with the subtleties of poets, such pointless sensitivities for which he reserved a detached disdain. He had caused a sensation when invited to a soirée in honour of the author Selma Lagerlöf, and in response to a question asking whether he had liked her book, he answered that he had read *The Surprising Adventures of Baron Munchausen* and that, surely, was more or less the same thing.

You can just imagine the laughter that erupted in the wake of his reply, and indeed the embarrassed smiles of those who feared they had been overheard by the guest of honour herself. It was all part of the character which the anecdote would come to feed, would emphasise. For Andrée, the main game was playing out far from such salons:

it involved action, it required being out in the field, a long way from the meandering digressions on the page of a book.

Perhaps it is these sort of moments he relives when casting a sidelong glance at his companions, their clothes identical to his own, praying fervently that he does not resemble them – those outbursts which set him apart from others, indeed made him a leader, the sort of man he is no longer quite sure he is.

They swim about in his head, the comments made at those social receptions, gently they unravel, lose themselves in the thick whiteness. All that for this, they niggle away. Those moments of glory and grace, those discussions, that laughter, all those years of self-construction just to find yourself here, frost in your whiskers, puffing and panting away on the deserted pack ice thinking about dark wood-panelled salons and cigars smoked in sprawling entrance halls filled with handsome polished furniture, surrounded by curious faces to whom he must have appeared as disconnected from reality as Selma Lagerlöf and her new book appeared to him, as mad as Baron Munchausen propelled into the sky by a cannonball.

Here he is, the failed baron whose only sky is now a limitless field of ice. Here he is, so attached to what is real, so rarely the dreamer, here he is, without even realising it, having slipped into the skin of the very fictional heroes at whom he would snigger, and it is precisely this iron-clad pragmatism, his calm level-headedness which, pushed to the extreme and never challenged, have led him to this place that is just a reflection of the extent of his madness.

Do his companions still see in him the fragments of that self-assured man with the resonant voice when, thigh-deep in snow, he cradles his long, calm face in his hand, looking like an exhausted walrus, eyes drooping, whiskers tangled, swallowed up by the collar of his woollen jacket?

*

Does Salomon August still see Knut as the solid companion? And Nils, still the eager, conscientious, young man in love?

And if there is no longer any certainty about that previous life, if it seems ludicrous, misleading, artificial, why not reconstruct them as they see fit, these lives for which there is no longer any evidence, except for the letters, the photographs, the locket containing Anna's image?

Any hierarchy, so often erased by the camaraderie between them, remains only discernible in a few details – a way of addressing each other, the position they adopt in the photographs. Perhaps Frænkel and Strindberg are sometimes tempted to create a new hierarchy, one that reflects neither age nor qualifications nor social status, but is based in this environment on new governing criteria, namely strength and youth, in which case, doubtless, they would emerge superior.

But they retain their respective positions, remain under the command, albeit benevolent, and barely authoritarian, of Salomon August Andrée. They remain mindful of the few markers of their circumstances, of the remaining indicators which distinguish them. Perhaps they are clinging on to their own positions as much as their leader is to his, as they might an empty armchair that could well prove useful once more. Were they to leave it outside, to let it fill with snow, they would no longer have anywhere to sit should they one day happen to resume their lives.

Only every now and again do they allow arguments to break out, as if to reassure themselves that some fault lines still exist between them, some disagreements, as if to remind themselves that they are not entirely carved from the same piece of wood or that it is still possible for it to cleave apart, to reveal knots and scars, its deep veins.

It probably starts over nothing, like couples bickering, a triviality that once pointed out will have to be refuted, its significance denied. That Andrée, he is a man incapable of admitting his errors, Strindberg and Frænkel probably mutter to themselves, a man incapable of admitting he has led them to this point notwithstanding the common sense which he so prized, if only he could utter one word, one single word, to voice his regrets, they could allow themselves the solace of a sacrifice suffered in silence. But Andrée jokes around, tries to put things in perspective, insinuates that they have always been in the same boat, always wanted the same thing and of course, they know, Strindberg and Frænkel, that this is what they wanted too, this ice, this immensity, this exhaustion that is breaking them, and the quarrels dissolve on the march or at least in the bear fat that must be heated before it turns solid.

As they abandon any attempt to defend their point of view, to plead their own case, once again they merge into that collective body, a being at once new and ancient, the only form in which together they might survive, gradually abandoning the men they once believed themselves to be.

Baron Munchausen sets off across the pack ice and it is as if he has three bodies, three faces, six feet planted in the powdery snow, three pairs of hands, empty and frozen.

ANDRÉE'S JOURNAL

8 August 1897

The wind right in our noses but it is cooling.
The ice has been about the same almost for the last three days.
I do not use spectacles excepting in bright sunshine.
I press my eyes together instead.

DREAM

In the middle of the night or perhaps in broad daylight

I ascribe this dream to Andrée:

A house. It is white, built on the edge of a lake. The leaves of the tall trees cast shadows that slip across its façade. He watches them lengthen across the pale plaster of its walls. It looks like a small house, from the outside. However, standing at the threshold, you can see down a long corridor leading off to several rooms.

Andrée has his back to us, he's wearing a suit, looking a little tense. The hair on the back of his head seems slightly dusty, like the fur of an old animal. Can you see yourself from behind in a dream?

He is happy to have chosen this house. It is like a happy surprise, this corridor which he does not recall being so long. He goes into an office where the sun is warming the mahogany. Branches sway at the window. There is everything he needs: a chair, a bookshelf, a pile of books on the desk. In the background, a door gives onto a walled garden overtaken by weeds.

He doesn't remember there being a garden. The door, on the other side, opens onto a bedroom – he doesn't remember this room either, with its heavy curtains filtering the rays of light which grow weaker as he approaches. Behind another door, he discovers yet another bedroom, this one is bare, and then a much bigger room with polished furniture. The surprise already feels less pleasant, less enticing, he begins to feel it is odd that all these rooms interlink without his having noticed it happening, odd that they are all multiplying, one after the other, without his permission.

His steps make a dull thud on the creaking parquetry floor. Another door, another room, the smell of furniture wax, then the strange sensation that the space is tilting, leaning towards the earth, and he thinks back to the splashes of shadow on the façade, and now there are no more shadows, only a single block of colour, with no contrasts.

He would like to see it again, that façade, because this is what he is struggling now to remember; the house is preventing him from seeing what doubtless still exists, on the exterior.

Outside, he hopes, there must still be a little street, a garden, a neighbourhood, people he doesn't recognise, there is probably still a town, and at its centre, this house. But he must admit, he is no longer certain of anything. The house is a barrier, a screen. It may well be that beyond its walls, there is no longer any sign of life.

Every door opens onto another door, the house never ends, he can feel the ill wind blowing through it, the age-old memories, no door is closed off and yet it is all closing in on him, the house is crushing him, and on waking, there are no more walls to protect him.

ANDRÉE'S JOURNAL

9–11 August 1897

3h00 Primus started
3h18 the steak ready and the coffee-making begun
3h29 the steak eaten
3h48 the coffee made
4h00 the coffee drunk
5h30 broke camp
Thickness of the ice, 1.6 metres

Frænkel thought he saw land and it was really so like land that we changed the course in that direction.

DORMANCY

Time travelling

They had never been cold, previously. If they stopped to think about the seeds of that sensation, they would have nothing to cling to. Not on that day, in Stockholm, waiting for nightfall beneath a lamppost, nor the day when they left home in the morning, with an acrid smell of chimney smoke in their nostrils, to take advantage of a sea that was still calm in the early morning. Nor on that night of drunkenness, emerging from a restaurant, walking arms linked, inadequately dressed for the winter chill.

That was a cold they recognised. A cold that had a start and a finish, bounded at one end by an evening spent in front of the fire, and at the other by the warmth of your sheets, a cold that made you rub your hands together under your coat, to walk a little faster, help yourself to a cup of coffee, just as soon as the door had closed.

But if there is no warmth to be had, what becomes of the cold? Is it still able to be recognised? Here, the cold, like time itself, has no boundaries. Few people have any notion of a cold such as this. It is a secret they keep to themselves, that will not be divulged.

In theory, the lowest temperature would be absolute zero, but it is impossible to reach it. Absolute cold does not exist. It has no limit, no boundary, they feel it every day. So, their bodies adapt. Their blood cools, their organs too. There are times, even, when they feel too warm, when they are pulling their sleds, when the sun is beating down on their tent, when the clouds of their breath become one around the Primus stove. Their bodies have found an utterly different measuring stick, like plants which become dormant as winter approaches, bulbs which store their reserves in the earth, shrubs which rid themselves of their leaves so the ice cannot weigh them down, nor cause them to burn in the sunlight, nor make the fibres of their woody branches collapse. The sap, then, seeks refuge in the earth, nourishing the plant's roots, with some plants becoming scaly to protect themselves from the ice, creating miniscule alveoli known as "dormant eyes."

The cold corrodes as much as it preserves, feeding fantasies of cryonics and eternal life and perhaps this is the stuff of their dreams, in their passing moments of wretchedness and discouragement, of falling into a long deep sleep, of abandoning themselves to that peculiar warmth which, it seems, takes over the body as it freezes, a furnace, and perhaps they even dare to imagine a miraculous awakening, if one day science should manage to revive dormant bodies.

Once their intact organs have been miraculously revived, they would get to their feet and, in 100, perhaps 200 years' time, they would open their eyes to a new world, where they would recognise nothing, where there would be nobody to remind them of the men they had been, with only their bodies as baggage, to be jumpstarted like an engine that had seized, and once more thrust into the world of the living.

Is this not how the nineteenth century imagined the Arctic to be: a veneer of ice concealing monsters and marvels, haunted by Jules Verne's explorers or by Dr Frankenstein's creation, where the secrets of magnetic force are revealed, where everything starts and stops, a place capable of upending the world, of flipping it like a crepe to show its hidden side – an immense, pale, dormant beast, that all of a sudden shakes itself, revealing the chasms in its body and, in the previously unseen stony flesh of its belly, something akin to the secret of life.

They know that night in these latitudes is immense and that in just a few weeks it will devour everything. Thanks to Nansen, they suspect that the North Pole is not a land, that it is nothing more than a dot to be marked in an ocean of ice. The dream has crumbled away but it remains just as intense, the beast just as enduring, that they might yet believe in a miracle, in this place which always seems both asleep and on the verge of wakefulness.

Around 500 kilometres from where they are marching, on the main island of Spitzbergen, one of the most brutal transformations ever to manifest in a landscape is about to take place: the violent eruption of a town, constructed in the face of all common sense in such hostile territory.

It will be called Pyramiden. Founded by the Swedes in 1910, sold to the Russians and then to a mining company in 1931, it will be abandoned in 1998 and will leave behind the deep traces of lives that will last only a few decades.

The mountains will return to their slumber. The apparition will have been brief, the beast will have roused itself, in only the flutter of an eyelid, time enough to glimpse the monumental plan to construct a city modelled on the heavens, a symbol of the power of the Soviet Union, a folly that will have pierced the ice, shattered the earth, and beneath the disembowelled mountains will have witnessed the spreading fingers of mining galleries. Men will have worked there, families will have moved in, unable to conceive of the imminence of its planned obsolescence, its return to a silence as brutal as its emergence from the earth. The town will be emptied, the mining operations will wind down, the residents will leave having barely embarked upon their dreams, the promise of a virgin territory to be tamed, evenings of drinking vodka with children playing in the snow, growing up, forming relationships, notwithstanding the cold, the depths of the night. They will leave behind them the green grass imported directly from Ukraine, the climate which is to be endured as some additional proof that the place is perfectly suited to socialism, that life, in spite of everything, is as banal as elsewhere, followed then by a premature nostalgia, the collapse of industries and hopes, the return to a previous world, where the way has been cleared, where it is comfortable, so much less vast and absurd.

Nowadays, Pyramiden is nothing but a relic, a ghost town where only tourists are heard walking the empty corridors. Were Strindberg, Frænkel and Andrée suddenly to be resurrected, were they to come back to earth and happen upon the vestiges of that town, they would raise their eyes, perplexed, to the statue of Lenin, erected triumphantly where the mountains meet.

What would they make of these remains hemmed in by an environment into which they appear gradually to be dissolving? In the deserted corridors of the Cultural Palace, in the company of a handful of tourists with an interest in ghost towns, they would see abandoned on a windowsill an accordion, a balalaika. They would cast their shadows across the swimming-pool blue walls and would head down a monumental mosaic-decorated staircase that could have them believe they are running their fingers over the ruins of some alternative Pompei.

The setting of Pyramiden is reminiscent of images of Chernobyl. The same vast, utilitarian buildings which seem to have been deposited there for the eyes only of phantoms, the same forlorn chairs left in otherwise bare rooms. Those who once lived there appear to have been evicted from their dreams, destroyed by radiation or by the black depths of the mines, and you walk through them as you might along the edges of contaminated spaces, abandoned to mysterious species and to the tracks of wild animals. This is precisely what appeals to those who continue to visit: the impression of desire and loss, the remains of worlds which have disappeared or the harbingers of worlds to come, as if, in this place, they might become one and the same thing.

Outside deserted buildings, where ivory gulls screech, in front of playground swings dangling in the wind, visitors try to capture it, this emptiness, try to grasp the desolation of the landscape, to sense the heaviness of the silence which will only resume when they have gone, at day's end, when the boat has departed.

In the photographs of Strindberg, Frænkel and Andrée, the pack ice is only a stage set, a background canvas against which any nuance is difficult to discern. It is their bodies they are keen to display in the frame, their feet on the white ground. This Great North is nothing but a progressive reduction of that which is able to be seen, so one stands out more effectively, there is only oneself in the frame.

They cannot know that one day, not far from where they are, towns will sprout up, or that one day there will be others who come to the Arctic searching for the very void they are trying to block out with their exhausted bodies.

ANDRÉE'S JOURNAL

13 August 1897

The instant after we had gone to bed we again heard a whale but could not catch sight of it.

SAVAGES

13 August 1897

I t rains on the 13th of August. It soaks into their clothes, the permafrost is already spongy beneath their poor footwear. At half past
three in the morning they head to bed. Huddled in the tent, they
hear the whistle of a whale and the drumming of the rain. And at five in
the evening, they set off again, in the same light.

"Three bears!" cries Strindberg suddenly.

They freeze, flattening themselves against the snow. Andrée advances,
exposed: better to serve as bait than to die of hunger. He creeps forward.
He whistles, trying to capture the bear's attention, then he too starts to
crawl on all fours – a curious pantomime seemingly enacted by this elegantly clad man, already looking tattered, yet still handsome, crawling
along like a wild animal, mimicking his watchful counterpart.

It is a female, with her two cubs. She advances, in that particular fashion
which marries a certain awkwardness with an almost spider-like grace
as she emerges from the water, thick fur draping her limbs, under-
scoring her well-developed muscles. She turns her head to reveal the
slender line of her burrowing snout that finishes in a sharp, gleaming
tip, black as the pads of her paws.

These dark spots are the only stains on the expanse of pack ice.
Andrée blinks. He ought to put on his dark glasses, but for some
strange reason does not. Waiting, his gaze lowered, his retina is filled
with the whiteness, even as he sleeps he can feel it gradually erasing
the details of his dreams and now, as he focusses, trying in vain to keep

his eyes open, he watches as the contours of the she-bear start to blur, almost nothing now distinguishes it from ice and sky, nothing but those small black spots, shifting: eyes, snout, the pads on its paws as it lifts them one by one, and wanders into the gaping emptiness stretching out before his failing eyes.

He rubs a frozen hand over his eyelids. He knows his companions are watching him, that they are waiting. The rifle trembles in his arms. He stretches his neck, lifts his head which had been drooping, slowly, towards his chest, under the weight of his exhaustion and the blinding light.

He wipes away a drop hanging from his pronounced nose.

The she-bear starts, she too sniffs and suddenly unfurls like a hollow puppet into which some enormous hand might have been slipped. Standing upright on her hind legs, she sweeps the air with her snout but, catching no scent of danger, falls back down, supple, into the glimmering snow.

Again, Andrée advances. Strindberg and Fraenkel are right behind him. Suddenly, they exchange a look, unfold their numb limbs as they bring themselves upright, and shoot as they leap. The strident detonations underscore the heaviness of the silence. It would be tempting to flatten their hands over their ears.

The two cubs turn back to their mother. They no longer have the fluffy plumpness of the very young, rather there is a sort of juvenile disproportion to their bodies. For an instant, they are stationary, then they start to run. Andrée fires a second time. The mother, having halted abruptly, hauls herself upright, as if the impact of the bullet has brought her to her feet one last time, and when he shoots again, abruptly, she falls back down.

Other hunters have described the reaction of cubs whose mother they have just killed, a reaction they describe as peculiar. Often, they say, the cubs make a run for it after recoiling, especially if the she-bear lets out a roar before dying. Then the cub will take fright and, very quickly, try to flee, howling also until it is caught. But it does happen, too, that the mother dies at the first shot, soundlessly. In those cases, they note, the cub behaves as if the she-bear were still alive, huddling between her paws, licking at her blood, suckles from her teats, trying to protect itself against her flank. The cub might survive days if nobody captures it, if the corpse is not removed, if she has not been killed for her flesh, but for the thrill of it, for a lark.

Andrée will not have the luxury of time to describe the behaviour of these young bears. He fells the closest of them with a single shot and it collapses gently, as if falling asleep, as if it had never awakened in the first place, as if there were nothing to differentiate it from the snow until a scarlet puddle sketches an outline of its body. Strindberg and Frænkel take care of the second.

The next day, after sampling the meat, all three of them will be delighted that the flesh of the cubs, unlike their mother, remained soft and tender for quite some time.

It is already becoming a sort of routine for them. *Today bear-tracks were seen and the day before yesterday two such traces were observed. This means for us that we have wandering butcher's shops around us.*

Every bear they sight is slaughtered if possible. For the most part, they are unable to carry all the meat with them, they are already over-burdened, so they content themselves with taking the best cuts, the lightest, brain, kidneys, heart, tongue, and in so doing, these refined men, these scientists, engineers, grow comfortable plunging their arms into those warm bellies, all the way up to the elbow, taking unexpected pleasure in playing at butchers, then rubbing themselves off in the snow in order to rid themselves of the colour and the persistent odour of the blood.

There is great joy in the caravan, writes Andrée after a good kill. They will use the fat to protect against chapping, the skin to line sleeping bags, favouring the lighter fur from the forelegs for this purpose. And should their meat supply be running low, they cut up what remains into small pieces in order to give an illusion of plenty.

On the 18th of August, while mending his drawers, Andrée exclaims: "See, there is another bear for us," before resuming his task and leaving it to Frænkel to kill without further ado.

They sketch a bloodied map of motley red patches mixed with clots and entrails as they make their way through the snow across the floating pack ice. These are their markers, their version of white pebbles, the gaping carcasses of bears and their bloody tracks.

One of the photographs shows Frænkel and Strindberg alongside a pale shape. They are looking down, each holding a rifle. Through the fog of the image, a bear can be seen lying at their feet – where the image is less grainy, the subject fluffier, one can make out its legs, folded back on its chest, like a cat in the sun, its mouth half open, one can see the miniscule stud of its eye.

They have curated the setting, tried several poses, Frænkel with a firm grip on his Remington rifle. It is the first bear they have killed, unnecessarily just at that moment, they still had plenty of provisions, any threat a distant one. They killed it for the training, taking advantage of the opportunity, so that others, later, might be killed. To make this place their own, to occupy it, with the new sensation of witnessing so great, so ferocious, so handsome a creature drop. To prove to themselves that they are still at the apex of the food chain, they are abundantly alive, more alive than the other animals, at the very top of the world, and of the animal kingdom.

They captured a bird, a young ivory gull: they butterflied it for the photograph, on what looks like a plank of wood, as one would nail a bird of ill omen to a farmhouse door.

The effect is peculiar. It is as if the animal has been carefully cut out from the background, ripped from the powdery material of a charcoal sketch. No other photograph has the precision of this pious image, this fallen grace. Its wings, nailed, are spread wide. On its feathers, small round spots trace dotted patterns.

It is hard to make out its head, its beak; its wings take up all the space, the image is concerned with flight, that is what they are trying to grasp, and to do, so they shatter it, first with the rifle's bullet and then with the shutter release of the camera.

A year earlier, in Stockholm, Nils took another photograph: grey hues of refracted light, and at its centre, a bright shape. You have to look past the seductive surface, beyond the velvety greys and fine lines, in order to discern, beneath the halo of white, something that looks like bones: in order to see the skeleton emerge beneath the flesh.

It is one of the first photographs taken in Sweden using X-rays. It is the hand of a man with fingers spread, a vanity that is at first beyond reproach. It is proof that photography no longer captures only the surface of things, rather it is capable of capturing what the eye itself cannot see: the traces of time much like the interior of a body, all that will die, all that is alive.

It is a time when the practice of taxidermy is spreading throughout Sweden. Had they been able to, no doubt they would have brought this gull back home to be able to admire it in a glass case, to grow old alongside it.

The world is a wide-open eye, an enormous diorama where the movements of animals are fixed like the indigenous people of distant lands before spectators at World Exhibitions. Photography, cinema, these are just the technical manifestations of this feverish gaze: there can no longer be any darkness harboured behind one's eyelids.

In order to continue being able to appreciate the majestic appearance of animals after having killed them, their skin must be sliced open in precise areas – along the inside of their limbs, their belly – it must then be peeled back with infinite care and, most importantly, well cleaned. No trace of life can be left behind, no organism, however microscopic, which would risk sabotaging the work, it must be completely stripped back, rendered utterly lifeless, so it might then be easily pulled back over the armature of wood and straw. Then, it must be tanned, soaked in chemical baths as meticulously as you would soak photographic film, and with a similar degree of expertise, for the purpose of conservation and remembering, in order to present an immutable, non-degradable skin, a gleaming sheen, but a skin that still reeks of dust, impeccable though it may be.

Collections of shells, of skins, of corpses, of images. In natural history museums, stuffed animals are displayed in careful reconstructions of their environments, which seem to lend them their shape, their colours. And so we are led to believe that the hue of their belly comes from the earth along which they have been dragged, the density of their plumage, from the shade where they nest.

Reindeer graze, immobile, in artificial forests, antlers pointing to the sky. In the hollows of painted rocks, gulls look sideways, cantankerous, suspicious, and hundreds of birds are displayed with their nests and freshly hatched fledglings. Predators are frozen mid-attack, mouths agape, talons deployed.

Indoors, nature is proliferating while outside, it grows increasingly rare. Sweden is industrialising, the silent fumes of factories, the glow of streetlights block out the night, compete with the sky. Scientists are constantly offering up new specimens to ever-growing numbers of city-dwellers, who are increasingly removed from their natural existence. The Swedes take issue with the Norwegians over the rights of people being chosen to open up the polar regions. The wilderness is being turned into a sanctuary, held up as an example. It is being exposed, it is being destroyed at the same time as it is being conserved, it is becoming the melting pot of a Nordic nationalism characterised by its cold, its purity, its whiteness.

Large corporations are still able to exploit the natural resources as they are the ones financing the celebration in the natural history museums of their chosen resources. Slender pines, snow-covered hills, gaping lakes form backdrops. The animals, just the bit players.

These days, the hunting of bears is prohibited on Svalbard. In the window of the supermarket in the town of Longyearbyen, a notice tells visitors how to behave in the event of an encounter with a plantigrade, warning that they should only fire their weapon as a last resort.

Bears are the holy grail of tourists, proof that something, here, is still wild and that it can be captured, if only in a photograph. Many of them are starving. They are thin, drawn to the lights. Their effigies haunt the town – painted wooden panels, fluffy toys in the windows, stuffed animals used to decorate the hotels, the small church or the gloomily lit bars. The torso of a bear presides in the corridor of a restaurant, its paws sporting boxing gloves. Customers stroke its yellowing neck, peer into its black glassy eyes.

Andrée, Frænkel and Strindberg hesitated before opening the bear's jaws for the photograph, before holding them up to show off their massive size in their diminutive human hands. In the end, they chose to leave the creature on the ground, preferring to pose in front of its fallen body.

The bear is the Polar-traveller's best friend, writes Andrée. Always this breezy, amused tone. It's as if they summoned what remained of their reason and strength to end up with these paltry, merry expressions, as if they had squeezed out their days in order to extract these few presentable drops you cannot help but read into, looking for the flipside: shouts, curses, insults, with nobody to witness it, the bear's own voice rising in their gullet, forcing open their mouths, making them bare their teeth in imitation of these pale creatures that all of a sudden haul themselves upright onto their hind paws, to look just like them.

Or perhaps the tourniquet tightened around their written words helped them to suppress the others, the cries of despair and the desire to kill, helped them to silence the sound of the bear's voice and preserve what must remain of their own – the voice of humour, of level-headedness, of distance.

Do they sometimes look askance at each other, spying each other's weaknesses, their wounds, do they think of those members of other polar expeditions who, worn down by hunger and illness, ended up breaching the ultimate taboo and sampling the flesh of their companions?

Do they sometimes wonder if they too would be capable of that, once their provisions have run out?

Would they bite right into the frozen skin so as not to have to taste what they are ingesting into their own bodies, or would they roast an arm, a leg, over a flame?

Do they start to mistrust the others as the days pass, the weeks, the months, do they keep an eye half open as they tumble into the darkness?

They wave away their nightmares with the flick of a wrist. They have hunting jackets, pompoms on their gaiters, checked caps, the memory of a lover or a mother at home, they write polite words, remain steadfast and assured: nothing can happen to them.

They must never tilt towards bestiality, it is the constant refrain of their words, their clothes, their etiquette. This, too, is the raison d'être of those natural history museums, the hunting parties, more than allowing us just to know, to understand: they offer us a way to protect ourselves, to reinforce the boundaries.

We are above all of this, say the words set out on the paper, above the suffering and the savagery, we are not animals, and so we are able to slaughter them and devour their heart, we are above the chilblains and the mad folly of the landscape, we write to come up for air, before sinking back beneath the water.

ANDRÉE'S JOURNAL

13 August 1897

*In a fissure found a little fish which was pretty unafraid and seemed
to be astonished at the sight of us.*
I killed him with the shovel.

DRIFT

Approaching summer's end

It is time to abandon any hope of reaching Franz Josef Land. The summer is progressing much faster than they are, night is approaching, they can see the daylight dwindling, fringed by dark ridges. They do not speak of it, or as little as possible, and together they agree on the fall-back plan of the closest supply depot: Sjuøyane, the "Seven Islands."

But they are making no progress, they are moving backwards. In addition to being a desert, in addition to being frozen, this place which they are crossing is shifting. It is not solid ground, but rather an agglomeration of forms that are constantly moving and reshaping themselves, leading them most often in the opposite direction to which they would like to go. You have to imagine the jigsaw, these thousands of rafts of ice, drifting, knocking into each other, depositing icy debris, forming fault lines, collapsed cliffs.

They are never allowed to forget that they are walking over a sea. There is water everywhere, underfoot, under their bodies, it rumbles against the ice, they can hear it bracing itself, straining, see it carry off slabs and slip its way in, everywhere, in the form of leads reminiscent of those drawn by the sea on a sandy beach, easily able to be stepped over, but these nothing-channels expand, swell, become crevasses hidden from the men's sight by the snow. No water is truly dormant.

If time is against them, so is the landscape, forever changing its face, just a moment's distraction, a few hours' sleep and, on waking, everything around them has been transformed, even the horizon appears to have shifted in the distance. It takes them a minute to adjust their gaze, their step, to believe what they see: it is not a dream, not even a nightmare. They are further still from their derisory goal than they were the previous evening, when they allowed their eyes to close. Ever since they landed, they have continued to move south, ever further from the Pole.

They are growing weaker. Frænkel is the most affected – an injured foot, diminishing sight, pain in his knees. He is struggling, the others must help him pull his sledge. He was operated on for sciatica prior to their departure: his sturdy constitution is cracking, and one single crack is sufficient to allow anything in.

They try to correct their drift as they continue their dogged march, relying on their calculations, their plotting, their unreasonable common sense, but march and struggle as they might, the pack ice carries them backwards like a current dragging swimmers out to sea, and they grow exhausted battling against the will of this landscape which is leading them wherever it pleases.

Several decades later, on the 31st of October 1968, in an entirely different world you might say, another man, yachtsman Donald Crowhurst, will set off on his impossible voyage across another ocean. His challenge? To circumnavigate the world under sail. Should he win this race, he will be able to save his failing business. The prize is significant, but it must be acknowledged that he gets off to a bad start, even at the preparatory stage. His equipment is utterly inadequate. His supplies insufficient. His trimaran, the *Teignmouth Electron*, named after the small town in Cornwall that is already singing his glory, is far from optimal, even though it is equipped with an inflatable buoy atop its mast to help prevent capsizing. He did not complete its fit-out with safety devices. He has never sailed this sort of boat. He sets off too quickly, driven by a sort of panic, by that intuition that brings one to act in haste fearing a change of mind.

Donald Crowhurst is not mad, not yet, but once he has set off, there is no question of returning to shore, of giving up on the money, of rediscovering, most significantly, that his life is taking on water at every point. Barely a few hours after his departure, he realises he will not win the race but neither does he resign himself to losing it. Somewhere, between these two possibilities, he must find a third option, a way out.

On a calm sea, with no land any longer in sight, he halts, in the middle of that infinite expanse that is carrying him along, causing the hull of his boat to roll left and right. He considers. He observes the pitching and rolling, this capacity of the sea to imprint on another entity its flux, its force, its direction. And it is this moment, when he is drifting, miniscule, in the middle of the ocean, which seems to be his tipping point.

He resolves to let it do the work, the water that is, to let himself be guided by his environment, to drift in his boat across the southern Atlantic, far from the main shipping routes, to remain hidden in this vast expanse where nobody will come looking for him. He sends false positions by radio, makes fake entries in his logbook, sets an imaginary course. Perhaps, from time to time, he truly believes he is following it, perhaps he even ends up believing it as he looks at the same thing day after day, ocean as far as the eye can see, with him drawing circles on the surface, with no other purpose than to wait, to endure. Days of watching the most minute variations in the waves, in the light, in the maddening sky with no protection from any of it to be had.

Five months after the race began, in March 1969, he docks near Rio Salado, on the Argentine coast, to repair one of his pontoons, to see at last an outline of coast, to abandon for a moment the madness of the sea. And then he sets off once again, reporting only infrequent locations which, for the most part, are scarcely credible. He makes false entries in his log regarding the sky, the stars, the precision of his notes seeming to indicate that they had required as much of his attention as any accurate readings would have done.

Deception becomes his landscape, more hospitable than the quantity of water pressing up against the hull and against the walls of his mind. He refines it, inhabits it, patiently weaves it, populates it with details – the position of the moon, of constellations, an entire written universe to counter the world surrounding him.

As the race is a circumnavigation of the world, a circular route, and he has remained almost stationary, his fictitious position ends up almost coinciding with his actual location. Perhaps he can no longer be certain, then, of having lied, his deception adhering so perfectly to reality, like a piece of fabric folded in half.

The final position which he bothered to log, on the 9th of March 1969, has him among the winning competitors. But well does he know that should he arrive in first place, his logbooks will be subjected to close scrutiny: his deception will be revealed. As victory draws closer, so the gap between lie and reality becomes ever more apparent, the walls of his deceit falling away.

A chasm into which he could well fall.

So, to his logbook he flees. He writes poems, jots down thoughts, makes obsessive calculations – the figure 243 appears over and over again, the number of days he had anticipated his circumnavigation would take, a number he will reach by choosing, very probably, the 243rd day to take his life.

The game is up, he writes, on the 1st of July.

Radio silence.

On the 10th, a liner comes upon the *Teignmouth Electron*, aimlessly drifting.

There is nobody aboard.

The artist Tacita Dean has based several written works and films on Donald Crowhurst. She has been to Teignmouth, has wandered along the seawall, delved into the relationship between the amateur sailor and this small village in dire need of notoriety – the generosity of those we would now know as sponsors, the glare of the spotlights of which he must have been so fond before being blinded by them.

Alone on his trimaran, surrounded by water, much like Andrée, Strindberg and Frænkel found themselves surrounded by ice, Crowhurst recognised, more than those men did, the discrepancy between the grandiose dreams of an entire town and his own wretched condition. He did not give any hurrahs or raise the flag. He tried desperately to become the opposite of what was expected of him, a no-hoper, brought to a standstill, in the middle of the ocean, as if within the four walls of a bedroom, writing verse and philosophising, watching time pass.

A question of character, perhaps, or of the times – no doubt previous role models had already prepared Crowhurst for the cynicism he could expect from his contemporaries, a cynicism which would prompt the good burghers of Teignmouth to rush to get over his death since this episode, in all its fantastic absurdity, would ultimately bring them more publicity than any victory.

In Teignmouth, Tacita Dean pays a visit to the small exhibition devoted to Crowhurst's circumnavigation. She contemplates the remains of the boat, washed up on an island in the Caribbean and then sold to the West Indies for a peppercorn. In one of the films she has made of the story, *Disappearance at Sea*, we see Crowhurst's face appear on the luminous face of a lighthouse, as one might imagine a man in the moon.

By the 1960s, we are no longer trying to reach the Poles. The deserts are known and maps redefined. It is the heavens that are calling us now. A need to conquer space has replaced our conquest of the seas. Soon, a man will set foot on the moon, not long after Crowhurst's disappearance. Two faces, both attracting and repelling each other. On the one hand, an image of Neil Armstrong, invisible behind his astronaut's helmet, flooding across television sets with families huddled around them, a night nobody will forget, in the crackle of black and white mixed with the graininess of space which is finally offered up to our gaze, and on the other, the face of the man lying somewhere in the depths of the sea, whose shadow, whose story, has been brought to light by an artist.

Perhaps Crowhurst has heard talk of the discovery of the bodies of Frænkel, Strindberg and Andrée and their expedition, which took place more than seventy years prior to his own. Perhaps he thought of them, launched on their impossible endeavour. Those men who no longer knew night or day and who marked off the dates, so as to stamp a place in time if not in space, as Robinson carved his notches on his island.

Around them, the landscape repeats itself. A mirrored splendour. Nothing looks more like a slab of ice than another slab of ice and everything is shifting, dizzying. Even the sky, from time to time, is reflected in the snow, is conflated with it. Lying stretched out, there is no distinguishing them, it is true, it's as if the world no longer has edges, neither horizon nor interruption, impossible to imagine that the whiteness one day might end, it is like a shroud draped over the eyes of the dead.

Perhaps, then, it is to escape all this that Andrée describes in such fine detail the tessitura of the gulls' cries, the hue of their wings, the bands of colour separating their feathers into two distinct worlds, the rings around their legs, their worn beaks.

Reading Crowhurst's fictitious journal, one might wonder at the extent to which Andrée's own journal – with its recounting of meals in minute detail, its observation of birds and rocks, the banter among companions – is not also intended to create an alternative reality, one they could have allowed themselves to believe. Not just to cling to their status as civilised men but, with increasing desperation, to carve into marble a reality which is little by little drifting off course, as the gap widens between the reality they are living and the version they are retelling.

Perhaps in this gap, so impossible to measure, there is another narrative of which we will forever remain ignorant, which only the precise, obsessive recounting of a daily existence increasingly removed from reality is still able to soften. Andrée's journal, peopled with characters becoming more detached from themselves, might be read then as is almost always the case with a survivor's story: a means of escaping the unbearable, of ordering a life which with every passing day grows a little more unhinged from its reality.

Every passage of every bird is noted, every presence. When they are able, they kill, everything is eaten, but before eating it, they observe, and perhaps they stroke it, because their fingers are seeking something other than the textures of their everyday, the snow, the ice, the ropes, their hands are black, so there is a softness to the feathers, something reminiscent of a woman's hair, or that of a child.

ANDRÉE'S JOURNAL

14 August 1897

The ivory gull has three cries:
Piyrrr with four soft and trilling r's
Pyöt-pyöt.
Resembling the croaking of the crow.

BIRTH

20 August 1897, a little further south

On this very day, as they march through the whiteness, a boy is brought into the world on a farm in Telemark, Norway. He is called Tarjei. Tarjei Vesaas. He is a quiet child who, soon enough, will want more than anything else to write. As a young man, he burns his first manuscript that is rejected, he perseveres, and is finally published. He is a writer already, this man born on the same day, only a few hundred kilometres from where the three explorers are wandering. A writer whose masterpiece, *The Ice Palace*, describes a frozen waterfall, a natural palace of complex, shimmering architecture, a place where you might lose yourself exploring a succession of gleaming, interlocking caverns.

The man who is born on that night, that night of bright luminosity tilting towards darkness, is the author who will erect from the ice the most fascinating of structures, *a magical world of sharp peaks and teeth, of rounded domes and frozen cupolas, of soft contours and intricate lacework.*

The waterfall captivates a young girl who skips school in order to explore it. She is keen to investigate this place which she feels must be harbouring a secret. In the dense translucency of the ice, she discovers leaves, stones, the delicate curves of ferns. She looks for her own face.

Slipping through a crack, she works her way towards the frozen cascade of water. She feels the walls, listens to the silence. She calls out and, trembling, hears the echo of her own voice. She is in a veritable forest where the water has *fashioned trunks and branches from the ice*. She has never seen anything like it. She moves from one cavern to another, slips through ever narrower fissures but each new chamber looks entirely unlike the previous one. Thinking she is retracing her steps, she buries herself deeper and deeper. She panics, turning in circles, calls out, grows increasingly cold, loses hope.

As she advances into the frozen depths, she stops trying to find a way out. Something within her is extinguished, a flame is blown out, a watchfulness gives way, and something else opens up, yet one more door leading her to an inaccessible heart, where she will succumb, entirely.

She no longer tries to escape, no longer resists. She stops looking behind her, stops trying to understand the configuration of the space, no longer notices the bluish light, the sound of dripping from the walls, it is all vaguely reassuring, vaguely familiar, it works its way into her head, plays the first notes of a tune in her mind.

Against this white backdrop she comes across a scrap of an age-old memory, which holds her, cradles her. And since the cold is an anaesthetic, since it is said to dull the senses and consciousness, you can imagine she is dying in much the same way as you might fall asleep, lying deep within this place of her desire turned tomb, bewitched to the end.

ANDRÉE'S JOURNAL

22 August 1897

One cannot speak of any regularity among [the hummocks] ...
Today a lead changed just when we had come across it (five minutes
later and it would have been impossible) ...
The floes came at a great speed and there was a creaking round
about us.
It made a strange and magnificent impression.

The day has been extremely beautiful. Perhaps the most beautiful we
have had. With a specially clear horizon we have again tried to catch
sight of Gillis Land but it is impossible to get a glimpse of any part
of it.

The clear air was utilized by Strindberg to take lunar distances.
He saw haloes on the snow: an inner more sharply defined with the
inner boundary red ... Observed from the ground these haloes seemed
to be the extremities of parabolas or of ellipses.
Magnificent Venetian landscape with canals between lofty hummock
*edges on both sides, **shimmering** water-square with ice-fountain and*
***glittering** stairs down to the canals. Divine.*

DAWNS

22 August 1897

S ome days they get up, they march, and they forget, both what they have already endured and what may still come, they forget to be sensible, no longer listen to their bodies or, rather, suddenly adjust the attention they give them, the landscape gnaws away at them painlessly then, no more than a hand firmly gripping their heart, the already distant sensation of a bow on the strings of a violin.

In those moments, they are no longer conquerors, nor even explorers. Suddenly they are using unexpected words, a vocabulary of wonder, to describe what they are seeing about them.

This morning, for example: hearing the cracking of the ice, allowing themselves to be carried by it and, suddenly, everything is fluid, the water such a vivid blue coursing between the floes, a lively fresh spring, pure as the salt crystals spreading across their skin – they wash themselves off then, cleansed to their very depths.

It happens more often when one of them finds himself alone, when he no longer has the others before him, forcing him to recognise in their faces his own feverish eyes, his sunburnt forehead.

They are the same now, all three of them.

Strindberg, Frænkel or Andrée, one of them is the first to emerge from his sleeping bag. He sniffs the frozen air like a bird, like a bear, attuned only to sounds, to variations in temperature. Emerging from their tent, the cold strips away the others' odours, the lack of privacy of the previous night. Colours seem inextricably intertwined with the sensation of the wind on his skin, on his tongue: it is no longer something he sees but a presence that stuns him.

This, too, is why the faces in the photographs are incidental. Why the men pay so much attention to the quality of the ice, to the pearl-like snow. Why, to the very end, they continue to make so many notes, to investigate, to observe. Because over and above the pride of being the first, and the solace of maintaining a link to the earth, there is, when faced with the intensity of the landscape, a curiosity which is never extinguished, and the folly of their desire to catch sight, at journey's end, of the white continent of their dreams.

Strindberg marches, or perhaps it is Fraenkel, or Andrée, alone as always – each of them will have experienced at least one such moment and will be able to hang it from his neck like a pearl – he heads off and the world no longer has any contours, any direction, no road nor path, it becomes this limitless thing, the whiteness of which he no longer even notices, it is a colour that does not even exist, no, to his downcast eyes, lowered before the light, there are only colours clashing or blending, the mint of still waters, brown ice so impossible to break, a surface of yellow clay, navy depths, orange sun, or that softer blue, bright milky slate, where everything is reflected, blended – sea, ice, horizon and endless sky.

There are no more mountains, no walls anywhere, everything is like him, in motion. And if it is Andrée we are following, as he embraces the dawn, perhaps his regret at having brought the others this far, the culpability at having led them to their end, melts away, and perhaps as he feels his chest swelling before the expanse of the landscape, he feels suddenly proud, unexpectedly content – a happiness that grips him in an instant, nourished by neither hope, nor plans, a happiness that is fed on the contrary by their very absence.

There are other moments. Feeling the warmth of skin exposed to the air. It steams. The flesh contracts, becoming stone.

Stopping when the body is crippled with exhaustion. Dividing up the daily chores – Strindberg prepares the meals, Frænkel erects the tent, Andrée makes his observations, takes down clandestine notes, inspects their surroundings – and then slipping under the canvas walls, around the Primus stove, temperature climbing quickly, 25 degrees, breathing the same air, listening to the wind whistle, sinking into sleep.

Sometimes, slipping across the sea on the boat, when there is a swell, as if on a fast-moving river, but there is no canyon ahead, no rapids, just an endless, flat body of water. Knowing that night will not fall, not today, not tomorrow, and that so long as there is no night, there can be no end.

ANDRÉE'S JOURNAL

23–24 August 1897

Sample no. 11 consists of driftwood which F. found sunk down into the snow. It was rotten but I took a part of it.

Sample no. 15 contains soup-algae.

Sample no. 16 contains the eyes of the young ivory gull that was shot, in order to be able to examine its construction against snow-blindness.

On the surface of a very large pure pressed piece of ice there was made a find no. 17 …
After this find I have observed that the ice is perforated everywhere and filled with things that are certainly well deserving of a special Polar-expedition merely on their account.
The natural philosopher would find the interior of the ice to be almost as rich in contents as that of the crust of the earth or that of the sea.

Find no. 17 was washed in a tea-strainer whereby, perhaps some small quantity (clay?) was sluiced away but otherwise everything was included. The leaves were dried by being placed in layers in a "bandage" and dried against the breast.

We have several times seen a black little bird with white on the wings like a black guillemot, but white under the belly like a little auk. It has a kind of twitter and we have not seen it fly but only dive.

What kind of bird is it?

SNAPSHOTS

A gradual slope

W hat do they look like now? The closer winter gets, the more silent the photographs, the greater the gap between what is seen and what is known.

Never at any point do they allow the camera to focus on their tired faces, or allow it to record the scars of their everyday existence. Do they take the time to adjust their clothing for the shot or do they march like that all day, *gentlemen-farmers* of the Arctic? In any event, they are careful to preserve their bearing intact, immortalising themselves at a distance, an action shot, always taken from a good angle, insisting, no matter what, on respecting nineteenth-century photographic customs – the same poses, the same meticulousness, the same distance.

Shortly before their departure, a student by the name of Carl Størmer, known for having studied the formation of the aurora borealis, took some curious photographs. He was able to capture his contemporaries without their knowledge using a small camera manufactured by the firm C. P. Stirn, which he could conceal under his jacket thanks to its round, flat case, with its lens poking through a tiny hole and a cable attached to the shutter release.

He would walk the streets of Oslo, greeting passersby in order to attract a look, a smile, a moment of surprise. These strangers captured by Størmer are wearing the same clothes, have the same bearing as any of their fellow countrymen and women posing in their studio portraits, and yet they are faces we have never seen.

That man in the bowler hat, pointing his finger at us, suspicious.

The young woman who is eyeing us, smiling, and that other one, cheeks round with laughter, who is clasping her hands shyly.

The hint of a smile from beneath the umbrella.

The heavy body of that woman in white, the weight of her day, her dangling hand.

The cautious small steps of the woman hurriedly crossing the tram rails.

The shadow of that child whose cheeks are glistening with tears.

The smell of rice flour foundation which lingers, certainly, on that peaceful, determined profile.

Another woman, this one captured from so close by that we see only the bottom half of her face and her dark dress against which she is clutching a small, restless cat.

Her mouth slightly open and her beauty spot.

The texture of her skin.

Remnants of light lost in her hair.

In the chance position of all these strangers, the contours of their bodies, we might be able to recognise those of the three explorers, their bodies bowed as the day draws to a close, their hands chapped as autumn approaches, and they are no longer formal records to be interpreted, rather it is a line that is tilting, acknowledging it might be mistaken.

That is what it would have taken, a clandestine photographer, paparazzi before their time, a watchful little mouse scurrying along in their tracks: finally to see them. To capture the flash of their feverish eyes, their teeth which are rotting and yet which are revealed in a burst of laughter, when they grimace in pain. The transformation of their skin, the growth of their beard. The weight in their gaze.

We shall never see any of it, ever. It is an image they will manage to construct, to the very end: this alternative vision of themselves, never entirely defeated, never quite done in, an image they will maintain, upright and glistening, a screen between themselves and our imagination.

ANDRÉE'S JOURNAL

25 August 1897

The sea-serpent was seen but looked different.
He still appeared to have his black band against a solid grey
background and when he dived a two-cloven fin was seen at the end.

A bird was seen, most like a skua.
He was quite black with the exception of underneath where he was
blackish-brown. Flew as silently as a spirit and dived down here and
there for food.
I shot one of those mystical little auks.

RE-RUN

1896

There is one thing about their elegant clothes that is out of place, slightly clouding the image: a grain of sand, a pebble in their shoes which sometimes abruptly sets them back on their haunches, and Andrée's face closes up, and he loses the spring in his step.

There is not a single jacket lining, not a chest, not the smallest tool, which does not bear the inscription: *Andrees pol. exp. 1896.* These labels, stamped onto the most insignificant of objects, none of which have been altered since their first attempt the preceding year, are a constant reminder that they are a year late, that their heroic departure has already missed its moment.

In 1896 when, for the first time they headed to Danes Island, they waited, they feasted, they experienced a rough first draft of their adventure, a wasted effort that allowed frustrations to take hold, resentment, where hope took root. That was the original attempt, the first experience, whose sequel would be nothing more than a re-run, unable to deviate from that initial course.

Frænkel had not yet joined the expedition. Together with Strindberg and their first team member, Gustaf Ekholm, Andrée had been watching out for the right moment, waiting beside the balloon for the wind that never blew.

Andrée had never come to terms with this aborted attempt. To make matters worse, he had to suffer criticism and vexations, those of the weather to begin with, since he was relying on a wind from the south and yet was continually faced with winds from the north, glacial, unpredictable, blowing so hard against the hangar that it had been necessary, and sadly prophetic, to deflate the balloon at that point already, reducing it to a flaccid envelope.

Then he had had to attempt to convince Ekholm, an older, more experienced man, who had been his superior and had retained something of a psychological ascendancy over him, Ekholm who kept insisting that the balloon would leak, that it would not hold air, that an aerostat, no matter how good the quality, was not comprised of a single piece of fabric, no, he hammered the point home, it was a complex patchwork of pieces that had been sewn together and those pieces, under extreme conditions, would necessarily reveal gaps, tiny holes which ultimately, notwithstanding the rubberised varnish and their every effort to plug the openings, would allow the hydrogen to escape and make it vulnerable.

Andrée swallowed his anxiety, his anger and fury, visible, however, in his diary: *Today,* he wrote one day, *we have ground the scissors with which the balloon is to be cut open.*

The unspoken implication of Ekholm's words, their unbearable import, evident in the man's thoughts, was this: the balloon was an example of shoddy workmanship, much like their expedition, like his entire dream. Ekholm, who had become an impediment, ultimately announced that he would not participate in the next expedition – Frænkel would be a more tenacious companion, more likely to turn a blind eye.

To cap it all off, Andrée was forced to witness the triumphant return of the crew from the *Fram*, who docked in Svalbard before dashing on to Norway, unaware that Nansen, their captain, was also en route to the same port. Their skin was tanned, their exhaustion immense, much like their happiness at finally finding themselves back on terra firma. They had made it so far north. They had returned. Their faces bore the stigmata of heroism which Andrée, with his pale colouring and cool cheeks, could only envy, shaking their hands mechanically in front of the useless sphere that was his poorly inflated balloon.

The heroic return of Nansen at least served to eclipse their own failure. In the shadow of their rival's glory, they pulled up stakes, packed up their bottles and Primus stove, sledge and tents, champagne and silk scarves, all bound together with the thread of their regrets and unused energy.

Like Donald Crowhurst making his solitary circumnavigation, like Franz Reichelt atop the Eiffel Tower, like Pilâtre de Rozier preparing to cross the Channel in the wrong direction, from that point onwards they were as bound to the considerable investments all Sweden had proffered to them as they were to their impatient, detained selves, waiting for one thing and one thing only: the next attempt.

But what Strindberg did not know, what Frænkel and he were still unaware of, was that prior to their take-off, Andrée was in the habit of waking up in the middle of the night. He would slip across to the balloon house, like a thief. All about him were dangling ropes, boxes lying around, the silent vestiges of their daily activities. A gust of wind would whip across his cold cheek, the shriek of a bird piercing the muffled sound of the outgoing tide.

The balloon had centre stage, its monstrous belly weighed down with dozens of sandbags, supported by the immense scaffolding from which you could look out to the sea, to the mountains. Andrée, on tiptoe, would rest his still smooth palm on the balloon's pink skin, stretched taut, in the glittering light of the night which never grew dark. He would feel it vibrating – querulous, knocking against his hand – and suddenly, they would become blindingly obvious, the breaches which Ekholm had so relentlessly pointed out, those miniscule cracks hinted at by the tiniest breath of air which in places tickled the pads of his fingers. The balloon, so majestic but so fragile, exhaled under his hand. He would feel it weaken, tremble: little by little, it was deflating.

Ekholm was right, Andrée realised, from that point onwards seeing his balloon as nothing more than a multitude of gaps covered up by what remained of the silk: a void poorly clothed in pieces of fabric.

It was not from bears that it needed protection, nor from the sharp beaks of the ivory gulls. It was from Andrée himself, the impatient and anxious leader who, under cover of night and taking advantage of the slumber of the designated guard, would secretly replenish the balloon with hydrogen to compensate for the leaks, so the others would find it intact in the morning, as proud and swollen as his own chest, and, having reinflated the balloon, repaired the illusion, would return to watch over his slumbering, trusting companions.

ANDRÉE'S JOURNAL

29 August 1897

Tonight was the first time I thought of all the lovely things at home.
S. and F. on the contrary have always spoken about it.
The tent is now always covered with ice inside.

RUNNING

In the middle of a similar night

Nils is dreaming. Later, he will recount his dream in a letter to Anna, like an excuse, like a prayer, but for now, he is dreaming. Night is falling, it is mild, he is warm behind the windows of his Stockholm apartment. He is going over the details of the night ahead. He is resting, the day has been long, tiring, his foot is hurting him, he gives it a good, long rub.

He sinks further into sleep. The dream anaesthetises the pain, turns his aching muscles into the promise of a well-earned rest, the mad yearning for a quilt. But something pierces the membrane of his fantasy, irritates his skin, suddenly carves a hole in his belly: a regret, remorse. Nils has forgotten something, he can't quite put his finger on it, it is not yet torturing him, but still, it is an irritation. It's Sunday, the day of rest, of peace. What could he possibly have forgotten now that is returning to haunt him, like a shooting pain?

He tries to chase the feelings away, this regret, this discomfort, he looks out the window and suddenly, just as he was finally about to slide under the sheets, he remembers: Anna. They were meant to see each other. She was supposed to meet him in Stockholm so they could spend Sunday together. She must have been waiting for him for hours.

It's nothing serious, it's a dream, and one can struggle against a dream, so Nils hastily dresses, leaves the apartment, now the cold truly clutches at him, a curious cold for the end of summer in Sweden, he buries his hands in his pockets, something is burning his cheeks and sore feet, he is overwhelmed by a panic that is greater than him. He is going to be late. She will have been waiting for him for hours, perhaps she has already left.

Everybody has had those dreams where you are running even though it is hopeless, where you catch trains, taxis, buses, all the while knowing deep down that it is too late. And still, you run. And still, Nils runs, down towards the sea, rushing towards Vasagatan, the boulevard in Stockholm where they were due to meet, bumping into other pedestrians, zigzagging between the trees.

Forgive me, he says, running.

Forgive me, he thinks, running.

This is what he wants to do: beg her forgiveness.

It is even more important than being on time, than taking her by the wrist before she leaves.

Forgive me.

He has forgotten the Sunday they were supposed to spend together, walking side by side, chatting in the summer, he has forgotten how her arm would slip through his, how her hand would attach itself to his sleeve, he has forgotten the way she breathes and how he moves faster as they approach one another, their bodies drawing closer.

That breath. In his ear.

He runs towards the dock, towards the sea, hurtles down the sloping street, a vertical street, a mountain, he wants to fly but falls, and he starts in his sleep. And yet he does not stop, too bad if he trips over his legs and too bad if he falls, this is doubtless what is known as strength born of despair.

At each section of the street where she is not to be found, Anna seems to retreat before his outstretched hand, a little piece on a chess board. Miniscule. She retreats. He holds out his hand. She is further away, still further away, perhaps at this intersection, standing outside those ornate façades, leaning over that balcony, at the back of that shadowy little shop, he enters, he leaves, turns this way and that. Lost.

She is here, somewhere. Buried in his shoe, a pebble, he leans over, he's wasting time, so he stands up again, keeps running.

This pain, in his foot, in his bones.

But where has she gone? This way probably, to that part of the city where it dips down.

He stops short.

The blue is there, before him.

The breeze.

The waves.

The absence, where one might sink down into its depths, dissolve within it.

The street plunges into the sea.

There is no more Vasagatan.

He wakes up.

Well then, that was foolish, he will write to Anna.

ANDRÉE'S JOURNAL

2 September

I have now begun to use wool-and-hair-stockings at night and tonight for the first time I shall creep into the sleeping-sack top.

DUSK

12 September 1897

The polar autumn has arrived, a season that does not last. After the endless light of the Arctic summer, autumn is a parenthesis. The days and the nights rediscover their changing rhythm and it is strange, so close to the end, being pulled already inexorably towards it, to renew their awareness of this division of time, so ancient, so ordinary, yet almost effaced by the daylight from which they are struggling to emerge.

The luminous intensity they have experienced, like its slow dissolution into the darkness, could have them believe they have lived through just one single immense day, its morning the months that have just passed, and then its sun-filled noon, its twilight the approaching autumn.

We have no images of the night's return. The best we can do is scour the surface of the darkest photographs. If you look only at them, look at them one after the other, it's as if you might detect a movement, bring to life a silhouette, much like when flicking through one of those little flipbooks a scene is brought to life. You can sense their presence then, which is no longer an outline of their body but of the little we know of it.

There they are, all three of them gathered around the Primus stove. They are rediscovering the shadows of evening and the memories slumbering there. Every memory. Let us wager we might have the same. That there are some we have in common, that we share without knowing it, with these Swedish men from another century. Let us wager we are all comprised of the same moments, scarcely faded, bathed in a slightly different light, and on their tongue that bitter-sweet taste which we are not used to.

Sweden, in some ways then, would always have been familiar to us, like every distant country conjured like the ghost of ancient memories, from the time when we recognised nothing, when we had no names for anything. The first shores, the first plains, the first bodies touched, probably all look the same and could spring to our mind as they spring to theirs, to these men holding out their hands to the stove as night reclaims its dominion.

They recite poems, preferably parodic verse, what matters is that they remain awake, provoke discussion, laughter. They roll the words around in their thick mouths, weaving them into witticisms.

When they stare at one another, from either side of the flame which renders half their face red, one cheek hot, the other frozen, like exhausted cowboys in the light of a campfire, when they see their eyes glow, we can probably touch with a finger the memories of home, of their bedroom, of a hand on a feverish forehead, of their first nights spent outside, under lamp-posts lighting their hurried steps, of dashing towards the harbour in Stockholm as a child or towards the enormous gleaming lake at Gränna.

It's as if time is doubling back on itself, there are months that feel like hours, hours like years, and towards the end of life it can happen that the past returns to swallow everything up, as neatly and sharply as the present itself starts to dwindle, relegated to nothing more than a tooth glass.

After these endlessly drawn-out months, these months hunched over their memories, long enough to make them forget there had ever been a life before this whiteness, this cold, their infernal triumvirate, it is possible they now feel like something is dragging them backwards at full tilt, towards these images of a previous life, images which could still be separated, one from the other, that you could pull out like tarot cards as the present stretches towards infinity.

The polar day, the constant activity, had allowed them to distance themselves from the memories, these reminiscences, had diminished their solidity. They probably require a smell, a touch, a different light, in order to bring them back to life. The polar day offered nothing, nothing to which those memories could attach, no jutting edge, no dark corner.

Now their bodies are each resuming their own rhythm, they are no longer able to continue the superhuman efforts they have thus far made. They stop wanting to paint themselves as heroes as they rediscover the memories of the men they once were.

During the night of the 12th of September, when they see their first stars, they resign themselves to wintering on the ice. Stretched out beneath the heavens, they can make out the constellations: the rough saucepan of the Great Bear, whose outer edge you must follow to find Polaris at the end of an imaginary straight line and, just below it, the W of Cassiopeia. They trace the outline of Pegasus and that of the now vanished Summer Triangle.

Somewhere in the Milky Way, the seed of the town of Pyramiden has been sown, which is still waiting to appear, and with it, the upheavals of the world they left behind. It is readying itself, this town, as the world, too, is readying itself, and they have no notion of any of it; all they see in the sky is the reservoir of their memories, their own immense, personal Pandora's Box.

A few days earlier, they solved a mystery: what they had assumed from their balloon to be sea serpents they see now are nothing more than walruses who had been keeping their distance. They no longer believe there are sea serpents. They have come back to earth for good. Something has been lost, and something has been found.

Around the flames, they recognise forgotten hues, the basalt grey of the black-fringed ice and the mauve of the horizon just before dusk.

In their tent, they burn their remaining candles one by one. They did not think to bring more. Perhaps they were not expecting to still be there when darkness returned.

It is a peculiar loop, which pins their fast-approaching end to the very beginning of their life.

On the 4th of September, Nils has been woken by the voices of his companions. It is his birthday, he is turning twenty-five, and as a final gift, he emerges from sleep with the breaking day and there, right in front of his own, are faces, memories, songs.

ANDRÉE'S JOURNAL

4 September

Strindberg's birthday. Festal day. I awakened him giving him letters from his sweetheart and relations. It was a real pleasure to see how glad he was. Today we have had some extra food on account of the day.
The breakfast consists of bear's-meat, beef with bread and Stauffer's pease-soup with bear's-meat and bear's fat.
Dinner fried bear's-meat kept warm inside our waistcoats.
Supper Bear's-meat, bread and goose-liver paste, Stauffer-cake with syrup sauce, syrup and water, speech for Nils, Lactoserin chocolate.

S. kept his birthday by falling very thoroughly, sledge and all, into the soup. We had to pitch our tent after three hours' march and then had a very troublesome and time-wasting business to dry him and his things.

On such a journey as this there is developed a sense both of the great and of the little. The great nature and the little food and other details.

ISLAND

The sun is shining for no more than a few hours a day, every now and again offering up spectacular phenomena, like that seen by Lieutenant Greely, who some fifteen years earlier had formed an expedition to Grinnell Land, and who had seen up to six suns appear, *almost as luminous as the real one*, taunting him before disappearing altogether. They are the last flames of the light, its final colours.

The brightest often start with a tiny glimmer, barely distinguishable against the black, barely more than a sparkle, spreading and quivering, a wave, as if the wind were suddenly to take on colour and substance, as if you might see it cross the sky, luminous, tangible. As if by reaching out your hand, you might catch it.

When the aurora borealis is weak, it is red: it flames. When it is stronger, it becomes green, electric, an extraterrestrial green because it is not the wind, it is the sun: particles of sun projected into space.

Several days earlier, an eruption ejected sparkling particles from the star's inferno, shimmering, incandescent lava projected at more than 400 kilometres per second, glittering like nothing ever seen before, setting alight the upper atmosphere of the earth and spreading out over their heads.

Just before disappearing, the sun erupts, spitting out showers of sparks that become phosphorescent-green liquid clouds, dancing in billows, there is no other word for it, they are dancing, at lightning speed, too quickly for their eyes or their brain to be able to register their trajectory, already they are gone, spectres of the sky, blindness.

Wind, waves, cyclones, tornadoes, black holes: it subsumes every known phenomena, every spectacle they have witnessed, it surpasses them, electrifies them, forces their eyes wide open.

Later the ice is new and red. Andrée writes: *The landscape is ablaze. The snow a sea of fire.*

Around these bursts of brilliance which give rhythm to their days, they allow the night to envelop them. This is where they will stop, on the threshold of their winter. For the first time, they settle, they stop, not yet aware of how permanent this halt is to prove. For the moment, they think only of how sweet it is: no longer to march, no longer to run, no longer to have to flee.

In order to construct their shelter, they select an ice floe more stable than the others, the thickness of which they regularly measure – 1.1 metres at its thinnest point on the 29th of September.

They are never quite able to forget that they are not on solid ground, that beneath them are shifting currents, tides, all the harnessed force of the Arctic Ocean. Despite it all, this is where they settle. As they have familiarised themselves again with the stars, they learn how to wake up again in the same place where they went to sleep the night before, how to colonise their new surroundings, the slightest shift in which is very quickly noted.

To begin with, it is an indistinct shape. Perhaps it is Strindberg who is the first to see it and perhaps he confuses it with the apparitions borne of the most recent displays of lights. Perhaps it is Frænkel who, on emerging from the tent to relieve himself, distractedly watching the yellowish meanderings of urine on the snow, makes out its silhouette in the distance. Perhaps it is Andrée.

Whoever noticed it must have first blinked then moved a couple of metres, to be certain he was not mistaken. He would have re-opened his eyes: yes, there it was. Then he would have called the others, and they would have registered a new level of excitement in his voice. They would have hurried over, looked in the direction of his outstretched finger: "There, I swear to you, there is something there."

They would have screwed up their eyes and suddenly made it out, this shape that does not quite dissolve as does everything else in the darkness. The shape of an island. A real island, fixed, a grey mass emerging from the grey water, from the mercury which the sea has become since night has expanded its reach.

White Island. Kvitøya.

The sole fixed point proffered up to them after their months of wandering, appearing miracle-like when they can march no more, when they are frozen, broken, spent. Much like the sailors who feel the ground pitching beneath them when first they go ashore, they would first swear it is the island herself that is shifting. The island, firmly anchored, only serves to emphasise their own pitching, their own instability.

They believed themselves to be approaching what, on the charts, was known as Giles Land, but they must face facts: Giles Land does not exist, unless it should be this polished island, of mineral and translucent ramparts. At night, a great, obsidian marble.

Every morning, upon waking, they fear it will have disappeared, but it is still there. Very quickly it becomes their companion, a support. We do not always measure the significance of those objects of relief in a landscape which carve out a place for us in the world – the mountains, the forests, even the buildings which slice up the sky into sufficiently modest pieces that we might not be crushed by it. We forget the extent to which these markers anchor us to the earth, create paths for us. Living in cities, in the mountains, in forests, as we do, nothing prepares us for living in a place where nothing is taller than anything else, where there is nothing to interrupt your gaze. This island is a vanishing point, reconstructing a landscape they can recognise.

*

They make the most of the last hours of light to look at it, to describe it. Andrée sketches it in his journal, in the approximate shape of an ellipse. Strindberg photographs it. Yet they do not see it as a place where they might stop, a place of hope. It is too steep, too inhospitable. They know, already, that it will offer them no salvation. But its mere presence anchors them in space.

There is an island: they are somewhere.

In the reflection of this outline of solid ground, they construct their haven, their shelter. It will have several rooms, a sleeping chamber, a common area, a pantry where food will be stored. There are only a few more blocks of snow to pack down before the walls are finished. Strindberg and Frænkel direct their remaining strength to the task, laying them one by one, before bonding them with frozen water.

They take their time. They are in no hurry. Before them, they have only the thought of the months of darkness which will be spent face to face with the others, in a claustrophobic space in which tensions and bitterness will fester. They have only the abscesses on their feet, the stiffness of their bodies. Their motivating force every day had been their onwards march; now they must become sedentary once more, rediscover daily acts of domesticity.

Their Primus stove is showing signs of failing. It is constantly going out. None of them thought to bring replacement parts. Without daring perhaps to admit it even to themselves, they fear soon not having any flame with which to warm their nights.

ANDRÉE'S JOURNAL

17–19 September 1897

Remarkably enough the fulmars seem to have disappeared.

Possibly we may be able to drive far southwards quickly enough and obtain our nourishment from the sea. Perhaps too it will not be so cold on the sea as on the land. He who lives will see.

The day has been a remarkable one for us by our having seen land today for the first time since 11 July.

[The island] presents a charming view in the sunshine which illumines the glacier both from the edge and from above, thus giving the island the appearance of being transparent. The edge of the glacier contains very blue glacier ice and also brown sections …
[T]he only dark patches one can discover are shadows. These together with the formation in general show the ground below the glacier is not altogether level.

There is no question of our attempting to go on shore for the entire island seems to be one single block of ice with a glacier border.

FEAST

18 September 1897

I t is the day of the royal Jubilee and to celebrate, Nils wakes his companions with a full-bellied blast of the hunting horn. They emerge
from the tent, happy, but still half-asleep. Unable to raise their flag
as far north as they might have wished, they hoist it now against an
untroubled sky and content themselves with looking at the colours of
its interlocking crosses, dark blue and bright yellow for Sweden, oxblood red for Norway, vibrant colours to which their eyes are no longer
accustomed.

On this Jubilee day, Stockholm's Royal Chapel is alive with rustling,
whispering, an air of expectation. The dark suits worn by the men create a curious mirror-play, as if the same person, in this immense space
decorated with frescoes and colonnades, has been infinitely multiplied.

The sunlight is as bright as it is on the pack ice, but more golden,
a honeyed glow that shines through the stained glass, carving up the
space into wide shafts of light. Oscar II, a descendant of Jean-Baptiste
Bernadotte, a soldier from Pau who was adopted in 1818 by the King of
Sweden in the absence of an heir, is continuing the rule of the French
dynasty that still holds the reins of Swedish society. One member of the
House of Bernadotte inherits the throne from the next, and the day is
one of welcome celebration at the constant renewal of their reign, and
the new faces representing it.

*

211

That same morning, Andrée killed a seal at point-blank range with a flurry of small shots in its back and remarked upon the fragile nature of its skull, *as thin as egg-shell.*

Once the seal had been cut into pieces and sliced up, they tried the brain, the lungs, the heart, the kidneys and liver, the intestines, the stomach, not to mention the blubber and blood. Andrée recorded it all, as was his habit as a curious observer and gourmet, much as he described the day of jollity which, for them, was their Jubilee.

Together they sing the national anthem at the top of their voices, into the great silence. Their legs are no longer able to carry them. Their beards are devouring their faces. They have layered their clothes, one item on top of another, their stockings are mismatched, their shoes lined with straw, they are no longer taking photographs, are no longer mindful of their appearance, they probably look much like the bear Nansen became, wearing the trousers he sewed by hand in his winter lair. Their lips are so chapped they are no longer painful but here they are, chatting like good friends at a dinner party.

An ivory gull simmers in wine, the sauce gives off a meaty smell, they sniff the ribbon of steam that escapes from the stove and disappears into the frozen air. By way of appetiser, they nibble on some Boström's cheese, butter and biscuits, and Schumacher's bread, they drink wine and port, propose a toast, sing, again, voices ever dwindling, shout hurrahs in the midst of the pack ice in honour of the King who is celebrating in the city, they feel the heady flow of the alcohol in their blood, the tensing of muscles just before they relax and doubtless they are drunk, it's such a rare occurrence, they make jokes and then something is released, *the general feeling was one of the greatest pleasure and we lay down satisfied and contented,* as Andrée writes, a raw joy which lodges itself also in the astonishment that it might still be possible, even here, against this white screen onto which they project the country of their birth, the lavish celebrations of its ruling classes, the glory of which they continue to dream.

Even if it's a fairly certain bet that nothing will remain of what has been accomplished and nothing of this moment, in spite of it all, they sing, and finish their meal with some Stauffer's fruit cake doused in fruit syrup and some chocolate. Sated, carried off by the sweet reverie of the alcohol, they re-create something of a house around themselves, a house whose wide-open windows will let in the cold.

Right up to the end, or almost, their accounts stand in sharp contrast to those of other explorers who ration themselves, make provision, economise. These men, however, allow themselves celebrations, treat themselves to some bear heart and crack open the champagne. This is why they have dragged their overloaded sledges all this way, because you must give yourself an excuse, some pretext, some perspective. So, what better time to make the most of it? Every now and again your stomach should be full enough to pop your belt. You must do all you can to observe dates, meals, to maintain some sort of variation.

They prepare some bear ham over several days which they judge to be delicious, showing themselves to be experts in culinary matters: *A little reindeer-hair in the food is recommended for while taking it out one is prevented from eating too quickly and too greedily*, writes Andrée.

They talk and sometimes doze off before reaching the end of their sentence. It is a lavish banquet, dwindling into silences, punctuated by the sounds of a mouth chewing, a sigh.

In Stockholm and well beyond, while waiting for their new heroes to drape in a new flag, much time was devoted to dreaming up fabulous lives for Andrée and his companions, imagining them as escapees, Robinson Crusoes, adventurers who had discovered a habitable island with welcoming locals building luxurious igloos and warming themselves in front of fires while devouring reindeer, or wondering if they hadn't returned to some savage state or if they had not perhaps abandoned the North for the South of their dreams – three cheerful fellows thumbing their nose at the entire world, dipping their toes into a warm ocean, surrounded by ripe fruit and Polynesian women.

These lives that had been imagined for them dissipated in the intervening years, lost something of their lustre, their exotic colour; at some point people become upset by the misfortune they suddenly imagine to have been sadly predictable, they swear never to have believed in the more optimistic of scenarios, they relish the shared notion that this crazy undertaking was never anything but hopeless. Nobody yet knows that in 1926, Amundsen and Nobile will be the first to fly over the North Pole in a dirigible airship, proving, too late, that Andrée's plan was not so absurd. Soon, then, will come the time to praise the audacity of these new explorers, their technical expertise, their good sense and their foresight. For now, though, thoughts are focussed on the disaster for which people always like to congratulate themselves on having seen approaching.

Somebody else, for certain, will pick up the torch, other men will soon be jostling, trying to push back the territorial limits; Oscar II, whom they are cheering in the Royal Chapel, knows it all too well – he can rest easy, there will be no shortage of them, of men who will give their lives for just a few more metres to be added to their nation's score card, the party can carry on in full swing.

In Stockholm, on the 18th of September, nobody can conceive of the possibility that Strindberg, Frænkel and Andrée's flag might still be fluttering in the sunlight, and that the men who have been carrying it are still seeking to expand the boundaries of a world that is already despairing of seeing them again alive.

ANDRÉE'S JOURNAL

1 October 1897

The 1 Oct. was a good day.
The evening was as divinely beautiful as one could wish.
The water was filled with small animals and a bevy of 7 black-white
"guillemots youngsters" were swimming there.
A couple of seals were seen too.
The work with the hut went on well and we thought that we should
have the outside ready by the 2nd.
But then something else happened.

M

2 October 1897

I t is the heart of the night, they are all fast asleep, the three of them nestled into their reindeer-skin sleeping bag, lined with bear fur, sheltered by the igloo they have just finished building and which they have named "home." For the first time in months, they have walls around them, a roof over their head. The ghostly, translucent silhouettes of their own abandoned homes hang suspended over their exhausted bodies.

It is the heart of the night, and they are dreaming. Of course, they're unsettled, they're snoring, sniffling, coughing, shifting their injured feet and their frozen fingers, but despite everything there are moments when they sink into a deep sleep, when nothing else exists, pitch-black beaches, rare and precious, prophetic, where they enter a place only they know, for which sleep is preparing them.

Suddenly, they are hauled from their slumber by the sound of something cracking. A dull noise, creeping upon them, a fissure of sound. They barely have time to haul themselves upright before water is drenching their clothes, their shoes. Forced hastily outdoors by the violence of the shock, stunned, sleepy, they try to hold themselves upright on their ice floe that has just split, sliced in two at the entrance to their "house."

They throw each other questioning looks. Strindberg and Frænkel wait for an injunction, some encouragement, an order. But Andrée remains silent. So, for the first time, overcome by discouragement or just because of their pressing exhaustion that sweeps away their fear and with it their tomorrows, they make no attempt to contain the disaster. They look at each other, true, but it is a look that brings with it no cry, no gesture, no vestiges of courage, unless that is precisely what courage looks like: a return to their beds, falling asleep on the floor once again, for a few meagre hours, their heavy bodies drawn to the sea, so close to the water, so close to the void, in their broken shelter.

They wake up in a nightmare that nothing can arrest, under their icy roof from which hangs the remains of a wall. They take a few steps, as if inebriated. Before them, darkness speckled with pallid patches and the cold, like a stone, battering their limbs. They try to gather their affairs which are floating atop the dislodged floes, powerless they watch the remains of the two bears they have just killed. The fragments like a map, an exploded continent.

And it is then they remember the island. Though steep, though impossible, it is still there, made of stone and ice, perhaps, but it is at least something, stone and ice, something tangible. Something solid on which to lay down their bodies and hope that one day they will be found. Land, hostile though it may be.

They will try to reach it, it is the only option they have and that, already, is a certainty, an exhaustion. It is a form of closure, the island, planted before them.

Once again they haul their boat and sledges across the pack ice, making their way towards the shore. But what shore when everything is topsy-turvy, when you are marching across the sea?

In the distance, tall, smooth rocks and the ground, like the sky, is a dark pea soup. The air feels as impenetrable as the water that is appearing now between the plates of ice, long stretches of leaden blue, opaque and unfathomable. Best not to wonder what is ruffling its glistening spine in the depths below, what giant squid, what fish from the abysses, nothing, it would be better to tell yourself, nothing could survive in that water that is as cold as it is dark and opaque.

They march, for an age they march, and finally they make out something that resembles, if not a beach, at least a mass of stones less sheer than the others. They go ashore at the southern tip, stumble, drag themselves along, gather up their belongings.

At last they allow themselves to collapse onto solid ground.

Their relief is short-lived. They must keep moving, get away from the waves which tumble the stones, strike at their shins. The light has changed, not just because the Arctic night is gnawing away at what remains of the day but because it is no longer reflecting off the same surfaces. The white of the pack ice, even at this time of the year, made the light softer, gave it that sparkle which transformed the faintest glow into an unearthly halo. Here on the island, though, the light strikes the dull grey of the rocks that the snow has spared, and is absorbed by the subdued tones of the stones which seem to trap its rays – even the rocky peaks are barely shrouded in a muted phosphorescence.

The smell of the sea is stronger here than on the ice, there is more seaweed, more life between the rocks and the moraines, in the tongues of water which lick the shoreline. To set foot on this soil is like rediscovering some small part of the places which saw them on their way, the shore of Danes Island and further away still, Gothenburg, the wind in their faces as the boat departed. But this piece of earth here is miniscule, ringed by frozen ocean. An uninhabitable replica of what they have left behind.

They are no longer marching, they are creeping, beating a way across the shore, gradually gaining height. The stones hurt their hands. They grope their way towards ramparts that might offer protection from the snow and wind. They want to be dry, in this place which is as close as they'll come to a safe haven. On the flattest terrain, the most sheltered they manage to find, they blindly erect their tent, securing it with driftwood and whale bone.

Between the 3rd and 4th of October, Nils notes: *Exciting situation.* Then: *Snow-storm Reconnoitring.*

And finally: *Moving*.

They still have some supplies of meat, use their net to fish for zoophytes and seaweed. They have enough equipment and foodstuffs to survive the winter, but they feel they have lost too much ground, too much hope. Having made it to the island, they stop. Once and for all. Their arrival on solid ground almost equates to the end of their tracks. As if the unstable character of the ice over which they had journeyed had forced them to maintain a sort of perpetual motion, as if only this much longed-for stability could defeat them.

In the fragments of Andrée's diary, it appears they gave a name to this final stopping place, this cranny on the island where they sought refuge. All that remains of it is a single letter: "M."

It is a place you might be tempted to call *nowhere* and yet the men have spent time wondering, arguing perhaps, over a name that nobody will ever know. A form of homage perhaps to the place they have come from, a qualifier for the land they have just reached, a huge joke, why not, the last, a joke only they could understand.

Certainly, by this act of naming, there is some vestige of what made them explorers, a dogged determination to possess a place which in fact already possesses them. But there is doubtless, also, the simple magnetic attraction of a piece of land, of a time now passed when there had been no question of stopping somewhere, anywhere.

The wind batters the canvas that is still protecting them, pushes it against their bodies. Do they fall asleep, is it possible to fall asleep?

They are in a cacophonous black belly, nestled beneath their collection of reindeer and bear pelts, under the tent that is affixed to the ground by whale bones, and above them, out of sight, is the dome of White Island, paler, more muted than the sky, more translucent than the snow, radiating every part of the summer that has been absorbed by the ice, the last immense night-light illuminating the darkened sky.

ANDRÉE'S JOURNAL

2 October 1897

No one had lost courage.
With such comrades one should be able to manage under, I may say,
any circumstances.

NIGHT

Approaching winter

On the 8th of October, they stop writing. The pages of their travel journals have been left blank. After the final remnants of legible phrases, silence. There are no words for what is to come. No account describes the manner by which they reached the island. It has had to be imagined.

Nils probably finds himself at that particular moment apart from the others. Perhaps he has just emerged, still stuffy with sleep, to carry out the simplest, the most everyday of tasks, attempting to light the Primus stove, protecting the flame from the wind, cupping his hands around its heat and, in the slit between the two flaps of the tent, perhaps he glimpses a movement, a presence. He stands up. He has forgotten to be cautious. They have probably blocked out the fact that they, too, are prey, increasingly vulnerable as they grow weaker, easy to identify now they are no longer on the move. Their fire, their tent, the flame they are maintaining, all of this attracts animals, hunger, craving. Nils probably does not have his shotgun on him, he has left it in the boat, a few metres away, yes, he has forgotten to be cautious. And suddenly the creature is there, immense.

Unless he is somewhere else. Somewhere on the shoreline, going for a walk so as not to go mad, pacing the beach. The light, even at high noon, is no longer the same. Every crevice of rock casts longer shadows that blur the view, the sense of distance, not to mention his burning eyes, his great exhaustion. He could almost be walking with his eyes shut, there is so little that remains distinct, tangible. The bear, then, hidden in one of those endlessly expanding shadows, resembling, from a distance, a rock, a hole in the earth, would uncoil at lightning speed, would be upon him already, unless he is attacked by something in an altogether different form, something carried by the wind, by the air, from the interior of the island or from the depths of his belly, something much slower, much more insidious than that white creature, beating a path to him before he had time to be on his guard as he bit into raw, contaminated, rotten flesh, a bacteria taking over every last one of his cells, one by one, or perhaps a great void that little by little expands to devour him, a cavity, a deficiency, an emptiness that burns away his remaining strength, a void as violent as a poison or maybe an excess of dark bile, that medical manifestation of melancholy.

Something has left him there, lying on the pack ice. And deep, deep within him, there is a flicker of something else, a flickering that dies, then resumes, a beat, a pulse, and if his eyes are wide open, and you were to peer right into them, you might make out this miniscule trembling, this pulsing in his pupil which is dilating, processing invisible images, finally relieved of the landscape before they too are consumed by the night, secret images, monstrous and profound, which no words can describe, which no camera can capture since they envelop and burrow into the same disintegrating body, drilling into its interior which is collapsing through and through, his heartbeat slowing, growing ever softer, and the images are falling silent, dwindling, subsiding, and whatever he is carrying within him, whatever remains alive is tracing out an ever narrower path, a gap is closing, a line disappearing, and his pupils fix, leaving only a very narrow circle of blue to emphasise the blackness.

It is over.

His watch stopped at 12.10 p.m, but on what day is unclear. Andrée and Frænkel probably kneel next to him, lean over him. Their young companion. They can hardly believe it, hardly dare touch him. It is over. Once and for all.

Perhaps they are under attack from the same threat, perhaps one of them is injured or unwell but they are still there, at that precise moment, even if it feels as if a considerable part of themselves has been amputated. Whatever was anchoring them to the earth has disappeared along with Nils and no doubt they utter a prayer together when they remove his jacket, when they discover there the locket containing the photograph of Anna. Andrée buries it in his own pocket, along with a charm of a wild boar, the key to a padlock, a pocket chronometer, a pencil, a few coins.

Nils was the first to die and yet, of the three men, his was the future that seemed so filled with promise, as if the weight of these possibilities, responsible for fixing him so solidly to life, were just as capable of pinning him to the ground once all hope was lost. Sometimes things we are deprived of can weigh too heavily, things, details, the house, the grove of trees, the smile, and it is the young man who collapses first, before the others, killed by the very things which had sustained him.

They drag his body several metres, lift stones which they use to cover his chest, his legs, his belly, and his face first of all so they no longer have to endure what remains of his gaze, that hard fixed darkness, a look that is so unlike him.

They try to gather their breath, their bodies still tense from the fear, from the effort. It has all happened so quickly. They have had to keep moving, not yet stop to think, to understand. One of them perhaps supports the other, I don't know which, Frænkel offering comfort to Andrée who finally allows himself to succumb to everything he has been holding in, grief, anger directed at his own blindness, Frænkel who breaks down, uttering outrageous accusations, or perhaps there is nothing but silence, both of them tight-lipped.

In any event, they pull themselves together, enough to fold Nils' jacket carefully and tie it up with some rope, because it may still prove useful to them or so that somebody, one day, might piece together something of the end of this life which they no longer think to record.

Nils is the only one to have been granted the right to a pile of stones on top of his body, by way of a grave: a sort of burial mound, a mausoleum. He has been granted a place, at least, where he might rest. By burying him in this way, they are sending us a message, too: we will know that when he died, they were still alive.

Andrée and Frænkel are left alone and you can imagine that it is then, finally, that something breaks within them. Until that point, despite the diarrhoea and the chilblains, the skin on their face ravaged by the cold and the sun – that skin which was no longer even skin, but a wound that had never healed – sapped by the monotony of the days and the infinite landscape, they were still there, all three of them, and so everything was still possible. They could wake up in the morning, at the end of a sleep-filled tunnel, with the humble perspective of a new day.

Strindberg's death smashes all of it to pieces. The days stop running on from one to the next, the thread is broken. Now, when they wake up, there is something there – in the dead angle of their field of vision, the feet of their young companion emerging from that makeshift mausoleum.

You could imagine that Andrée and Frænkel might stop fighting then, or that they are no longer expending the same effort, possessed of the same confidence, and that this is a sufficient explanation. In order to carry on, they had relied on an unusual combination of every man's limbs and spirit, and they had been astonishingly capable of working together, that much they had proven. It all had to intertwine, muscles set to work in unison, each one bringing along the others, activating nerves, and the moods they harboured within. Curbing thoughts or allowing them, when necessary, to dissipate, with the tears perhaps, of which there is no visible trace in their journals. But one suspects that the slightest doubt would be enough to reveal what they already were, carcasses that were barely animated by the marvellous machinery of their hopes.

For the time being, they are still there, both of them. They are looking more and more alike: two aged twins, similarly spent. As the end draws nigh, their faces take on the same brick-red hue, the same craggy texture, dulled by the night which little by little floods the sky and the ice, now barely illuminated by thin shafts of light. They'll not have the time to truly know the impenetrable darkness of the polar night, they will stop at its threshold – their end narrowly preceding that of the day.

In Gus Van Sant's film *Gerry*, two young friends, handsome and strong, set off on a hike through the American desert. They both have the same given name, Gerry. It starts off as a day hike, and soon they no longer know where they have been, nor where they should be heading. They never say it out loud, but they are lost.

Days turn into nights, how many is unclear. The faces of both Gerrys change, imperceptibly. Their skin reddens, their voices grow hoarse, their lips crack. They speak less and less. In the end, the salt pans of the desert look like ice and a frontier disappears, in time as in space: the searing expanses start to resemble the pack ice of the Arctic, and these American teenagers, ancient explorers.

White on the ground, an unseemly blue, pale and violent, overhead.

They lie down to sleep.

One of them, who senses he does not have long now, touches the arm of the other who, out of mercy or despair, finishes him off. Only one Gerry remains. The one who is dead, wrist folded over like a claw on his chest, already has the fossilised look of the skeletons on Kvitøya.

Suddenly, the remaining Gerry hears a noise. He gets up. He is weak, walking like an old man for all his twenty years. And then he gathers his remaining strength, because there on the blurry line of the horizon he can make out little bobbing black dots. He walks faster, he's almost running, heading for the road where cars are driving past.

The last shot shows him in the back seat of a car. His face is ravaged but he is alive. The car is driving, everything is normal. Through the window, the desert has once again been reduced to the dimensions of every landscape marked by roads, flight paths, railway tracks, any attempt to subdivide space. Once again it is harmless. The few days they have just experienced are already unimaginable. Gerry made the mistake of stepping out of his life, out of our familiar lives with their rules, their maps, their borders. It had taken no more than a blink of an eye and suddenly he had found himself in the wilderness. And half of him had perished as a result.

In the distant era in which they are living, where soon they will die, there are still dead zones. It is not enough simply to retrace your steps in order to stumble back to civilisation, for it still to be there, intact, just over a mountain, in an extended line of traffic.

The paths which today run from one end of the earth to the other have been sketched out by Andrée, Strindberg and Frænkel and their ilk, it was they who first drew a line, a road, a map which others would take up after them, as it is the work of many to draw the world and, gradually, to possess it. They have participated in this great undertaking to domesticate the landscape and will never know that once the task is complete, it will compromise the very thing they were so ardently seeking – the possibility of adventure.

But there are not yet enough of them, these paths, there is not yet a dense enough network to save them, so there they remain, at the very end of the road, undone by the scope of an unfinished yearning.

Do they speak to each other? Does Andrée try to reassure his companion, talk to him of winter's end, of the open sea where they will set off in springtime in their boat which is disappearing under the snow as did the fabric of their balloon so long ago?

Does he remind him of Nansen's story, of Johansen, surviving winter in their snow-cave, stitching clothes by lamplight, of all those men before them and the miracles which saw them extricated from the world of ice into which they had so passionately, so eagerly plunged themselves, or does he speak instead of what he will rediscover back home, those faces we will never know anything about, which Frænkel will carry with him but of whom, perhaps, he remains just one part?

Does something akin to a lullaby spring to his lips, words made incoherent by fatigue, by the night, something you might sing to infants, a song that blends with the short breaths of the other before he succumbs, does he close the man's eyelids, lay a hand on his forehead, or does he feign not to see, not to hear, just to make it last that bit longer, this final companionship?

Sitting on the edge of a rock, clutching his rifle, ammunition in his pocket, sitting ramrod straight as he did in the train that brought them north, Andrée must acknowledge that everything is indeed over.

Perhaps he grabbed the heart-shaped locket containing Anna's portrait and the lock of hair in the hope of bringing it back to Nils' family or for less noble reasons, on much stranger grounds: there, on his piece of rock, in the black of night, he might open the delicate hinge with his numb fingers and look at the photograph of this woman who is almost a stranger to him, for whom he has never been anything other than a threat hovering over her love, a woman who, at the start of this month of October, will learn too how to abandon all hope. He might look at this face he has never touched, just because he needs to hold in his hand the oval shape of a face, the lost scent of hair, as he senses death's approach. And then he would close the locket again, carefully, just as he bundled his diary into a pullover padded with hay, all of it then wrapped in a scrap of balloon fabric. They have come full circle, the vestiges of that flying contraption which brought them here, this sphere filled to bursting that hung there mid-air, these remnants will protect the single thing which remains: their story.

In winter, on Svalbard, the moon never sets. It is there, somewhere, the only vaguely familiar shape reflected by the sea, by the ice. There is no

227

more breath to be heard in the camp apart from that of the bears who will soon come to take what is there to be taken.

Maybe Andrée gulps down all the morphine that remains.

Maybe he is content to wait, to watch.

Maybe the pack ice has burnt his retina before burning his skin, it may be he has been blind now for weeks. Maybe the ice has already closed those eyes that were so keen to see it, maybe it has defeated him.

Does he ever admit, even subconsciously, to the failure of his undertaking? Or rather does he continue, right to the end, to admire White Island, in the silence broken by the cries of gulls and barnacle geese, happy to the last to have made it to where so few men had set foot.

ANDRÉE'S JOURNAL

Fragments of the final pages
October 1897

.... *897*
.... *with cutti*
.... *beginning of a*
.... *in the hut hung*
.... *the day passed*

.... *the low land. The question*
.... *here with everything*

.... *only* .... *us*
.... *on the island*

along the glacier ....
from the glacier ....
our hard .... *not* ....
even if late at night ....
the day's energetic labour ....
middle of the night ....
for the in (flaming) .... *outside* ....
northern lights neither ....
warmed .... *heavy wind*
.... *could not* ....
much .... *undertook however a short*
.... *we at last* .... *Swedes*
.... *to be the* .... *icy*

.... *from the sea found*
.... *All the ground*
.... *stone-brash*

.... *Darkness*
.... *on the snow –*
hut .... *when* .... *transport of the goods*

mon with .... *and intestine*
.... *envious*
now give .... *impression*
.... *innocent*
white doves but of .... *ul carrion*
birds
.... *bad weather and we fear*
.... *we keep in the tent the whole day*
.... *so that we could*
.... *on the hut*
.... *to escape*
.... *like*
.... *out on the sea*
.... *crash* .... *grating*
.... *driftwood*

.... *to move about a little*
.... *Is [pos]sible*

III
WHAT REMAINS

CONSTELLATIONS

From earth to the heavens

Night devours metal.

Night and all it comprises: air, starlight, damp winds, invisible particles, fear, waiting, hope.

Alcohol.

What is the night made of? This is what he wants to know. For several days, he has left light-sensitive plates out under the stars. Slowly they oxidise, consumed by the moisture, the rust – maybe the sky. They end up resembling his sleepless nights, his desires, his nightmares.

Can it still be called a photograph?

It is 1894, three years before their departure. It is another Strindberg who is leaning over plates that have been exposed to the night sky, who is running his finger over their meandering lines and tallying their traces. This one is the cousin of Nils' father, a famous playwright, a poet, an artist: August Strindberg, with his clear, wild eyes, and faun's beard.

In the marks left on the plates, he imagines the shape of constellations, the immensity of the cosmos, the flickering of lights. August is convinced. He calls them *Celestographs*, thus according them the status of works of art.

He wants to go beyond the power of the human eye, to be able to affix nature directly onto paper. He wants to grasp the clouds, spectra, the ice crystals on the windowpane of his Stockholm apartment, their fine veins resembling those of a leaf or the outline of waterways on a map.

Patterns repeat themselves, he has always been certain of it, in the infinitely large as in the infinitely small, this snowy fragment melting in his hand suddenly similar to the archipelago stretching out before his eyes as he lingers, in the evenings, body heavy with alcohol, on the terrace of Stockholm's Mosebacke cabaret restaurant with the city a miraculous cluster of light.

You can observe on the crater of a planet the same pattern which decorates the thorax of an insect; it is something that has always fascinated August, this mysterious repetition of symbols which he also reads as a harbinger of his own downfall. Some consider him to be mad, a mad scientist, to be precise. Others say, well, what do you expect, he's artistic.

On a sheet of paper which he carefully unpeels from his window, the ice has made wave-like shapes, yes, it's like the sea which only some kilometres to the north, at about this time, is being painted by Edvard Munch, that deceptively calm sea with its treacherous waves, it is visible in the very forms of the ice itself – the signs do indeed exist and there is, always, some common thread between what we are looking at and the thing with which we are obsessed.

Nature has manifested itself in August's hands. Not content to mimic it, he has conceived and produced it himself, a skill which he recognises as belonging to women and which, until now, has always evaded him. To celebrate, he downs a bottle of akvavit.

These far-flung expanses, this snow, the skies, these immense trees, this very night, this radiance, these northern lights, appear to him now as materials, ingredients, and the artistic act, like the act of exploring, becomes part of the same impulse pointing in the one direction, an impulse that originates with men, who are both its creators and owners – until that which they have set in motion leaves them in its wake.

Most of the plates exposed by August Strindberg to the sky continued to oxidise until the cosmos reflected in them was nothing more than a memory, a disillusioned hope. Without ever realising it, he achieved a result that was astonishingly similar to the images Nils was to leave behind, images which sought to describe the confines of the earth and which, unbeknownst to him, ended up portraying some curious Milky Way – a constellation that does not come from the sky, that does not herald the night, a script in braille that is constantly escaping our fingertips.

It is not always easy to grasp what we are seeing, but what we would prefer not to see is always there, threatening to engulf the surface of the picture. Slowly, slowly, the invisible reasserts itself.

At the campsite on White Island, something is at work, within them, just as it is working away at the heart of the images. As time turns their bodies into a frigid and desiccated mass, the images too are transforming. Within the copper canisters and inside the camera itself, they are starting their second life – subsumed by ground water, oxidised, erased, no longer leaving a copy but an impression, marked in turn by the cold, by time, by the landscape.

Doubtless they were worried about the conditions in which they were being stored, Nils, especially, who was preoccupied not only by the legacy all three of them would leave to the world in general, but by the message he, personally, would be leaving for Anna. He took as much care protecting them as August Strindberg took exposing his images to the heavens, outside, to the night sky. He did his best, to the very end, to preserve them, before acknowledging that they, like the men themselves, would be ravaged, soaked, caught in the ice which would leave its own grey patches, its scratches, its marks.

There is another side to heroic tales, something that falls and takes root, something that mutates, in the slow passage of time. Soon, there will be nothing more to make out in some of their photographs. Tarnished mirrors in which they were briefly reflected, the images will have nothing to recount and yet they will capture everything, the slightest deposit of sand, the slightest drop in temperature, things which escape the otherwise accurate lens of the camera: the shadow of the nights, the empty spaces between exposures, the silence of the frozen sea, that which sparks the optic nerve, any nerve in fact – the shifting matter of stories.

They have a message for us, these images, a message from the men, which they will continue to convey to us, for while we have no way of deciphering it, nor do we have any way of defining it, of stopping it. It will continue to find us, just as it continues to escape us, a liquid that spills, an ink blot that spreads, the dark side of sharp images, of abandoned clothes, of markers left by the wind and stars.

While they intended to create with each image a moment of fearlessness, a small feature to obliterate their days and afford them some meaning, the images themselves will change shape, be easily moulded, will shift, become elusive, like this place which drew them to it like a magnet and consumed them.

We will never know if the shapes able to be made out are the traces of August sunlight or just a hand over the lens, if that brighter patch is the remains of a face or the shape of the stone on which it was resting.

All their efforts, their kills, their pride, all of it will be erased. All that will remain is the fact itself of their exploits, the impression of what took place both on the images and on the men themselves, in the same approaching night.

There will be nothing they can do about it: one day, the images will reveal what they themselves would never have dared say, they will turn the men into the ghosts they feared they would become, adrift in the silver fog of the film. The images will become the account of their adventure and then of their loss, the account of a place still capable of consuming the men who remained determined to reach it, the most secretive of the Poles, the final landscape – tomb and darkroom.

MAUSOLEUM

1947

All we know of her is a bust sculpted by her father, Tore, when she was a child, hair cut into a bob with a straight fringe, small round face, biting her lower lip, large vacant eyes. When Ulla Strindberg, Nils' niece, visits Anna at her home in Torquay, she is thirty-four years old. Anna is sixty-six. They have not seen each other for years.

Ulla probably removes her hat, Anna takes her in her arms – after all, Nils' family, whom she still sees from time to time even fifty years after his death, must have come to feel a little like her own, so she hugs the young woman to her breast, to her lace blouse.

Ulla takes a few steps forwards. On every wall, carefully framed photographs of her uncle Nils, and in front of her, the silhouette of the old woman Anna has become, moving further into her house, turning back, offering her a seat in this British interior whose impeccable décor matches its clear message of ennui, as comfortable as it is hopeless.

Anna seems always to be resolutely elsewhere, the corners of her lips are defined but her smile is pleasant, heavy eyebrows overshadow her attractive, hazel eyes. They talk. From time to time, Anna's husband, Gilbert Henry, comes into the room, almost shyly he casts an eye over the house plants, the knick-knacks, the two women's animated, lively faces, Anna's especially so, which he is unused to seeing so illuminated by a far-off glow; she raises her hands, and her ringed fingers flutter in front of her. He slips away, as if fearing he might break a spell, afraid he is bursting in on a scene that belongs to her alone, this wife of his who just now looks like a stranger sitting in that armchair, smiling, vivacious, suddenly impressive as she pronounces particular words, returns to her origins.

Soon, Ulla will walk back down the corridor in the other direction, close the door again, leave the house, a little relieved perhaps to be leaving them to themselves, these three ghosts who share that space, Anna, Gilbert Henry and Nils' face in the photographs. Anna's hands will busy themselves once again with their few pastimes, and nothing more will be said.

On her return to Sweden, Ulla will acknowledge the gentle and unflinching humanity of Anna's husband as she considers the irrevocable impossibility of any forgetting, as one might ordinarily know it, this so-called resignation we call mourning. And she will make this observation in particular: that there is some part of Anna, perhaps a significant part of her, that is still wandering the streets of Stockholm, in 1897.

Anna is an old woman now. An old woman who still loves a young man, photographs of whom still portray him with regular features, full cheeks, a proud moustache. If she imagines herself still at his side, does she picture herself as she used to be, stuck with him in their artificial youth, or does she see the odd couple they now are, he so young and she bearing the signs of the years he has not lived?

Nils and Anna are each now almost as detached from the world as the other and, in their abandonment, perhaps there is a place where they might once again find one another, a place to which she retreats, every evening, with her husband keeping watch over her.

Two wars have washed over her and have left her there, bewilderingly untouched, her body scarcely heavier, wearing great black hats adorned with feathers, her gaze more fixed even if you can still make out, through the filter of photography, a sort of double layer, an internal screen onto which other images are projected.

*

Seventeen years earlier, she received the letters that had been written there, on the pack ice, letters in which Nils recalls how sweet the evenings were that he spent with her, how mild the weather must be in Sweden, her birthday, her patience, such delicate letters, attentive, in which he enquires before anything else, after her own feelings.

She has followed his journey, but she is over thirty years too late, she has seen pictures, doubtless read the travel logs, matched the most inconsequential of facts to every hour that passed, imagined the taste of polar-bear-blood pancakes and the last bubbles of champagne on their tongue, trembled when he fell into the leads between the ice, she has restitched with thread and needle, woven together the missing pieces, she has caressed his body, a thousand times, in her thoughts, first to exhaust her desire and then, later, to keep vigil over him, to soothe him with her patient, tireless, distant hands. Almost everything has become clear, except for the moment of his death which is still uncertain, there is nothing to stop the film playing on loop, over and over she sees those black scenes, there is nothing to confirm which is the correct one, where his last breath was drawn, in which position, suffering what pain, she has kept flicking from one version to another, hoping that some light that is bearable will emerge from the uncertainty, unless ultimately she has decided to settle on one, at last, to stop the proliferation of images, a calm, quick death, as if carried off to sleep, not feeling a thing, not knowing. An exhalation. Nothing more.

Reading his letters surely sharpened something else within her, something sufficiently acute to prompt her to action, to make a plan. Having exhausted the meanderings of her imagination, faced by the blank spots that remained, she made a choice which was still open to her to make, and nothing diverted her from it.

It was a choice that doubtless sprang from the first time they fell asleep, head in the crook of the other's arm, when her face was resting on Nils' chest, giving her the very real sensation that this was where she came from, somewhere there, somewhere close to his neck, to the smell of his hair, that she had always been there without ever quite knowing it, as if reliving this old, old memory meant that, for the first time, her body was at one with her surroundings. Next to him she had felt aligned, she had felt in her place, so there is only one thing to be done in order to feel that certainty once again: she must ensure that one day a part of her own body will end up next to his, regardless of whether it can happen only after her death – this simple knowledge is enough ballast for her body, enough to keep her here on this earth until her heart stops beating.

Whom was she able to convince, which family doctor, which stranger, perhaps, did she persuade to open up her aged body to perform a ritual previously reserved for the cadavers of certain queens, their heart extracted and embalmed, plunged into turpentine, slipped into an urn before their chest was carefully sewn back up?

Nobody has kept any record of her death in 1949. All we have is a note that says everything and nothing: she passed away following a long illness. She returned to the place of her birth in order to die, surrounded by familiar scenes from her childhood while in her mind, the pack ice continued to stretch out before her, uneven, brutal, invisible to those who placed a hand on her forehead and closed her brown eyes, extinguishing along with her the persistent reflection of the adventure that was lived and relived, and the cold creeping up through her limbs, she recognised it immediately.

After her death, Nils' brothers, who have never strayed far, return to keep the promise made to this woman who once posed at their side in the photographs at the turn of the twentieth century, a fierce look to match theirs, reconnecting a brotherhood whose links had been severed but was still proudly there.

They are older now, these men, mature, come to fulfil a wish that springs from their shared youth, from that distant crucible in which they all learned how to lose, how to exist apart. They revert, for the occasion, to the stubborn lads who posed mid-summer of 1897, for the family photo in which their older brother was missing.

Perhaps they have the same dark look, the same lascivious and determined posture when they slip into the cemetery, one of them clutching to his chest the silver urn, when they open Nils' tomb, with no official authorisation of any kind, and slip in the small silver box containing the ashes of Anna's heart, right next to his own funerary urn.

They leave the cemetery. They have done what they came to do. The paths of box hedge trimmed into a maze close in around them once again, along with the blue shadows of the hundred-year-old trees. I would like to see the look they reserve for Andrée's tomb which is very close by, to know if they acknowledge him, if they harbour a grudge, if, after all those years, they still believe in his project or if they always considered it a folly, a flight of fancy that embroiled them all.

They will resume their life where they left off. And far away, in England, in the small cemetery of Devon which flanks the sea where soon she will be joined by her husband, Anna's remains will be laid to rest, her body sewn back together over an empty chest.

RHIZOME

1990–2013

There are some stories which awaken something of which we were previously unaware, until it makes its presence felt. A hunger, a desire, a loss, a process that can't be stopped, and we don't always understand why they resonate. Perhaps they are more recent than they seem, these stories, something quite disconnected from our own lives but firmly linked to others, lives we have not ourselves lived but which prompt in us feelings of fear or regret.

In the early 1990s, amid the alcohol and laughter of a party where she is a little bored, a young Swedish woman by the name of Bea Uusma idly picks up a book from a table. In it she discovers Andrée's expedition. She will never let it go, neither the book, nor the story. She will spend the next fifteen years and more gathering the information to answer this question: how did they die?

She uses the knowledge gleaned from her medical studies to dissect autopsy reports, to study the photographs of the bodies, to examine the evidence along with a crime scenes investigations expert. One hundred years after the events, she will decode the clues, and from every fragment of bone, from the precise position of every last object, she will recreate their actions, their struggles, their exhaustion.

Decades after Hertzberg unwound the films and dipped them into the developing baths, Bea Uusma cautiously unfolds what remains of their clothes, every now and again coming across scraps of nails, skin or traces of blood in the folds of woollen fabric. It's as if this will never end. In another ten years, another hundred perhaps, somebody else will find other remains, will examine them with the same patience, will snatch other adventurers by the collar who are prepared to dive head-long into a chasm just so long as there is a witness standing on the edge to watch as they fall.

Nothing has changed since their disappearance: there are mysteries to be unravelled, lives to be imagined, black boxes to be recovered from the bottom of the ocean, and many are required for the task, another chain of people, that does not rise up to the sky but that sinks down into the depths, an underground chain comprised of scientists, computer experts, writers, the curious who in that enquiry find some convoluted way of looking deep within themselves, scratching where they didn't know there was a wound.

From her careful consideration of Nils' clothes, of the tears, the dark marks, Bea Uusma determines there is evidence of claw or tooth marks and blood. On discovering a hole in the bone of his forehead, she thinks first of a bullet which would have finished him off from point-blank range before measuring its diameter and discarding that hypothesis. Which is what hypotheses are made for: firstly to reassure us, to settle upon a much sought-after answer, only to dismiss it when it is not possible to incorporate every detail into the chain of events that they would have to construct in order to confirm them, and so they splinter apart, losing themselves in other possibilities, bifurcations, metamorphoses.

From the chain with its three charms – the anchor, cross and heart – discovered inside one leg of his long johns, she ascertains the injury that not only breaks his neck but simultaneously the fine links of the chain which slipped down Nils' chest, past his stomach, and ended up settling there, between his legs. To her, this can mean only one thing: he was attacked by a polar bear and, more particularly, he died standing up.

*

She examined everything, assessed it, recorded it. She spent more than half of her adult life trying to re-enact the expedition. She even went so far as to have sent to her by post the bone that a photographer had uncovered at the camp in the 1930s, hoping to find in it fragments of human tissue that had not yet been analysed. She found herself queuing up at the counter, like the dozens of other Swedes there to pick up a parcel, in the feverish, slightly incredulous hope she was about to receive a fragment of a man with whom she was obsessed. She opened the packet, analysed the bone, and realised it had belonged to an unusually large bear, perhaps some distant relation of the abominable snowman.

Having exhausted the resources of scientific methods, she decided to consult a spiritualist, notwithstanding her own rationalist tendencies, who suggested she look for the final letter thrown overboard by Nils from the balloon – perhaps the missing letter contained a piece of the key to the mystery. She paid for her own expedition, chartered a vessel, every day scrutinised the coloured zones marked on the maps so she could familiarise herself with the area of open sea before receiving the green light for departure. She experienced the Arctic, the ice, seasickness. She did not find the letter but, thousands of kilometres from any tree, at the supply depot on Sjuøyane, she did find a piece of wood with a fingernail embedded in it. She gathered up other items whose significance was equally opaque, in the hope that some hint of meaning would rub off them.

And then she set off once more. This time heading further away still. At first, on approaching the island, she remained huddled under her covers, too nervous to emerge. Fifteen years she had been waiting for this moment. Something that to her seemed too big appeared at the bow of the boat.

White Island. Kvitøya.

She walked towards the prow, looking straight into the blinding light, and described this place she had carried in her heart for so long:

the white wall of the glacier, the wind bearing particles of sand, the sensation of walking she herself harboured within.

At first she was astonished at the place they had chosen for their final campsite – there were other places along the way that would have been far more sheltered. Then she came up with a hypothesis: the rocky outcrop where they had set up camp was the only place that offered protection from the wind from the south. Thus, in all likelihood that was the direction of the wind at the time. She had even determined, then, the last wind that had swept across their faces: that same wind from the south whose fateful arrival had allowed the balloon to take off.

She sat at precisely the spot where Andrée had sat himself down to die, on the same rock, and she saw, then, what he had seen: Strindberg's grave.

He was looking at it, rifle in hand.

Bea Uusma did not look for any explanation for her obsession. The enigma of their adventure, of their wandering march, and then of their death, probably proved sufficiently vast to encompass the echoes it would carry with it into the future, the mysterious driving forces behind all those who would so doggedly persist in decoding their traces. She devoted herself entirely to deciphering the images, to understanding the maps, to examining the bones, to surveying that white desert, and no doubt her own yearnings, her own fears, both dissipated and, at the same time, were revealed, to her alone, in the shock wave that follows any disappearance.

Frænkel, Strindberg and Andrée's disappearance prompts a thousand echoes and responses, a loss of bearings, a drawing into the void, vertigo in the face of the interval that separates us from that era when an adventure such as theirs was possible, when it seemed to have some meaning, and it is this disjuncture too, this absence that we probe.

Their world disappeared well after them, but it died in their wake – and this world has become ours. The world that is coming bears no comparison, something has broken.

WONDER

2016

I arrive in Svalbard on the 23rd of July. Through the windows of the small airport at Longyearbyen, the dramatic cut of the fjord, a repetition of straight lines: the sea, the sky, the rounded mountains, striated with white, with black.

Summer, here, has never felt so much like summer. At three o'clock in the morning, the sun is shining as brightly as if it were midday and it is not some strange, sickly glow, it is a vast afternoon light in the middle of the night.

I am not looking for the answer to any mystery, just a point of contact: the threshold of the place where their story began to break down into the landscape, to melt into the excessive light that brings out every detail before effacing them altogether.

In 1906, a certain John Munro Longyear, originally from Massachusetts, arrives at the same fjord, the same patch of land ringed by mountains. He intends to mine there for coal and, while he is about it, to establish a town. In the absence of any indigenous people, there were no spoken words to be heard in the surrounding landscape. He thus had the satisfaction of naming the virgin territory after himself, territory that ever since has been sold to the highest bidder – Americans, Russians, and most recently to the Norwegians.

For years people would come there to mine, to extract the natural resources and to use up the strength they had garnered for the journey as they bored into the mountain. People came for its proximity to the

Pole, to be able to imagine the shore of this final continent: we know now that such a place does not exist, that where we have imagined the North Pole to be, there is nothing.

Following the closure of most of the mines, people come here now for research purposes, to breed sled dogs, to endure a winter, to rediscover some distant era, a place as unencumbered as their childhood, and to which they might miraculously still be able to return. It is a place where births and deaths are forbidden, but a place where citizens from many countries rub shoulders, refugees from previous lives, who are seeking its particularly weighted nature of time. Svalbard is one of the few remaining places where people choose to settle, a laboratory for some other form of territorial occupation, of an attachment not borne of inheritance or descent but of a continuing fantasy that there still exists such a thing as a map with a vanishing point.

So it is from here, then, that they departed, from here or nearby – Danes Island is a little further to the north. I recognise the shape of the mountains, that skeleton-like landscape, reduced to its essence, as if everything which would otherwise form part of the setting had been stripped away, leaving nothing but a bare matrix, a frame. This necklace of islands, that for so long would have been submerged by the sea, would have shifted from the equatorial region towards the tropics, would have made their way across oceans before finding themselves stranded here, at the frozen top of the world, rudely laying bare the traces of every creature that has lived and died there – Iguanodons, Allosaurus, marine reptiles from the Triassic, Placodermi, primitive blue-green algae – life which took root far from the gaze of men, leaving markers on the landscape of a time with no scale, of mysterious hidden depths.

For so many years, the sun reflected off the ice, which in turn cast its radiating light back into space. But the ice is melting, and the fjord is darkening, the earth and the ocean are absorbing the sun's rays, their heat, their light, their energy, and they are growing ever warmer.

The absence of vegetation on Svalbard makes it an open book, a book that is increasingly legible as the ice thins out, gradually exposing the deepest layers of the archipelago. Like a picture exposed to the light, it is revealing itself just as it starts to disappear. It's a form of involuntary archaeology cracking open for us the earth's memory as it readies us for its transformation, and the details are starting to surface, the fossils, the imprints, the different shades of colour that have been hidden by the ice, and the more irreversible the destruction, the more we become alive to the loss of what we are only just now seeing.

I thought I had come to find something of them but there is something else that strikes me, holds my gaze: the magnetic pull of this place and its metamorphosis that is on full display.

A sense of vertigo takes hold, here, at the thought of all that the rock is revealing, the various states it has passed through, that have passed through it, and suddenly, everything in the landscape seems equally in suspense, as if some immense tide were very gradually pulling back, engulfing all that has been deposited by the preceding influx, every sign, every trace, one after the other, site machinery, gigantic reels of cables, Evergreen shipping containers, snowmobiles reluctantly abandoned the previous winter or in anticipation of the next, soil ploughed up by the wheels of 4WDs, buckling bitumen, a mountain scarred by mine infrastructure creating its own exoskeleton, guardrails, pylons, houses coloured oxblood, blue, ochre and green, four colours, always the same, nothing distinguishable to suggest any sort of progressive urbanisation but rather the remnants of an order that soon enough will have lost any meaning, the triangular shape of wooden roofs against a sky that severs the peaks from the mountains, that sky already cloud, mist, vapour, a memory of snow, the ravines it creates so close to the summits, this engraved pattern, the pattern left by the absent snow, and below, on the plains, the floods of mud it becomes, the riverbed constantly hollowed out by machines and the water that sweeps through, spreading underfoot.

*

For so long we thought that absence was white, that it resembled the pack ice, the sheets of ghosts, the light that floods in when life comes to an end, this is how we imagined all we did not know, all we longed for, the departed, our loved ones, and the inaccessible continents, but well might one say that the white is disappearing, that it too is fading. Absence has changed colour, it has several hues now, this cameo of grey turning bistre, fawn, this coal black, the hues of peat and bracken, the rust brown of this secret skin, restive in the bright light of day, which the snow has left behind in its wake.

On looking more closely, there is something else evident in the photographs of the expedition. If they harbour such a sense of urgency, of melancholy, it is because we are not just seeing Strindberg, Frænkel and Andrée, in the process of fading away, but that through the ruined gelatin, we can sense the crumbling away of the place where they are trekking, this far-off land we assumed to be untouchable and whose transformation weakens, by osmosis, every other agreed truth, all our accumulated images.

Every slab of ice that calves prefigures the erosion of the mountain, every drop that falls into the calm sea, the receding waters and the forest fires. The place we assumed to be distant, far removed from everything, from ourselves especially, has become a sort of parable, a mirror, linking their wandering march, this distant era which is theirs, and which bears them along, to everything that comes after it, this dangling ribbon to which we cling.

The bridge connecting us is gradually disintegrating, so we must hurry, run before it collapses, or instead stop, take stock and, it is our turn now: take photographs. Record it, what little remains.

There are no more men in these images. No more proud silhouettes to screen out the place just discovered. There is the black matter that is covering the mountains, the planks falling off the houses, the spreading light and suddenly, everything freezes, something of their wonder is lost, their wonder at the smallest details, the feathers, the seaweed, the plants drying against their skin, the herbarium on their chest, we no longer recognise the thirst for discovery but the terror of loss which nonetheless pushes us towards the same gesture, with the same urgency, to see, to capture, to catalogue, to press down once again on the shutter release, without coming any closer to knowing what these images will have to say to the future, what they will tell us of the era when they were taken, of the desire still to hold close these flayed mountains, this mercury sea, this pebbly earth, to spill forth there a light that nothing will dim, a brightness from which there is no shelter, and by this illumination, by opening one's eyes wide, the details are lost, this bay, this inlet, this shore, everything is overexposed, with a dangerous, sharp clarity, we would have to close our eyes for years, centuries, until the world seeks relief from our gaze, until these places are reborn as myths, living on as memories within us, or possible illusions, until we can no longer be certain they ever existed.

THE AMERICAS

November 1876

Andrée is twenty-three years old. He is probably already sporting a moustache, his eyes already crinkly, mischievous, squinting, his hair a lighter blonde and combed back off his face. There are some faces that do not change, children who already have the face they will have when they're old.

It is night-time. Andrée is on duty. Around him, a curious cardboard world – monuments and statues have sprouted up like perennials across Fairmount Park, in north Philadelphia: a make-believe, spectacular town, illuminated all night. Shadows slip across Andrée's face. He battles to stay awake. Sometimes his head droops, his chin drops onto his chest.

He has crossed the Atlantic, left Europe behind. It is too small, Sweden is too constrained, he needs more, something bigger, something to match his youth. America is a draft, a sketch of the Great North, the beginnings of an adventure.

The nights are oppressive on the crossing, over the endless ocean, a great pocket of tedium radiating beneath the hull, making his heart leap when he leans overboard, but he has found a book on the wind, he is immersed. He starts to notice the different feel they each have on his face. Each has its own smell, its own distinct power. He would like to be able to recognise them by name, to work out their direction, their provenance, to recognise the dust they swept along on their breath, to guess where they came from, these cool particles stinging his cheeks, dampening his whiskers – from the now-distant Europe, from the East, perhaps, from America already, straight ahead.

Andrée is not yet quite as old as Strindberg and Frænkel will be when they take off alongside him. He does not know that he has already lived a little over half of his life.

At the Universal Exhibition in Philadelphia, in that enormous city re-created for the curiosity of the entire world, he has picked up a job as janitor and night watchman. He sweeps the footpaths of all the cities, symbols of every civilisation. He polishes, monitors, maintains this dream that he, too, shares: to bring together the marvels of the world, in miniature.

Here, in just a few hours, you can cross every ocean, explore every continent, admire a tower of steel that Eiffel himself would not have disavowed, sophisticated weapons beneath soaring glass ceilings, curious animals and marvellous machinery of war. There are precious substances, delicate fabrics, glassware and jewellery, bell towers, rose windows, Chinese pavilions.

Andrée likes being able to hold the world in his hand, even in this lowly position, wielding his broom, night and day, without fail.

In Philadelphia, he met the balloonist John Wise, one of the men who used balloons as a surveillance tool during the Civil War and who then himself mysteriously disappeared, a few years later, mid-flight, over Lake Michigan.

Sweeping up the dust, monitoring the empty boulevards of the city at night, the young Andrée likes to scroll through in his head, like the Hollywood films which will lend their colours to these youthful flights of fancy, images of the Battle of Bull Run: combatants rendered harmless – suddenly nothing more than statistics, pins on the maps at military headquarters – by the bird's-eye view provided by Wise's balloon. The great expanses of America reduced to a scale model, to a sketch. Andrée sails through his dreams of being aloft in the air as he walks the streets that are so much more attractive than their real-life counterparts, passing through halls sparkling like Christmas windows, while he contemplates his future conquests.

As he comes to the end of one such night, he meets another aeronaut who is organising flights in a hot-air balloon. This is his opportunity: Andrée is determined to abandon his broom and his work as a janitor. He wants to leave the earth behind.

The flight costs $75. Andrée has only fifty in his pocket. The balloonist is unswayed, he takes off, and Andrée is left there, his two feet still on the artificial ground that is the Universal Exhibition. Up there, where the balloon is ascending without him, there is an inaccessible world that is already beating away like a pulse in his clenched fist, there is the extent of his longing, his burning sense of urgency, all of it compressed into this moment which, like a piece of paper that has been crumpled for too long, will always be trying to unfold, long after this moment has passed, well beyond, impossible to stop, a desire that gets passed around like a ball and as it grows, just as it starts to spread, Andrée curses and watches the balloon float upwards.

SOURCES

This book is inspired by and is a liberal interpretation of available sources on the Andrée expedition.

The extracts from Andrée's diary are all authentic, despite being cut and reassembled, and were initially published in *En ballon vers le Pôle; Le Drame de l'expédition Andrée*, based on the notes and documents discovered on White Island, published by the Swedish Society of Anthropology and Geography, translated from the Swedish by Cécile Lund and Jules Bernard, with a foreword by Charles Rabot, Librairie Plon, 1931.[1]

The letters of Nils Strindberg to Anna Charlier were initially published in English in *The Andrée Diaries*, The Bodley Head Ltd, London, 1931. They have been translated from the English into French by the author of this book.

The enthralling book by Bea Uusma, *The Expedition*, published in Swedish by Norstedts Förlagsgrupp in 2013 and in English by Head of Zeus in 2014, has been an important source of information and reflection. It has not yet been translated into French.

---

1   **Translator's note:** Extracts from *The Andrée Diaries*, along with the letters of Nils Strindberg to Anna Charlier quoted by the author, were first published in English as *The Andrée Diaries, being the diaries and records of S. A. Andrée, Nils Strindberg and Knut Frænkel written during their balloon expedition to the North Pole in 1897 and discovered on White Island in 1930, together with a complete record of the expedition and discovery.* Authorised translation from the official Swedish edition by Edward Adams-Ray, London, John Lane The Bodley Head Ltd, 1931. Accordingly, wherever possible the translator has relied upon that authorised translation of the diary extracts and letters used by the author.

BIBLIOGRAPHY AND REFERENCES

Italicised extracts within the text have been quoted from these works

Arctic, Catalogue of the exhibition of the same name at the Louisiana Museum of Modern Art, Copenhagen, (September 2013–February 2014), curators: Poul Erik Tøjner and Mathias Ussing Seeberg.

Chasse et chasseurs arctiques, duc d'Orléans, Librairie Plon, 1911.

L'Expérience photographique d'August Strindberg, Clément Chéroux, Actes Sud, 1994.

L'Instant et son ombre, Jean-Christophe Bailly, Seuil, Fiction & Cie, 2008.

L'Odyssée de l'Endurance, Sir Ernest Shackleton, Libretto, 2011 [translated from English into French by Marie-Louise Landel].

Le Palais de glace, Tarjei Vesaas, translated from the New Norwegian by Jean-Baptiste Coursaud, Cambourakis, 2014. Published in English as *The Ice Palace*, Tarjei Vesaas, translated by Elizabeth Rokkan, Penguin Random House, 2018.

Le Voyage de l'ingénieur Andrée, Per Olof Sundman, Gallimard, Du monde entier, 1967 [published in English as *Flight of the Eagle*, translated by Mary Sandbach, Pantheon Books, New York, 1970].

Les Effrois de la glace et des ténèbres, Christoph Ransmayr, Points, 1991.

Les Fusils, William T. Vollman, translated from the American English by Claro, Actes Sud, Babel no°832, 2007 [published in English as *The Rifles*, Viking Penguin, 1994].

Les Vies multiples de Jeremiah Reynolds, Christian Garcin, Stock, 2016.

Message from Andrée, Joachim Koester, The Danish Arts Agency, Lukas & Sternberg, Pork Salad Press, 2005.

Ninety Degrees North, Fergus Fleming, London, Granta Books, 2002.

Pyramiden, Portrait d'une utopie abandonnée, Kjartan Fløgstad, Actes Sud, Aventure, 2009.

Voyage d'une femme au Spitzberg, Léonie d'Aunet, Actes Sud, Babel n°149, 1995.

With Nansen in the North: A Record of the Fram Expedition in 1893–96, Hjalmar Johansen, Cambridge University Press, 2011.

Zones blanches: Récits d'explorations, collection edited by Hélène Gaudy, Le Bec en l'air, 2018.

ACKNOWLEDGEMENTS

Thank you to Håkan Jorikson, of the Grenna Museum, for sending photographs and the translation from the Swedish to the English of letters from Nils to Anna.

Thank you to my publisher, Marie Desmeures, for her support during the writing of this book, marked by the sharing of images, books and films on various polar expeditions.

Thank you to Maison Gueffier, Pôle littérature du Grand R, Scène nationale de La Roche, for two years' residence as an associate author which allowed me to consider different and mixed forms for this work.

Thank you to the museum at La Roche-sur-Yon and in particular to Hélène Jagot for the shared commission of the exhibition *Zones blanches*, bringing together contemporary artists addressing the topic of the journey of exploration based on the photographs from the Andrée expedition. Thank you to Fabienne Pavia and to Éditions Le Bec en l'air for their publication of the eponymous book gathering the texts of writers inspired by works from the exhibition.

Thank you to the Villa La Brugère Association in Arromanches, and in particular to Marie-Thérèse Champesme and Daniel Foucard.

Thank you to the Centre National du Livre for its invaluable support.

Thank you to Xavier Mussat, for so many things, and for helping to lend this work its lyrical quality during the musical readings, which helped me harness sounds and images, and certain atmospheres and textures of the Great North through our working together with the words.